Murder Shoots the Bull

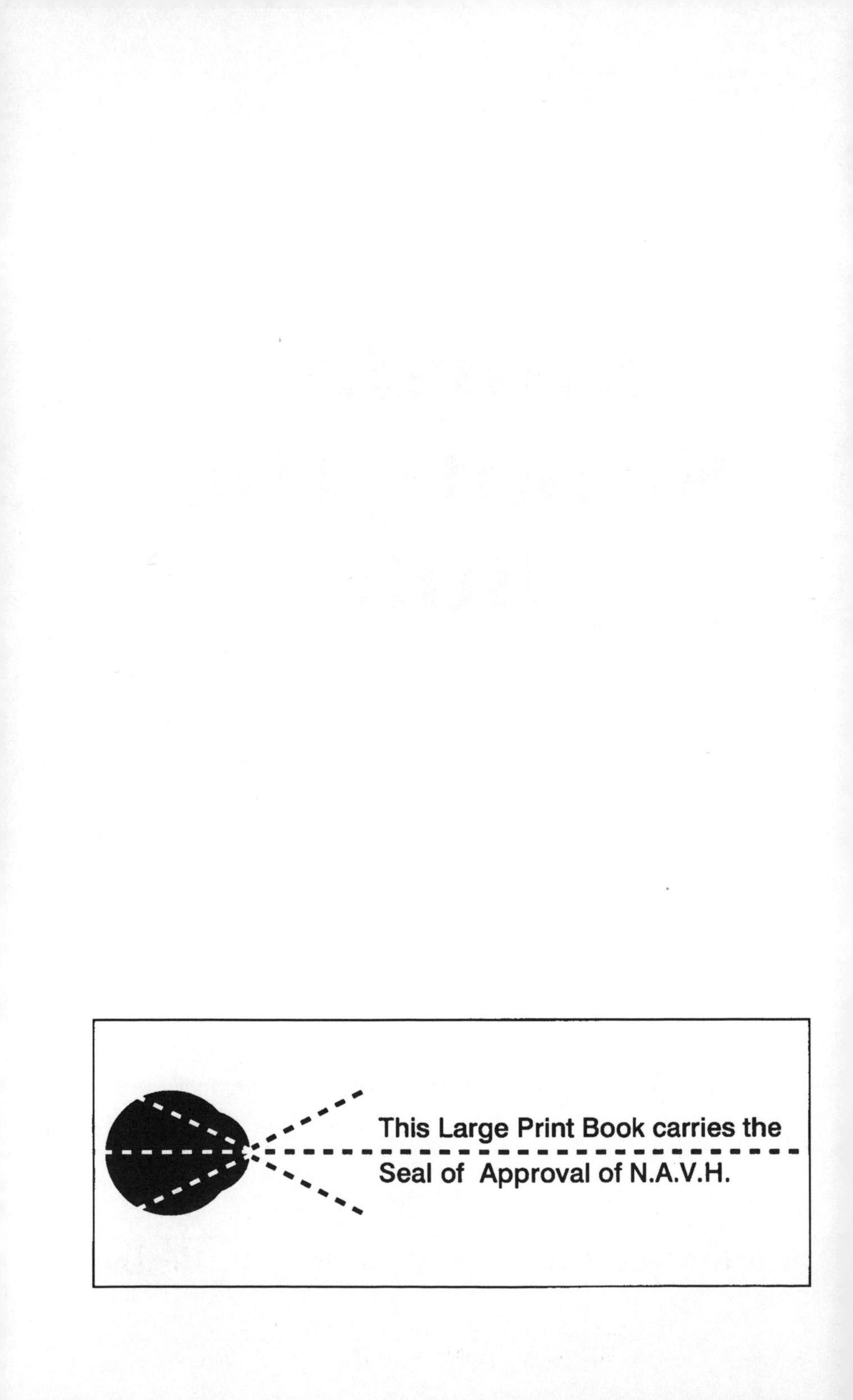
This Large Print Book carries the
Seal of Approval of N.A.V.H.

Murder Shoots the Bull

Anne George

Thorndike Press • Thorndike, Maine

Published in 1999 by arrangement with Avon Books,
a unit of The Hearst Corporation.

This is a work of fiction. Names, characters, places and incidents either are the product of the author's imagination or are used fictitiously. Any resemblance to actual events, locales, organizations, or persons, living or dead, is entirely coincidental and beyond the intent of either the author or the publisher.

Thorndike Large Print® Americana Series.

The tree indicium is a trademark of Thorndike Press.

The text of this Large Print edition is unabridged.
Other aspects of the book may vary from the original edition.

Set in 16 pt. Plantin by Al Chase.

Printed in the United States on permanent paper.

Library of Congress Cataloging-in-Publication Data

George, Anne.
Murder shoots the bull / Anne George.
p. (large print) cm.
ISBN 0-7862-2222-0 (lg. print : hc : alk. paper)
1. Patricia Anne (Fictitious character) — Fiction. 2. Mary Alice (Fictitious character) — Fiction. 3. Sisters — Southern States — Fiction. 4. City and town life — Southern States — Fiction. 5. Investment clubs — Fiction. 6. Large type books. I. Title.
PS3557.E469 M875 1999b
813′.54 99-045076

For my friends,
Malu Graham and Fran Boudolf,
whose words help shape my world

One

The way my sister Mary Alice got us arrested was simple enough; she hit the president of the bank over the head with my umbrella. Grabbed it right away from me and "thunk" let him have it. I think he was more surprised than hurt. There was hardly any blood, and everyone knows how much head wounds bleed. There wasn't even a very big knot. Probably wouldn't have been one at all if he'd had any hair. But he screeched like she'd killed him and the security guard came rushing in, saw Mr. Jones staggering around holding his head, and pulled a gun on us. He looked like Barney Fife, the guard did, and chances were the bullet was in his pocket, but you just don't take a chance on things like that. At least I don't. Sister said later that she might have hit the guard, too, at least knocked the gun out of his hand, if he hadn't looked so pitiful standing there shaking like a leaf. She also said she was surprised that Alcorn Jones, being a bank president, didn't have a higher threshold of pain.

This sounds like my sister is aggressive, and she is, a little bit. For sixty-six years (she says sixty-four) she hasn't bothered a lot of times to knock on doors. Things like that. But she's not aggressive as in going around hitting bank presidents with umbrellas aggressive. Not usually. In fact, the whole time we were waiting at the jail for my husband, Fred, to come get us, she was worrying about whether or not the ladies of the investment club would think she was common as pig tracks for having hit Alcorn. I assured her that they would consider her a heroine, a true steel magnolia who had been protecting her honor.

"You reckon?" she asked, looking up hopefully.

"Absolutely. You were protecting the club, too. After all, he was doing all of us wrong."

"That's true." She was beginning to look downright cheerful. "He got what he asked for."

I didn't know about that. It had landed us in the Birmingham jail. I had lived for sixty-one years with nothing but one speeding ticket on my record and here I was, incarcerated.

"Mouse," Sister said, "let's ask the lady that put us in here for some stationery. We could write Haley a letter from the Birmingham jail. She'd love that."

She probably would. Haley is my

daughter who is currently living in Warsaw, Poland, with her new husband. She'd think it was funny that her mama and Aunt Sister had landed in jail.

"All sorts of famous people write letters from the Birmingham jail," Mary Alice continued.

"We're not famous." I was beginning to wish for my purse and some aspirin; I rubbed my temples. "Why do you think the police took our purses?"

"They have us on a suicide watch."

I looked at my sister in amazement. I swear she's half a bubble out of plumb. In fact, if our mother and father hadn't sworn that we'd been born at home, I'd have been willing to bet that we had been mixed up somewhere. We don't even look anything alike. Mary Alice is six feet tall (she says five twelve) and admits to two hundred fifty pounds. I'm a foot shorter and weigh in at a hundred five. She used to be brunette with olive skin; I used to be what Mama called a strawberry blonde, more wispy blonde than strawberry. Mary Alice also used to be five years older than I am, but she's started backing up. This day in the Birmingham jail, she was Beach Blonde and I was more gray than strawberry. But I still had better sense.

"Why would they have us on a suicide watch? They don't even have us locked up." This was true. A very nice police lady had put us in a small room and closed the door with a "Y'all want anything, just holler."

"That's what they do routinely." Mary Alice sat down across from me at a small table and looked around. "If these walls could only speak."

"Lord." I rubbed my temples harder. "You know you broke my umbrella."

"I'll get you another one."

"But that was my kitten one. The one where you could see the kittens like they were looking through stained glass. Fred paid thirty-eight dollars for it at Rosenberger's just because I was admiring it so." Tears welled in my eyes. "We were eating supper at Chick-Fil-A and I spotted it in Rosenberger's window."

Sister sighed. "I wish I had a Chick-Fil-A chicken salad sandwich."

The door opened and a policeman came in holding a clipboard. "Patricia Anne Hollowell?"

I looked up. "Yes."

"And Mary Alice Crane?"

Sister nodded.

"Your lawyer is here."

Our lawyer?

"My husband's coming to get us," I said. "We don't need a lawyer."

"Oh, yes you do." Debbie Nachman, Sister's daughter, stood in the door, looking very lawyerly in spite of the fact that her briefcase was clasped over a significantly pregnant belly. "What have you two done now?"

"It's all your mama's fault," I said without a moment's hesitation and with no guilt.

"I don't doubt that a minute." Debbie laid her briefcase on the table, sat down, and pulled her shoes off. "Lord, I think my feet are swelling already."

Mary Alice didn't miss a beat. "My feet swelled like balloons before you were born. I had to stay in bed for the last two months."

Debbie grinned. "Point taken, Mama." She pulled out a legal pad. "Now how about y'all tell me what happened."

"It's a long story," I said. And it was.

Sister grabbed my arm. "Just the highlights, Mouse. I'm starving."

Two

This was November, so to explain exactly how we got into this predicament, I would need to back up a couple of months, probably to an early September afternoon when I was sitting in the den practicing smocking. I had signed up for a class at the Smocking Bird, thinking I would smock dresses for Debbie's two-year-old twins for Christmas. Christmas trees and little drummer boys. I love hand-work, but I'd never had the time to do much of it when I was teaching and raising a family. Now that I was retired, though, I was going to dress every child in the family with beautiful embroidered clothes. Of course the kids would rather have jeans, but that was beside the point.

So I was practicing happily on an old soft blouse of mine, smocking and thinking about spending Christmas in Warsaw with Haley, which Fred, Mary Alice, and I were going to do, when Mitzi Phizer knocked at my back door. Mitzi is my next door neighbor, has been for almost forty years. She's also one of my favorite people, a pretty woman with no pretense about her.

We've helped each other through a lot of things during those years.

"Hi," I said. "Come on in and tell me what you think of these stitches."

Mitzi pushed her bifocals up on her nose and examined my work. "Looks good."

"Come on in the den. Oprah's fixing to tell us what to read this month. You want some tea or something?"

"No, thanks."

"It's Milo's. I bought a jug of it yesterday at the Piggly Wiggly. Sweetened."

"Sounds good. But I just need to talk to you for a few minutes."

"Sure. Anything wrong?"

"No. Everything's fine."

Oprah was holding up a book. I jotted the title down and turned the TV off. "What's up?" I asked.

"You remember Joy McWain?" Mitzi sat on the sofa, reached across to the coffee table and took a lemon drop from the candy jar.

"The name's familiar."

"Connie Harris's cousin, the pretty blonde one who used to work at Rich's cosmetic counter. Married the McWain fellow who owns the Chevrolet place in Alabaster. She made a commercial for him once. She was a cheerleader."

"In the commercial?"

"I'm surprised you don't remember it. She's got great big thighs. I mean really out of proportion. Those saddlebag things." Mitzi sucked on the lemon drop thoughtfully and then pushed it back to her cheek. "I don't think she did another one."

Sometimes Mitzi has to be encouraged over the finish line.

"What about her?" I asked.

"She wants to start an investment club. You know, like the Beardstown ladies. She called Connie, and Connie thinks it's a great idea. She's the one who called me. She said they're going to get about fifteen or twenty women that they know they can depend on. I told her I'd love to get in something like that and could I ask you, that you're dependable. And she said sure." The lemon drop came back to the middle and Mitzi pursed her lips.

"Sounds good," I said. "I don't know a thing about the stock market but I'd love to learn. As long as we don't have to invest much."

"You think Mary Alice might be interested?"

"Hell, Mitzi, she already owns the stock market." An exaggeration, but thanks to being widowed by three husbands who were all rich as Croesus, Mary Alice is not wanting in the money department.

"But she might help us out with which stocks to buy. Tell us what her brokers are advising."

"I'll mention it to her," I said. "But she needs an investment club like she needs a hole in her head."

"But you're definitely interested."

"Absolutely. Just let me know when to show up for the first meeting."

"We'll go together," Mitzi promised. She stood up and stretched. "I've got to go to the store. God knows what I'm going to fix for supper. Arthur has suddenly decided he should be a vegetarian, says it's better for his health. It probably is, but, Lord, sixty-four years old and Mr. Bread and Potatoes becomes a vegetarian." She smiled. "I told him I'd help him, but it's going to be as hard for him as giving up smoking. Chances are he's at Burger King right now downing a Whopper."

"I got some fresh asparagus at the Piggly Wiggly yesterday. Cost an arm and a leg. Came from Mexico. But it was delicious."

"That sounds good." She stood in the back doorway for a moment. "You're so lucky, Patricia Anne, to have Fred. He'll eat anything."

I took this as a compliment. "And you're lucky to have Arthur even if he is a vegetarian. More veggies would be good for all of us."

"I know." She gave a little wave and went down the steps.

I watched her cross the yard, a plump, pretty woman who looks younger than her sixty-four years. Something about the way she had said, "I know," hadn't sounded quite right. For a moment, I wondered if everything was all right next door. But then I shrugged and went back to my embroidering. Of course it was.

I was smocking happily a few minutes later when the back door opened and Mary Alice called hello.

"In the den," I called back.

"I'm getting me some tea."

When she came into the room, I was surprised to see she was dressed in a cream colored pants suit that I had never seen.

"You look good," I said. "I like that outfit. Where've you been so dressed up?"

She sank down on the sofa. "To Elmwood Cemetery. It's Roger's birthday."

Roger Crane was husband number three. "Did you take flowers to all of them?" I asked.

"Of course I did. I wouldn't want one of

them to get their feelings hurt."

Mary Alice's three husbands are buried next to each other. And, like she says, it's convenient and they haven't complained.

"That's why I'm dressed up," she continued. "I like to think it makes them feel better."

And I'd like to think she was kidding, but I didn't think she was. She ran a paper napkin over her forehead. "I'm sweating like a whore in church, though. Damn it's hot this year."

"It's September. What do you expect?" I handed her the blouse I was embroidering. "How does that look?"

"Strange. How come you're putting Christmas trees on an old blouse?"

I snatched it back. "I'm practicing. I'm going to make your granddaughters Christmas dresses."

"Oh. Well, that's nice." She turned up her tea and chug-a-lugged half the glass. "Lord, I'm hot. I took Bear Bryant some flowers, too."

"Why?"

"I just hadn't taken him any in a while."

This was not as off-the-wall as it sounds. If you're from Alabama, a visit to the Bear's grave is like a pilgrimage.

"How was the Bear?"

"Dead, Mouse. Just like he's been for twenty years."

"Only his body, Sister. His spirit lives on."

Mary Alice looked at me appraisingly to see if I was serious, decided I was, and said, "True."

"Mitzi Phizer was just here," I said, getting back to my sewing. "She wants to know if we'd like to get in an investment club some friends of hers are starting. I told her I would, but I didn't know about you."

Sister finished the tea and put the glass on the coffee table. "What kind of investment club?"

"You know. Like the Beardstown ladies. We pool a certain amount of money and invest it in the stock market. Everybody studies the market and makes suggestions."

"Coca-Cola's done fine by me," Sister said. "Tell them to buy Coca-Cola."

"Tell them yourself. It would be great to have someone in there who already knows something about the market." Actually, I knew that Sister didn't know diddly about the market, but her broker was sharp.

Sister seemed pleased. "Who all's going to be in it?"

"Mitzi said it's a woman named Joy McWain's idea. A friend of Mitzi's, Connie

Harris, called Mitzi."

"Joy McWain with the big thighs?"

I put the smocking down, looked at my sister, and asked her a simple question: was I the only one who missed out on things like big thighs in commercials?

"Probably. Those thunder thighs were hard to miss, Mouse. And the woman had on a cheerleading outfit, a short white pleated skirt and red satin underpants. Lord. Cheering for used cars." She reached over, got a piece of ice from her glass, and popped it into her mouth.

"Don't you dare chew that."

"I'm not." Mary Alice smiled. "Mercy, you sound like Mama sometimes."

"That's not bad."

"No."

I picked up my sewing again. I heard a suspicious crunching sound and Sister reached for another piece of ice. I swatted at the air since I was too far away to reach her. "Quit that! What's the matter with you?"

"Nervous, I guess. I've got a blind date who's picking me up in —" she glanced at her watch — "two hours and fifteen minutes."

"How come that's making you nervous? You have blind dates all the time."

"But this one's really blind. As in can't see."

"You mean he's visually impaired?"

"No. He's blind as a bat. He said so himself. When he asked me out, he said, 'It'll take a little getting used to, Mary Alice, I'm blind as a bat. But I'd love to take you out tonight.' " Sister reached for another piece of ice. "His name's Judson Murphree. I met him at a benefit party for the museum. He's a sculptor."

"Well, he sounds great. Sounds like he's got his act together."

Sister nodded. "He's also forty-three and handsome."

"Crunch" went another piece of ice. I got up and took the glass away from her. I was beginning to get the picture here.

"How old did you tell him you are?"

"Well, when I found out he was really blind, I sort of lost my head. I said I was forty-five."

"Anything else?"

"I said that I was tall and blonde, but that's the truth, Mouse."

"And he asked you out."

"Well, of course he did. A forty-five-year-old slender blonde with a good personality? Of course he did."

"Slender?"

"He's blind, Mouse. Like I said, I sort of lost my head."

"And now your conscience is hurting you?"

Mary Alice looked at me, puzzled. "Of course my conscience isn't hurting me. I'm just worried that I'll say something about remembering World War Two."

I swear talking with Sister is like playing ping-pong. I returned the serve. "Why would you say something about remembering World War Two?"

"Because I'm worried about it. I'll for sure say something like, 'Remember the air raid drills during World War Two?' "

"Why would you do that? How many dates do you ask if they remember the air raid drills during World War Two? Get real. It just doesn't usually come up in a conversation." I paused. "You really shouldn't have lied to him, though."

"I know. But it was such an opportunity." She flicked something from her pants leg. "I think that was a flea. Has Woofer been on the sofa? Or Muffin?"

I jumped to the defense of my old sweet dog and of Haley's cat, Muffin, who was staying with us while our newly married daughter, Haley, was in Warsaw. "Woofer and Muffin don't have fleas. If it was a flea, you brought it with you."

"Bubba doesn't have fleas, either."

Which was probably true. Sister's cat spends most of his time snoozing on a heating pad on her kitchen counter. A normal flea would want a more challenging environment. I got back to the subject at hand.

"About the investment club. Are you interested?"

"Sure. I'll bring Shirley Gibbs."

"Your stockbroker?"

"The one I've told you about. She's the one who told me to buy Intel stock when it first came on the market."

"She's a professional, Sister. The fun of the club is that it's a bunch of amateurs learning about the market, talking about the stocks and reading about them. Of course we could check it out with her later about the stocks we've chosen. I doubt she'd want to come anyway."

"Sure she would. We could decide what stocks to buy and Shirley could just nod yes or no. Besides, we're going to need someone to buy the stocks when we decide."

"That's true. I'm not sure how these things work. I'll check it out with Mitzi."

That answer seemed to satisfy Sister. She got up to leave. "Okay, but did I tell you about the condoms?"

"What condoms?"

"Shirley was recommending condom stocks back when everybody thought they were just for emergencies."

Condom emergencies? I decided not to pursue it. "I'll mention it to Mitzi," I promised.

I put down my sewing and followed her to the back door. "You have a good time tonight."

Frown lines appeared between her eyes. "Do you think I ought to offer to drive?"

"Play it by ear."

I stepped outside into the sunlight and watched Sister drive away. The large crape myrtle tree in the Phizers' backyard was still in late summer bloom, the color of watermelon. The smocking could wait, I decided, and reached behind the kitchen door where Woofer's leash hung. A good walk was what we both needed.

Woofer's igloo doghouse is the best of things and the worst of things. I purchased it for peace of mind. Woofer is nobody's spring chicken and I worried about him in his old doghouse. If the weather was very hot or cold, I'd bring him into the house which he really didn't like very much. Woofer's a yard dog. He can't dig holes or bark at squirrels in the house. So, after reading the brochure about the igloo with its promise of warmth and heat, I was sold. So was Woofer. He moseyed in, sniffed around, figured he'd found dog heaven, and settled down. Even on beautiful sunny mild days, he has to be coaxed out, and for a few minutes he acts as if I've insulted him. So I don't have to worry about him getting cold or hot. I have to worry about him forgetting how to move.

I coaxed him out with a couple of dog biscuits, put his leash on, and we headed down the sidewalk. The September smell of kudzu-covered hills and knotweed followed us and became mixed with the smell of cut grass; yellow butterflies were everywhere. I sniffed appreciatively. There was a tea olive blooming in someone's yard.

We had strolled for several blocks and had turned to go back home when a white Buick LeSabre pulled up beside us. A handsome man who looked to be in his early sixties let down the passenger window and leaned over.

"Ma'am," he asked, "what breed is your dog? He's so unusual. All those colors."

"Thank you. He's a Norwegian possum hound. One of a kind."

"So they have possums in Norway?"

"Must have."

Woofer headed toward a utility pole pulling me along. The car followed.

"Ma'am?"

"What?"

"Anybody ever tell you you have a cute butt?"

"My husband told me this morning."

"I'm glad to hear he appreciates the finer things in life."

"He's an appreciative man."

"Right now he'd appreciate knowing there's a cold beer in the refrigerator."

"There is. And Milo's sweet tea."

"I'm appreciative."

I laughed. "Get, you fool. I'll be home in a few minutes."

"I'll be waiting." He twirled an imaginary mustache and drove off.

I patted Woofer. "Your papa's a nice crazy man, Woofer."

Woofer wagged his tail in agreement.

Mitzi was out in her front yard picking a bouquet of daylilies as we went by. "Wait, Patricia Anne," she called. "Take some of these."

The flowers she brought to me were almost a rust color with a yellow throat.

"These are gorgeous," I said. "What kind are they?"

"I don't know. I got them a couple of

years ago from a lady out near Wildwood shopping center who has a whole field of irises and daylilies. I wanted some that bloom late. They are pretty, aren't they?"

"I've never seen any this color. All mine are orange or yellow."

"It's unusual," Mitzi agreed. "Did you ask Mary Alice about the investment club? I saw her car at your house."

"I did, and she wants to join. She also wanted to bring her broker."

"She did?" Mitzi frowned. "A broker's input would be nice, but wouldn't we just figure the broker knew more than we did and not really study the stocks?"

"That's what I told Sister, but she reminded me that we would need a broker to buy the stocks."

"Connie said something about doing that through a bank. Some banker who Joy McWain knows has volunteered to help."

I looked at Mitzi and grinned. "We've got a lot to learn, haven't we? Do you know anything at all about the stock market?"

"Lord no. My checkbook isn't even balanced."

I thought about Sister's condom stock. "It's going to be interesting to see what stocks Mary Alice suggests."

"I'll bet they'll be good ones."

"Don't bet the farm."

I thanked Mitzi again for the flowers and hurried next door where there was a lovely man waiting who thought I had a cute butt.

Three

When I walked into the house, Fred was already stretched out on his recliner with the *Birmingham News* open, a beer on the table beside him, and Peter Jennings on TV. I put the flowers in a vase, and went in to join him.

"Hey," he said. "What are we having for supper?"

"Your choice. Salisbury steak or stuffed peppers." This was going to be a Stouffer's night. I had, however, added some fresh lettuce to the salad left over from the night before.

"Stuffed peppers."

I knew which he would choose. He's easy.

"Did you and Woofer have a nice walk?"

"Some old fool accosted me. Said I had a cute butt."

"Maybe old, but no fool. You want some of the paper?"

I took the Metro section and settled down on the sofa. This is my favorite part of the paper, the part that shows how eccentric, kind, sad, violent, and funny the people of Birmingham are. I guess it's that way in every city, but Birmingham is still trying to live down its reputation from the Civil Rights' movement of the 1960's. Consequently, we miss no opportunity to show the world that we are nice people who shouldn't be judged by the goings on thirty years ago of, as Sister claims, all those outside agitators from Mississippi and Georgia. Here is our symphony orchestra, we say. Cultured people have symphonies. Here are our colleges, universities, medical centers, museums, planetariums, botanical gardens, libraries. We are erudite, sensible people living in the most beautiful place God ever created among rolling mountains and rivers.

The lead story in the Metro section was about a minister's wife who wanted to put wings on the tremendous statue of Vulcan that stands on Red Mountain overlooking the city. He would be our guardian angel, she declared. The story was accompanied by an artist's rendition of the statue with wings.

The reporter had asked several people on the street what they thought about the idea. The answers ranged from "good idea" to laughter to "what would we do about his butt?" The latter question is a reasonable one since Vulcan, the god of the forge, symbol of Birmingham's steel industry, wears an apron that covers only the part of his anatomy that no man would want to have hit by sparks. His prodigious, muscular backside moons the whole valley behind him.

Those of us who live under that moon are used to it and are startled when first-time visitors invariably look up and say, "My Lord! Look at that!" Then they want to go up to Vulcan Park to the gift shop and buy tee shirts and beer huggers with the rear view of the statue and "Buns of Iron" emblazoned on them because their friends in Seattle, Denver, etc. (just fill in any name) won't believe this.

Well, at least when you're at the park it's a beautiful view from Red Mountain overlooking the city.

"There's a lady here wants to turn Vulcan into an angel," I told Fred. "Put wings on him."

Fred didn't even look up. "That's dumb. Vulcan's too much a man."

"Men can't be angels?"

"Not Vulcan."

"Why not?"

"He just can't."

I suppose he considered this an answer. When I realized he wasn't going to elaborate, I continued reading. It was a slow day, though. The only other story that struck me as unusual was one about Alabama ostriches being exported to China. Their meat had less fat and more protein than beef and their body temperature of 103.2 degrees was high enough to resist Chinese parasites.

"Fred?" I asked. "Did you know they grow ostriches in Alabama? They're going to export them to China."

"Sure. A bunch of them down around Demopolis."

"You'd have to have a huge Brown 'n' Roast bag and oven."

"Hmm." He turned to the next page.

Muffin had joined me on the sofa. I moved her aside, got up and went into the kitchen to get some tea. When I looked out of the window, I noticed Mitzi was sitting by her daylilies, not working in them, but just sitting, her head bent over as if she were studying something on the ground. Something was definitely wrong.

I went out to the chain link fence that separates us. "You okay?" I called.

She looked up, startled, and then smiled. "I'm fine."

"The girls okay? The baby?"

Mitzi and Arthur have two daughters, Barbara and Bridget, who, like our children, have taken their time producing grandchildren for us. Bridget had recently given birth to Andrew Cade, though, the most beautiful child ever born according to Mitzi.

"They're fine. Why?"

"You look sort of down."

"Just thinking." She picked up a trowel. "Wondering if there's enough sun here for chrysanthemums."

"It's a good place." It was, in fact, where she had had a big bed of them last fall. I remembered how many butterflies the bright yellow flowers had attracted. So this wasn't what she was wondering about.

"I guess so." Mitzi pushed the trowel into the dirt in front of the daylilies.

"Did you get some asparagus?" I asked.

"Yes. Thanks for telling me about it."

"Sure. You're sure nothing's wrong?"

She smiled and shook her head. "I'm fine. Really."

She obviously wasn't, but whatever was wrong, she wanted to work it out by herself. She knew I was here if she needed me.

Fred was looking in the refrigerator when I walked back in, worrying about Mitzi.

"Tell you what," he said. "Let's go eat at John's."

"The Stouffer's doesn't suit you?"

"It suits me fine. I just decided I've got a hankering for some of John's slaw."

"There's all sorts of stuff here I could fix."

Fred closed the refrigerator. "I want fried snapper throats. I want slaw. I want key lime pie."

"You want a bait of cholesterol."

"You got it." He patted me on the behind as he walked by. "Come scrub my back and I'll take you downtown for some high on the hog good eating."

"Fried snapper throats and slaw."

"Doesn't get much higher on the hog than that."

And as simply as that, worry about Mitzi slipped to the back of my mind.

The neighborhood where Fred and I live was Birmingham's first "over the mountain" neighborhood. It's also the neighborhood where Mary Alice and I were born and raised. When we were growing up, if anyone asked where we lived and we said, "over the mountain," everyone knew we were talking about over the crest of Red Mountain, below the statue of Vulcan. Now "over the mountain" stretches all the way into Shelby County over Red, Shades, or Double Oak Mountain.

When we were growing up, living over the mountain had a special advantage. Jones Valley, where Birmingham is located, was also the location of the great steel mills and foundries that were responsible for the city's birth. Smokestacks poured pollution into the valley like coffee into a cup. It seldom spilled over the rim that was Red Mountain.

It's surprising how many of us have lived in this neighborhood all of our lives. I walk Woofer and run into old childhood friends out walking their dogs or pushing grandchildren in strollers. There are bridge clubs and reading groups here that our mothers began decades ago and which are still going strong. But young people are moving in, too, delighted with the sidewalks and old trees. With the stability and the closeness of downtown Birmingham.

We drove over Red Mountain and down into Jones Valley in a deepening twilight. The sun's rays no longer glinted off Vulcan's rear end, but God forbid that we should miss such a majestic sight. Strategically placed spotlights lit up those buns of iron. Below the statue, the city sparkled, beautiful and bright. The mills have cleaned up their act. No more descending into a dark cloud as you come down the mountain.

We stopped at a red light at Five Points, the center of Birmingham's nightlife. It was a warm evening, and the streets were already crowded with teenagers hanging out, business people who had stopped by a bar on their way home, as well as early customers for the many fine restaurants in this area.

"Mary Alice has a blind date tonight," I said, noticing a couple going into one of the restaurants. The woman was much older than the man, maybe his mother. "He's really blind, like can't-see blind. She told him she was forty-five."

"Should be an interesting evening. Did she tell him she was skinny, too?"

"Slender, I believe."

We grinned at each other. Fred has always said Mary Alice has the nerve of a bad tooth.

"She was hoping she wouldn't forget and say something about World War Two."

Fred laughed at this. "That's not her biggest problem."

"True."

We left Five Points, passed University Hospital, and entered what I call "old" downtown. Malls and suburbs have done a number on it, but recently some of the buildings have been converted into loft apartments and condos, and businesses are moving back to serve the new residents.

John's Restaurant has been a mainstay of

downtown for over fifty years, constantly doing a brisk business. People come in from the suburbs for its good seafood at reasonable prices. Tonight was no exception, and we had to wait a few minutes for a table. As soon as we were seated, slaw and hot cornsticks were placed before us.

Fred slathered butter on a cornstick and practically inhaled it.

"Chew," I cautioned him.

He chewed and managed to ask at the same time if there had been any messages from Haley today.

"Debbie got an e-mail. She printed it and said she'd bring it over tomorrow."

"Anything special?"

"She's happy." She was also thousands of miles across the Atlantic Ocean in Poland with her new husband, Dr. Philip Nachman, who was teaching a seminar at the University of Warsaw. She'd only been gone a few weeks and there was a huge empty space in Birmingham, Alabama.

It was time to change the subject. I told Fred about the investment club Mitzi was helping to organize.

"Computers," he said, leaning forward and reminding me of the man in *The Graduate* who told Dustin Hoffman, "plastics." "You can't go wrong with computers. We need to buy one ourselves."

I couldn't agree more. E-mail. I needed my own e-mail.

"We should have bought a bunch of Intel when it first came on the market," he continued. "I don't know why on earth I thought it was some kind of fly-by-night operation."

Fortunately, the snapper and baked potatoes were put in front of us at this point. I've heard the Intel bemoaning before. Many times. Fred owns a small metal fabricating plant, and a customer of his in Atlanta had recommended Intel stock. Fred had considered it too risky.

The food was delicious. Conversation came to a screeching halt while we enjoyed it. I finally sighed with contentment and pushed my plate away.

"Good thing you're anorexic," Fred said. "You left the bones."

He was referring to the fact that Mary Alice is always claiming I have an eating disorder. I'll eat one sandwich and she'll eat three and swear I'm anorexic.

I smiled at him. "That was delicious. Thank you, sir."

"Anytime."

"You know what? Mitzi told me today that Arthur's become a vegetarian. Vegetables are great, but I'd hate to give up a meal like this."

"Arthur a vegetarian?" Fred's left eyebrow shot up. It's a talent I've always coveted. I can wiggle my ears, but somehow it doesn't convey the sense of sophistication of a raised eyebrow. To tell the truth, ear wiggling just looks stupid, even if I can do one ear at a time. Only grandchildren appreciate it."

"Why?" I asked. "What's wrong with being a vegetarian?"

"He was at Shakey's Barbecue today at lunch scarfing down a plate of barbecue big enough to kill a horse."

"Arthur was?"

"Yes, indeedy. Arthur Phizer and a very attractive young woman. At one point, unless I was having a sudden slight stroke, I saw her slip a sliver of dill pickle into his mouth."

"Slip a sliver?" All this sibilance was confusing.

"Slip slowly. Fingers definitely involved." Fred motioned for the waitress, ordered each of us a slice of key lime pie, and then turned back to me. "Unless I was having a sudden slight stroke."

"Shut up," I warned. I thought about what he had said for a moment. "Maybe it was Barbara or Bridget. Bridget's blonde now."

"Nope. This woman was redheaded. Very attractive."

"You said that."

"Worth repeating."

"You're sure it was Arthur?"

"With a silly grin on his face. Or maybe it was a grimace from the dill pickle."

I frowned at him. "This isn't funny. Mitzi wasn't acting right today when she was over at the house. Surely Arthur isn't mixed up with another woman."

Fred shrugged.

The waitress placed our pie before us. As Fred reached for his fork, I grabbed his hand.

"You do understand that if there is ever a hint of you looking sideways at another woman, your voice will be so high you'll be eligible for the Vienna Boys' Choir."

"Lordy! Cutting off your own nose to spite your face."

"I'll find a good plastic surgeon."

Fred grinned. "Eat your pie. Your nose is safe."

I knew it was. Forty years of marriage and I was absolutely sure that Fred had been faithful to me. He might have lusted in his heart like Jimmy Carter but, like Jimmy, that was as far as it had gone.

I squeezed his hand, let go, and ate my pie. For the millionth time, though, I thought about how different men and women are. If I'd been the one to see Arthur with a silly smile on his face being slipped a slice of dill pickle by a good-looking red-head, it would have been the first thing I would have told Fred when he came in. After all, Mitzi and Arthur are our dear friends. Instead, he hadn't even thought of it until I mentioned Arthur's name. For some reason, and I haven't quite figured out why, I think this is why there are so few women politicians.

We finished our pie, had a cup of decaf, and declared ourselves stuffed to the gills.

"Don't worry about Arthur, honey," Fred said as we walked to the car. "If you were going to have a rendezvous with someone, you wouldn't take her to Shakey's where everybody in the world would see you."

There was some sense in that, but I couldn't erase the picture of Mitzi sitting by her daylilies, staring into space.

"You got a Tum?"

I reached in my purse and handed him a couple. One wasn't enough to do battle with five cornsticks.

The September evening was still warm as

we drove back over the mountain past Vulcan. I wondered how Mary Alice's date was working out. I thought about how happy Haley had looked when she and Philip had said their vows. And when we turned into our street and our lights flashed across Mitzi and Arthur walking down the sidewalk, obviously out for an evening stroll, I didn't even mind Fred saying, "See. I told you. Everything's fine."

A couple of nights later when Mitzi woke us up beating on our door and screaming, I remembered how easy it had been to believe Fred's words. They were what I had wanted to hear.

Four

"It's me!" Mary Alice called the next morning as she came into the kitchen. I was in the bedroom changing the sheets, and she paused long enough to pour herself a cup of coffee before she came down the hall. "You need a cleaning service," she said, standing in the doorway. "You could use some new sheets, too. A hundred percent cotton. I swear, Mouse, you can see right through those things you're putting on the bed."

"Don't you buy me any hundred percent cotton sheets." It may have sounded ungrateful, but my days for ironing sheets are long gone. Blends suit me just fine. I pulled the sheets around the corner of the mattress. Not a wrinkle anywhere. "And I don't need a cleaning service, either. Not with just Fred and me."

"Tiffany is mighty nice."

"She's a doll. But I don't need any help."

Tiffany came to Mary Alice from the Magic Maids. It was supposed to be a one-day cleaning deal, but Tiffany is taking on more and more of the chores at Mary Alice's house. A cute young blonde, she looks as if her hands have never touched a mop. But they have. Tiffany is as hard-working as she is pretty. And, according to Sister, she's a whiz at finding lost library books, a talent everyone could use.

I shook a pillow down into its thin blend case and asked how the blind date had gone the night before.

"Pretty good. I didn't talk to Judson about World War Two."

"Just pretty good?" I plumped the pillow and pulled the spread over it.

"I felt a little bad about taking advantage of him. You know. About what I'd told him."

If I could have raised my eyebrow, I would have. "That's a surprise. Let's go in the den," I suggested.

Sister put her coffee on the coffee table and sank onto the sofa; the springs screamed. "There's something wrong with this sofa," she said.

"Just getting old," I lied. "Tell me about your date."

"Well, he picked me up in a cab, and we went to The Club for dinner. Which was nice. But like I said, my conscience was bothering me. Just a little." She stopped for a sip of coffee and sighed. "I just couldn't believe it. My conscience seldom bothers me."

"And?"

"We were eating our salads and I was about to tell him I was fifty-three and pleasingly plump when his girlfriend showed up, wanted to know what the hell he was doing." She hesitated. "I assume it was his girlfriend. Unless it was his wife."

"Really? What did you do?"

"Finished my salad. Then I had leg of lamb."

Sister's answers frequently miss the bull's-eye. You just have to help her aim again.

"I mean about the girlfriend."

Sister looked at me as if I were the one missing the mark. "I didn't do anything about the girlfriend. But Judson went chasing after her." She finished her coffee and put it down. "I swear, Mouse, you'd never have known he couldn't see. He didn't bump into a thing."

"And he never came back?"

"Nope. Sent a waiter with his apologies."

"Well, that's terrible."

"No. It worked out fine. A real nice man at the next table asked if he could join me. He's English. Visiting his daughter. And guess what, Mouse. He was at Dunkirk during the war." Sister leaned back and smiled. "We had a wonderful evening. I'm seeing him again tonight."

I had to smile back. I swear this woman could swim a mile in Village Creek and come out smelling like a rose.

"She was ugly as sin, too," she giggled.

"Who was?"

"The girlfriend. Little beady eyes."

We were both laughing when the phone rang.

"I saw Mary Alice's car over there," Mitzi said when I answered, "and I just talked to Connie and she said they want to have the first investment club meeting Wednesday morning at the Homewood Library. Does that suit y'all?"

I turned to Mary Alice. "Wednesday morning for the investment club?"

"Sure."

"Sure," I said into the phone.

"Good. Connie said to tell you there's room for a couple of more people if there's somebody else you think might be interested. I'll call you back and tell you for sure if it's Wednesday and what time."

"Mouse, ask Mitzi if she wants to have lunch with us," Sister said.

I relayed the message.

"Thanks, but I've got a lot to do today.

I'll talk to you later."

I hung up the phone. "We're having lunch?"

"You need to get out more often. There's a lot more to life than cleaning house."

I couldn't argue with that. "Let me grab a shower," I said. "How about Chinese?"

"I'll call Bonnie Blue and see if she wants to go. I need to look for a new outfit, anyway."

Bonnie Blue Butler is the manager of the Big, Bold, and Beautiful Shoppe. She came into our lives when Sister made the mistake of buying the Skoot 'n' Boot, a country-western night spot out Highway 78 where Bonnie Blue was working.

"Good, clean fun," Sister had said. "Line dancing, sweet country music, good company."

The band's name was The Swamp Creatures which should have clued her in on how sweet the country music was going to be. But she and her then boyfriend, Bill Adams, were into line dancing, the place was for sale, and she's got more money than she has sense. What she bought was a passel of trouble.

We met Bonnie Blue, though, and she is a delight. She's as large as Sister with skin like smooth milk chocolate. I love to see the two of them together because they have many of the same mannerisms. I remember the first time I saw Bonnie Blue I thought it was like seeing Sister's negative.

Except there's nothing negative about Bonnie Blue.

"Girl," she said to Mary Alice an hour later when we walked into the Big, Bold, and Beautiful, "I don't know why in the world you come in here. You ought to go to New York and buy you some of those Versaces." She hugged the two of us. "I mean it."

I watch *Style* on CNN. There's a whole lot more to wearing a Versace than being able to pay for it. Let's face it. My sister is not a runway model.

"Put the shovel down, Bonnie Blue," Mary Alice said. "I think I'd like a nice pants suit. Something I can just throw on."

"And off." I thought it was funny, but the other two simply looked at me.

"Well, you said you're going out with a nice Englishman named Cedric tonight."

Mary Alice gave me what I swear was my own schoolteacher look. "And Englishmen are noted for their reticence, Patricia Anne."

"But you're not." Bonnie Blue put her arm around Sister's shoulder. "You come on back here. I think I've got just the thing you want. Got it in today. Little gold braids on it like medals."

They went toward the back of the store giggling. I resisted the urge to stick out my tongue and sat down with a magazine. I can't resist magazines that have tests in them, and this one was a good one — Are You Ready For Marriage? I got a pencil from my purse and passed the test with flying colors. The only question that threw me was "Are you turned on by his/her intimate wear?" I couldn't say that Fred's striped boxers that come in packages of three from Sears really turn me on. Particularly from behind where there's that triangular gusset that Fred calls the ballroom. I did okay on the rest of the questions, though. I was definitely ready for marriage.

"You like this?" Mary Alice had on a navy pants suit trimmed with wide gold braid around the lapels and across the shoulders.

"You look like an escapee from *H.M.S. Pinafore*."

"I do not." She walked over to a full-length mirror and studied herself from several angles. "I kind of like it."

"I do, too." Bonnie Blue had walked up.

Sister turned, trying to get the rear view. "Patricia Anne said I looked like I'd jumped ship."

Bonnie Blue turned to me. "You taking your estrogen?"

"Yes, I'm taking my estrogen. I just think all that gold braid is a bit much."

"You couldn't get away with it because you're too little," Bonnie Blue said. "But God blessed Mary Alice with the size to wear things that make a statement."

The pants suit was paid for and in a hang-up bag before I could think of an answer. Given all the women in Birmingham that God has similarly blessed, I realized Bonnie Blue was not going to be a store manager for long. She's heading for bigger things.

"Going to lunch," she called to someone in the back, probably Katrinka, her assistant, who is a wisp of a girl. "Want me to bring you something?"

"No thanks. I brought some yogurt."

"That girl doesn't eat enough to keep a bird alive," Bonnie Blue whispered.

We walked down the street to the Hunan Hut which had at one time been a Pizza Hut. It's hard to make a Pizza Hut look oriental, and the new owners were smart enough not to do much to change the decor. They had hung a couple of stylized prints of big waves and long-legged birds on one of the walls, and painted the salad bar gold and red, a jaunty effect.

People were crowded around the salad bar where the luncheon buffet was served. We staked out a table, ordered iced tea, and joined them.

"Get a lot of rice," Sister cautioned. "Some of this stuff will take the hair off your tongue."

I played it safe and started with a bowl of egg drop soup. I took it back to the table and started eating. Might as well. It would be cold by the time the other two finished heaping their plates.

"Arthur Phizer's over yonder in the corner booth," Mary Alice said as she put her plate down and pulled out her chair.

"By himself?" I looked toward the booth but could see nothing but the top of a bald head.

"With some woman."

"Redheaded?"

"Grayheaded. That streaked yellow gray they put bluing on. Lord, that looks good, Bonnie Blue." This last remark was accompanied by the pointing of a fork toward Bonnie Blue's loaded plate. "What's that stuff with the peanuts? I didn't see that."

"Don't know, but it looks good." Bonnie Blue settled down for some serious eating.

"I'll bring you some, Sister," I offered.

I sashayed back to the buffet table, getting

a good look at Arthur and the lady who appeared to be in her sixties and who did, indeed, have the kind of gray hair that has yellow streaks in it. She and Arthur were deep in conversation.

I found the peanut stuff that Mary Alice wanted, put some on a salad plate and helped my own plate to a little bit of everything with a big mound of rice in the middle. By this time, I noticed, Arthur was holding the woman's hand. Not just holding it, stroking it.

Trusting that Mitzi would have done the same thing if she had seen Fred stroking some woman's hand, I headed for their booth. Arthur stood up when he saw me, not an easy trick in a booth. Actually he was sort of hunched.

"Patricia Anne," he said, not flustered at all. "I'd like for you to meet my friend, Sophie Sawyer. Sophie, this is my nextdoor neighbor, Patricia Anne Hollowell." He sat back down, figuring, I suppose, that he had given politeness its due.

Sophie Sawyer smiled, a lovely smile. "Patricia Anne."

"Hello, Sophie. It's nice meeting you."

"Sophie has just come back to Birmingham," Arthur volunteered.

"I've lived in Chicago for thirty years. Birmingham's home, though." Sophie Sawyer eyed the plate I had fixed for Sister. "Watch that peanut stuff. It's a killer. You should have seen Arthur's eyes watering."

"It's for my sister, but thanks, I'll tell her."

Sophie was a very pretty woman, I realized, with wide-set brown eyes and high cheekbones. She must have been a dramatically beautiful young woman.

I said my goodbyes and headed back to Bonnie Blue and Mary Alice.

"Who is she?" Sister wanted to know. "And did you bring me some of that peanut stuff?"

"Here." I handed her the plate. "And she's a friend of Arthur's. That's all he said. 'My friend, Sophie Sawyer.' "

Sister took a bite of the peanuts and reached for some water. "Whoo."

"I told you." Bonnie Blue pointed toward some Parker House rolls that the waitress had placed on our table along with our iced tea. Like most Chinese restaurants in Birmingham, the Hunan House is eclectic. "Bite into one of them."

"Whoo," Sister said again.

I decided I'd stick to rice.

"He's holding her hand," I said.

Sister nodded toward Arthur's booth. I

assumed she was asking.

"Yes. And yesterday he was having lunch with a redhead at Shakey's. Fred saw him. Said Arthur was being very chummy with her, too."

"Chummy's about all you can get at Shakey's and the Hunan Hut." Bonnie Blue speared a dark brown morsel and held it up. "Reckon this is a mushroom?"

I had no idea. "Yes," I said.

"Bonnie Blue's right." Sister had recovered her voice though it sounded raspy. "You can't get too much hanky panky going in a barbecue place and a Chinese restaurant."

"Best hanky-panky I ever got was at Dreamland Barbecue."

Mary Alice and I both looked at Bonnie Blue, but she didn't elaborate, just smiled and popped the mushroom or whatever it was into her mouth.

Arthur and Sophie Sawyer got up, walked toward the door, and waved to us.

"She's very pretty," I said. "I can't believe Arthur's messing around, though. I mean, surely not."

Mary Alice and Bonnie Blue smiled at each other.

"This child needs to get out of the house more," Bonnie Blue said.

"Don't be so cynical." I watched Arthur and Sophie as they slowly crossed the parking lot. He had his hand under her elbow. Supporting her, I realized.

"That lady with Arthur's having trouble walking," I added.

Bonnie Blue and Mary Alice turned to look.

"Hmmm," Bonnie Blue said. "Maybe she's got osteoporosis. Broke her hip."

"Could be," Mary Alice agreed. "That's what's going to happen to Patricia Anne. We were at the movie the other day waiting in line and I noticed she's already getting one of those dowager humps." She curved her shoulders. "Like this."

"I was trying to sneak your popcorn in."

"Well, I couldn't take the popcorn and the Cokes both."

"It's tacky sneaking food into a movie."

"Well, folks wouldn't do it if they didn't charge an arm and a leg."

"It's not like you couldn't afford it."

"Y'all look." Bonnie Blue brought us back to the subject, Arthur and his lady friend. "She's having trouble getting in the car."

Arthur helped Sophie Sawyer sit sideways on the seat, then picked up her legs and placed them in the car.

"I hope he's not selling her any life

insurance," Sister said.

I don't know why, maybe it was the gentleness of the way Arthur was helping Sophie, but I had a sudden memory of a weekend camping trip that the four of us, Arthur, Mitzi, Fred, and I, and our five children had taken years before. The children were still small, and we had rented two pop-up camper trailers, packed practically everything we owned in and on them, including the kids' bicycles, and gone to Wind Creek. It was summer, but after supper we built a fire to toast marshmallows.

The children, worn out from a day of swimming and playing, didn't complain when we washed the stickiness from them and put them to bed in the campers. The four of us sat by the fire talking, tired and happy. A slight breeze came up, and the smoke kept following us.

"Let's go swimming before we go to bed," Mitzi said. "Wash off this smoke."

And, daringly, we stripped to our underwear and walked into the warm water of the lake, our young bodies firm and beautiful.

Sister poked me. "She's having one of her fugues," she explained to Bonnie Blue. "Does it all the time."

"Must have been a good one, the way she's smiling."

"It was." I could still smell the campfire.

Sister pushed her chair back. "I'm going to get us all some bread pudding."

Bread pudding is one of the specialties of the Hunan Hut, moist, with just the right amount of raisins, and a lemon sauce on the side. Southern Chinese, I suppose. And delicious.

"Tell Bonnie Blue about the investment club while I'm gone. Both of you want lemon sauce?"

Bonnie Blue and I nodded yes.

"What investment club?" she asked.

I told her what Mitzi had told me.

"Joy McWain?" she asked. "The cheerleader with the big thighs in the commercial?"

Where on God's earth had I been? I admitted that I had never seen the commercial.

"Those red satin underpants would put your eyes out," Bonnie Blue said. "It was something."

It must have been.

"Here you go." Mary Alice set bowls of bread pudding before each of us and sat down. "What do you think, Bonnie Blue?"

"It looks great."

"I mean about the investment club."

"It sounds like something I need to get into. I don't have any more sense than

Daddy does about money. Somebody comes in, says, 'Abe, I'll give you ten dollars for that picture you're working on,' he grabs the money and growls. Buries it in the backyard in a Mason jar."

Bonnie Blue's father, Abe Butler, is one of Alabama's foremost folk artists. If he was really doing this, and Bonnie Blue seemed serious, his backyard would be loaded.

"That could be dangerous," I said.

"Nah. He's got him a great big Rottweiler out there. Calls her Sugar Pie." Bonnie Blue took a bite of her bread pudding. "Umm. This is good."

"Maybe you ought to unearth a couple of jars and invest it for him," Sister suggested. "It's not drawing interest out there in the yard."

"Sister!" The woman has the morals of an alley cat.

"What? It's going to be hers one day anyway."

Bonnie Blue took a sip of tea and looked at her glass thoughtfully. "You remember *Jaws*?"

We nodded.

"Remember Jaws's teeth?" She paused while we remembered the teeth closing on the boat with Richard Dreyfuss in it. The look on his face.

"Now think Sugar Pie."

We got the picture.

"Like I said, it sounds like something I need, though. When's it meeting?"

"Wednesday morning at the Homewood Library."

"Now y'all give me a break. You know I've got to work."

"You could take off for a little while," Mary Alice said.

Bonnie Blue pointed a fork at her. "No way. I get commissions."

Our table was near the front door. When it burst open and a man rushed in yelling for someone to call 911, we jumped a mile.

The restaurant was instantly quiet.

"911! I need some help!" With that, he turned and ran out.

It took only a second for the shock to wear off and for me to realize it was Arthur.

"Call 911!" I was out of the door, running behind him across the parking lot toward his car. The passenger door was open and I could see Sophie Sawyer lying across the front seat.

He tried to crawl across her, tried to lift her.

"Wait," I yelled. I ran around and opened the driver's door. As it opened, Sophie convulsed, her back arching high.

By this time, several people from the Hunan Hut, including Mary Alice, had come up.

"I'm a doctor," a man in white tennis shorts said. I moved away from the door and he took my place. Someone had called 911; we could already hear the sirens.

"What's wrong with her?" Mary Alice asked me.

"Something bad."

Something terrible. By the time the paramedics got there, Sophie was no longer convulsing or breathing. But her body was still contorted.

"Do, Jesus," Bonnie Blue said watching the ambulance drive off carrying Sophie's body and Arthur who still clutched her hand. "I hope it wasn't the peanut stuff."

"Heart," the doctor in white tennis shorts said, tapping his chest.

There was a collective sigh of relief from the lunch crowd.

"Should we follow them?" I asked Sister. "Take Arthur's car home?" I had the shakes. Sudden death tends to do that to me.

"We'd better leave it here. I don't know of anything we can do."

"Lord, lord," Bonnie Blue said.

We walked back to the Big, Bold, and Beautiful Shoppe in silence, each lost in her own thoughts.

"Call me tomorrow and let me know how Cedric turns out," Bonnie Blue said, handing over the plastic hang-up bag.

"Did I tell you he's got a little mustache?" Sister asked. "One of those little pencil-thin ones."

Bonnie Blue grinned. "You go, girl."

Which we did.

The day was September warm, but I was cold. I wasn't ready to go home, to think about Sophie Sawyer dying as I watched. I suggested to Mary Alice that we run by both our houses, get our tennis shoes and go to Overton Park.

She frowned. "For what?"

"Just to walk some. Maybe play a little tennis. Nothing strenuous. We could just bat the ball back and forth."

Mary Alice looked at me as if I had lost my mind. "You want to play tennis?"

"Sure. I need to move around some. I've got the shakes."

"I don't do tennis. People who do tennis have heart attacks and die like that woman Arthur was with."

"They do not."

"Bucky Jasper did. Ran up to hit the ball and just quit running. Fortunately he fell into the net."

“Who’s Bucky Jasper?”

“You mean who *was* Bucky Jasper. This man who lived down the street from me. I went to Savages and got the family a cheesecake.” Mary Alice turned on her left turn signal for my strcct. “Thc ncighborhood sent flowers. A big wreath of gladiolas and Gerbera daisies.”

“That was nice.”

“Actually, it was kind of tacky. Shaped like a heart.” She pulled into my driveway. “He’d still be around if he’d been doing aqua aerobics instead of tennis. He’d have better knees, too.”

“Bucky had bad knees?”

“How should I know, Mouse? I hardly knew the man.”

“But he shouldn’t have been playing tennis.”

“Obviously. He should have been taking a nap instead.”

She and I grinned at each other. I got out of the car after making her promise that she would call me, too, to report on her date with Cedric.

“Just don’t let him get in your hot tub,” I cautioned. “You nearly lost Buddy Johnson that way last spring.”

“But Buddy’s old.” She gave a wave and put the car in reverse.

And Cedric had been at Dunkirk.

She started to back out of the driveway, let down her window and called, "I forgot to give you this. Debbie sent it."

It was the e-mail from Haley.

"She's doing fine," Sister says. "Got roaches. Wants you to send her some of those Combat things. She can't find them in Warsaw."

I simply had to get my own computer.

Five

"I'm telling you, I've still got the shakes. I came home and sat in the sun for about an hour just to warm up. I went over to Mitzi's but she wasn't home. Not that I know what I would have said to her. They've got real problems, Fred."

Fred and I were sitting in the den. We'd had the Stouffer's we hadn't eaten the night before and watched *Wheel of Fortune*. He'd read Haley's letter (which contained a lot more than the information that there were roaches in Warsaw), and had heard all the details of Sophie Sawyer's death.

"I'm sure she was just one of Arthur's insurance clients, honey," he said.

I shook my head. "Arthur was stroking her hand like this." I brushed the fingers of my right hand across my left to demonstrate.

Fred said, "Rich client."

I said, "I don't think so. You should have seen the way he helped her to the car like she was a piece of precious glass. He was hovering."

Fred said, "She probably told him she was

having chest pains. Where's the TV zapper? It's time for the ballgame."

He could have at least *acted* interested.

After the ten o'clock news, I got him up from the sofa where he was snoring, and we went to bed. Sometime during the night, I woke up and went to the bathroom. The lights were on over at Mitzi and Arthur's. I wondered sleepily what was going on, and felt bad that I hadn't called to see about them. I'd check in the morning, I told myself.

But in the morning, I put off calling. There had been such an air of intimacy between Arthur and the woman, I wasn't sure what was going on between the two. Regardless of what Fred said, Arthur was not just selling her insurance.

I fixed coffee, microwaved some oatmeal, and handed Fred a can of Healthy Request chicken noodle soup for his lunch as he went out the door. Wifely duties done, I settled down with my second cup of coffee and the *Birmingham News*.

I usually glance over the front page, read "People are Talking" on the second, and then turn to the Metro section. Which is what I did this morning. I was reading about a local judge who claimed he couldn't help it if he kept dozing off in court because of narcolepsy when Mitzi knocked on the back door.

"Have you seen it?" She pointed to the paper in my hand when I opened the door.

"Seen what?" I was so startled at her appearance, it took me a moment to answer. Mitzi looked rough. She had on a pink chenille bathrobe which had seen better days and she was barefooted. No comb had touched her hair. It was totally un-Mitzi-like. I might run across the yards looking like this, but not Mitzi. She's the neatest person in the world.

"About the death."

"What death?" I don't know why I asked. I knew, of course. I moved aside and she came into the kitchen.

"Sophie Sawyer's poisoning."

Mitzi walked to the kitchen table and sat down as if her legs wouldn't hold her up anymore.

"Sophie Sawyer was poisoned?"

"Arthur said you were there yesterday."

"I was." I sat down across from Mitzi, my heart thumping faster. "She was poisoned?"

"Second page. Crime reports." Mitzi propped her elbows on the table, leaned forward and put a hand over each ear as if she didn't want to hear my reaction.

I turned to the second page. The first

crime report, one short paragraph, had the words — SUSPECTED POISONING DEATH — as its heading. Sophie Vaughn Sawyer, 64, had been pronounced dead the day before after being rushed to University Hospital from a nearby restaurant. Preliminary autopsy reports indicated that she was the victim of poisoning. Police were investigating.

Goosebumps skittered up my arms and across my shoulders. Sophie Sawyer murdered? Someone had killed the lovely woman I had seen at lunch the day before? I read the paragraph again. Since it was so brief, the news of the death must have barely made the paper's deadline.

"God, Mitzi, I can't believe this. It's awful. Who was she? One of Arthur's clients?"

Mitzi's head bent to the table. Her hands slid around and clasped behind her neck.

"His first wife."

"His what?" Surely I hadn't heard right. Her voice was muffled against the table.

But she looked up and repeated, "His first wife."

The words were clear, but they didn't make sense. Arthur's first wife? Arthur and Mitzi had been married forty years. Fred and I had lived next door to them for much of that time, and no one had ever mentioned a first wife.

So I said something incredibly stupid. I said, "Are you sure?"

Mitzi smiled, not much of a smile, but her lips went up at the corners.

"I'm sure. They were high school sweethearts, and the day after they graduated they ran off to Bremen, Georgia, and got married."

"But why haven't you ever mentioned it?"

"They never even lived together, Patricia Anne. Their parents had fits when they found out. Arthur's folks thought he was too young and wouldn't go on to college like they had planned, and Sophie's folks were the Vaughn Foundry family. I'm sure they thought Sophie had married way down the social scale." Mitzi looked around. "Where's the Kleenex?"

I handed her a paper napkin.

"So what happened?"

She wiped her eyes. "So they had it annulled. Arthur went to the university and met me, and Sophie married a man from Chicago." She paused. "They really were too young."

"Of course they were," I agreed, still in shock.

"So it was just something we didn't talk

about. You know?"

The phone's ring made me jump. I got up and answered it. It was, of course, Mary Alice.

"His mustache is not the only thing pencil thin," she chortled.

"I'll have to call you back." I hung up.

Mitzi looked up. "Mary Alice?"

"Just wanting to tell me about her date last night."

I picked up the coffee pot, surprised to find my hands shaking. I poured us each a cup of coffee and sat back down. "Is that why you've looked worried the last few days? Because Sophie's been back in town?"

Mitzi seemed surprised. "Have I looked worried?"

"Worried to death."

"No. Sophie's never been a problem for me. Truthfully. That was over a long time before Arthur and I got married. I guess if I've looked worried, it's because Bridget and Hank are thinking about moving to Atlanta. I just can't bear the thought of not seeing Andrew Cade every day."

Every day? The thought zipped through my mind that this might be the reason for the move. But I dismissed it. Mitzi would never be an interfering mother-in-law.

"Anyway," Mitzi put a teaspoonful of

sugar into her coffee and stirred it around and around, staring into the cup, "the phone rang about midnight last night. It was Arabella, Sophie's daughter, saying the police thought Sophie was murdered." She looked up with tears in her eyes. "It's awful, Patricia Anne. I've never seen Arthur so upset. When he came in from the hospital, he was crying like a baby, and Arthur doesn't cry. You know that." She shivered, took the spoon from the coffee and laid it carefully in the saucer. "God, my teeth are chattering."

What could I say? I nodded, remembering the gentleness of the hand-stroking and the helping into the car. Maybe first loves really do stay with us.

"He went over there, to Sophie's apartment, when Arabella called. Bless his heart, he felt like he had to. But there wasn't a thing he could do. Arabella and Sue were there."

"Sue?"

"Sue Batson, Sophie's other daughter. I think she's the reason Sophie came back to Birmingham. She was in real bad shape, you know."

"Sue?" Some pronouns needed clarifying here.

"Sophie, Patricia Anne. She was diabetic

and was having all kinds of circulatory and eye problems. And Sue's husband is a doctor."

"Lord, Mitzi. I'm so sorry."

"And facing it so bravely, Arthur said." Mitzi held the paper napkin to her eyes. "I guess that's the only blessing in this whole thing. She won't have any suffering to go through."

"Not much of a blessing."

Mitzi shook her head no.

"Do they have any idea what happened? The doctor at the Hunan Hut said it was her heart."

Mitzi shook her head no again. "They haven't come up with a final report, just that they think it was poison."

I thought of Sophie lying across the seat of Arthur's car, the convulsions wracking her. Poison? I felt cold again.

Woofer came out of his doghouse and ambled over to the oak tree that he has left a white line around over the years. He marked his territory again, stretched, and lay down in the sun.

But Mitzi wasn't going to let me escape. She took several sips of coffee and continued.

"I said, 'Lord, Arthur, maybe it was something she was deathly allergic to, especially with her diabetes.' "

I nodded. "Arthur was eating some peanut stuff. A lot of people are allergic to peanuts, just being around them. And there's all kinds of stuff like monosodium glutamate in Chinese restaurants."

"He said no. It was some kind of poison." Mitzi put her cup down. "And you know what was ironic? Sophie had told her girls that if anything happened to her, they were to call Arthur, and he was the one who had to call them."

"Sounds like she was scared something was going to happen."

Mitzi shrugged. "She knew she was sick."

"True."

"But he said that last night he felt like he was just in the way. There wasn't anything he could do for Arabella and Sue. Maybe comfort them a little. Sue and her husband live down in Pelham. She pretty much fell apart."

"That's understandable." I looked at the newspaper again. One tiny paragraph stating the fact that a woman had died a violent death. Somehow there should be more. There were sixty-four years here of loving, and child-bearing, of work and fun, and, yes, suffering.

The phone rang again. I ignored it. The

answering machine would pick it up.

"Mary Alice again, you think?" Mitzi asked.

"Probably. Let me pour you some more coffee."

"No, but thanks. I have to go. I need to go get myself cleaned up. Get myself pulled together." Mitzi pushed her chair back. The phone quit ringing; the machine picked up.

I followed her to the door. "Where's Arthur this morning? Is he at home?"

"He's gone to the office. He said he had some work he had to do. I don't think he'll stay long, though. He's too upset, and neither one of us got a wink of sleep last night." Mitzi turned and hugged me. "Thanks for listening."

"Anytime. Call me if you need me to do anything. And, listen. Don't worry about Bridget moving to Atlanta. It's just a couple of hours drive."

"Two hours too far."

I watched her go over and pat Woofer before she opened the gate and went into her own yard. Amazing. I had lived next to Mitzi and Arthur for almost forty years and thought I knew the basic facts of their lives. Well, scratch that belief.

The phone rang again. I almost didn't answer it because I needed time to sit down and digest what Mitzi had told me. But, figuring it was Mary Alice and that she would call every five minutes, I picked it up and said hello.

"Aunt Pat?" Debbie whispered.

"What's the matter? Why are you whispering?"

"Because Lisa's in the bathroom."

"Lisa who?"

"Lisa, your daughter-in-law Lisa."

"Lisa? What's she doing here?"

"She's left Alan."

Granted, my nerves were already shot from Mitzi's visit. Now, with this news, I was so shocked, I couldn't think of anything to say. Alan is our middle child and he and Lisa were married the week they graduated from college. They have two sons, Charlie and Sam, and a nice house in the suburbs of Atlanta. They are our good yuppie children who are leading the great American middle-class life.

"Aunt Pat? You okay?"

"She's at your house right now?"

"In the bathroom. She's real upset. She may be throwing up."

"What happened?"

"I don't know. Do you think you could come over here, though? Just act like you're dropping in?"

While I was trying to absorb this information, Debbie whispered, "Gotta go," and the phone went dead.

And there I was on the horns of a mother-in-law dilemma. If Lisa had wanted me to know about their separation, she could have come to my house. Instead, she had gone to Debbie's. On the other hand, what in the world was she doing in Birmingham, anyway? Just a few weeks earlier, she and Alan had been at Haley's wedding and had seemed lovey-dovey. Maybe too lovey-dovey?

I didn't balance on the horns long. Resisting the urge to crawl back in the bed and pull the cover over my head, I brushed my teeth, combed my hair, checked on Woofer who was enjoying rolling over and scratching his back in the grass, and was off to Debbie's in all of five minutes.

Debbie answered the door with a bright and loud, "Why, Aunt Pat, what a surprise. Come in. You're not going to guess who's here."

This child will never be standing with an outstretched hand saying "You like me! You like me!" on Oscar night. Sally Field is perfectly safe.

My performance wasn't any better.

"Oh?" I said, just as brightly. "Who?"

"Lisa. She just came in from Atlanta."

"Lisa? Why how wonderful."

I walked past Debbie into the living room where my daughter-in-law was sitting on the sofa. Sitting isn't the right word. More like crouched into the corner.

"Well, this is a surprise, honey. How are you?"

Stupid question. She looked like hell. Her eyes were almost swollen shut from crying, and her hair, usually a smooth, shiny reddish brown, was white and standing up in spikes.

I'd heard of this, someone's hair turning white overnight because of a trauma. It had happened to the father in *Twin Peaks*, still one of my favorite TV shows. But this was my first time to witness it.

"I'm fine," she said, reaching over to the coffee table for another Kleenex and blowing her nose. "I've left Alan."

"I'll get us some tea," Debbie said in her fake cheerful voice.

"You have any Tums?" I asked.

"Always." Debbie disappeared into the kitchen, and I turned to look at Lisa.

"Is Alan okay?"

"I reckon."

"You want to talk about it?"

"No." Then the polite Southern child. "No, ma'am."

I sat in a chair facing the sofa. “What about the boys? How are they?”

“They’re fine. They’re in school.”

“What about when they get out of school?”

“They’ve got keys.” A reach for another Kleenex.

Un huh. I digested this news for a moment. Charlie and Sam were borderline, as far as I was concerned, for being left totally unsupervised.

“I left them a note,” Lisa volunteered.

Great. The kids would come home from school and find a note saying their mother had left their father. And them.

“What about Alan? Does he know you’ve left?”

Lisa sighed and burrowed deeper into the sofa corner. “He will when he gets home. Whenever that is.”

“But you don’t want to talk about it?”

“No, ma’am.”

“Excuse me a minute, Lisa.” I got up and went into the kitchen where Debbie was pouring tea into three glasses.

“Did she say anything?” she asked.

“Just that she left the boys a note saying she’d gone and that Alan would find out whenever he got home.”

“Whenever?” Debbie raised an eyebrow.

I shrugged. "I can't imagine what's going on. I don't know whether I should call Alan or not. He really needs to know where she is." I looked at my watch. "She must have barreled over here."

"You want me to call him? I don't care if he thinks I'm butting in."

"Would you?" I handed the job over to Debbie without a moment's hesitation. Fred's mother, the only woman in the world who could put the fear of God into Mary Alice, had taught me the hard way to stay out of my children's marital problems. "You have the number?"

She pointed to a bulletin board and handed me a bottle of Tums.

I took a couple and chewed them gratefully. "Find out what's going on if you can. Just ask him."

"I will."

I rubbed my forehead. "This is turning out to be the day from hell. Mitzi Phizer's just been over to the house telling me about Arthur's first wife getting murdered."

"My Lord, Aunt Pat. Whose first wife?"

"Arthur Phizer next door's, Debbie. It seems that he was married when he was a teenager to a woman named Sophie Vaughn. The police think she was poisoned yesterday. In fact, your mama and I were there when she died. Right outside the Hunan Hut."

"What, Aunt Pat? I'm confused."

"So am I. I'll explain it later. Where are the twins?"

"At the park with Richardena."

"Every mother should have a Richardena."

"I'm blessed."

I picked up two of the glasses and started back into the living room when I realized Debbie probably shouldn't even be at home.

"You working at home this morning?" I asked.

"I have to be in court in an hour."

"Well, don't let this hold you up. I'll try to find out what's going on."

Lisa was scrunched down even farther in the corner of the sofa.

"Here's your tea," I said. "Sit up and drink some of it. It'll make you feel better."

"Alan doesn't love me any more," she sniffled.

"Of course he does."

"No, he doesn't."

I was in no mood to stand there holding cold glasses.

"Well, be that as it may, here's your tea." I put Lisa's glass on the coffee table and sat down. I glanced at my watch. Not quite 10:30. If I hadn't retired from teaching last year, I would be in my AP Modern British Lit class. September. We'd be doing Yeats, the silver apples of the moon, the golden apples of the sun, and the smell of frying chicken would be permeating the building. I wouldn't have met Sophie Sawyer at the Hunan Hut or found out about her murder this morning. I wouldn't be sitting here wondering what was going on with my son and his wife. I'd be insulated in a classroom. Just me and twenty sweet, well-behaved teenagers, all of whom had been cleared by the metal detector at the front door.

I swear I felt tears in my eyes.

Lisa sat up and reached for her glass. It was my first close look at her white spikey hair which I realized immediately was the result of peroxide, not trauma.

"My God! What have you done to your hair?"

It just popped out, and I could have bitten my tongue. But Lisa didn't seem to take offense.

She patted the spikes. "This beautician in Atlanta did it. I'm supposed to look like one of the Spice Girls. I don't know which one."

I didn't either. I'd seen the Spice Girls on Regis and Kathie Lee and didn't remember a Spike Spice.

"Alan hates it. I told him, I said, 'Tough titty, Alan. It's my hair and my head.' "

"And what did Alan say?"

"He said my brains are scrambled." Lisa put the tea back on the table without drinking any. For a moment she stayed hunched over.

"He may be right," she added.

"Of course he's not," I assured her, trying to be a good mother-in-law.

The phone rang and Debbie answered it in the kitchen. I hoped it was Alan calling back, but in a moment she stuck her head into the living room and told me her mama wanted to speak to me.

"Did you get him?" I whispered as I went past her.

"Not yet."

I picked up the phone and said hello.

Sister informed me that she had had a terrible time finding me, that I really needed a pager.

Right. For all the emergencies that come up while I'm at the Piggly Wiggly.

"Listen," I said, "I can't talk now. We're trying to get in touch with Alan."

"For what? What's wrong?"

"Lisa's here. She says she's left him. We're trying to find out what's going on."

"What does Lisa say is going on?"

"She says she doesn't want to talk about it."

"That means she does. Call me back as soon as you can. You've got to hear about Cedric."

I was suddenly exhausted. "Listen," I said. "I don't want to hear about Cedric. I don't want to hear about some Englishman's pencil thin whatever when serious things are happening like people getting poisoned."

"Lisa's poisoned?"

Lord. I hung up the phone, marched back into the living room and told Lisa that she was going home with me, that Debbie had to go to work, and that the nanny would be back in a little while with the girls.

"Okay," she said and stood up. I had expected some argument, but she seemed to be beyond arguing. Which suited me.

The phone rang again.

"If it's your mama, tell her it's Sophie Sawyer who got poisoned, I'm sorry I hung up on her, and I'll talk to her later." I gave Debbie a hug, and ushered Lisa out to the car. So here I was, on a beautiful late summer, early fall day, with Spike Spice for a daughter-in-law, a next-door neighbor whose husband was attracting disasters like fleas, and a loony sixty-four- (really sixty-six) year-old sister who was sleeping with every Tom, Dick, and Cedric. Lord.

Six

When we got home, I suggested to Lisa that she lie down on the guest-room bed for a while.

Again there was no arguing. She asked for a couple of aspirin, took them, and disappeared down the hall. When I checked on her a few minutes later, she was already asleep, curled up like a child, her hand cupping her cheek.

I spread a light blanket over her and saw tears at the corner of her eyes. Lisa has long, dark lashes, and their shadows made the circles under her eyes seem even deeper.

Damn it. Alan had better have some good explanation for this.

I closed the door, went back to the den, and called Debbie.

No, she hadn't gotten Alan, and she was about to leave. She had left word on his voice mail, though, that Lisa was at my house. And her mama had wanted to know who Sophie Sawyer was and she had told her Mr. Phizer's first wife. That was what I had said. Right? Mama hadn't believed it.

I told her it was, and thanks. Then I went

out and sat on the steps to wait for Mary Alice.

But I was wrong. She was a no-show. I finally went in, fixed some tuna fish salad, decided that wasn't what I wanted and ended up with a peanut butter and banana sandwich and a glass of milk which I ate while I watched *Jeopardy!*

Lisa slept.

I called to see if Mitzi was okay and got an immediate pick-up on her answering machine which meant she was on the phone. Busy, probably, helping to make arrangements for Sophie's funeral, something Mitzi would be nice enough to do even though Sophie had had first dibs on Arthur. Maybe, I thought, I ought to carry some food over. After all, it was a death in a neighboring family. Sort of.

I looked in the freezer to see if I had something like a squash casserole that I could take over. Wishful thinking. I did have two packages of Stouffer's spinach souffle, though. I dumped them into a small casserole dish, added a little butter, and stuck them into the microwave. In ten minutes I was headed across the yard with a neighborly offering of hot food. We do live in good times.

But no one was home at the Phizers'. I got

back to my driveway just as Mary Alice pulled in.

"You're late," I said.

"Don't be tacky." She unstuck herself from between the steering wheel and the seat and climbed out. "What's in the casserole?"

"Spinach souffle."

"Stouffer's?"

"I added some butter."

"Remember how gritty spinach used to be? Mama would wash it over and over and it would still be gritty. The only thing that saved it was the sliced hard-boiled egg on top. Lord, I hated spinach. You could pick it up and look under it and there was green grit."

"There was not. Mama washed it better than that."

"There was, too. Green grit. Made funny noises on your teeth and we thought we had to eat it because it made Popeye strong. He always ate the canned, though."

"The canned's bitter."

"Put a little sugar in it. In fact, Henry says the secret to all good cooking is a little sugar."

"Really?" I was in awe of Mary Alice's new son-in-law's culinary skills. Sugar. How about that.

The spinach conversation had gotten us to the back door.

"Okay," Mary Alice said, holding it open for me, "Who's dead and who's getting divorced? I think Debbie was a little confused."

I set the casserole on the stove. "Nobody's getting divorced. The dead person is the same lady we saw yesterday with Arthur Phizer. She was murdered."

"That's what Debbie said, but I can't believe it. What happened?" Sister sat down at the kitchen table and pulled off her shoes. "Lord," she said, reaching down and squeezing her foot. "These shoes are at least a size and a half too small. Cuts off the circulation. But it was the only pair they had in this style."

"Somebody poisoned her is what happened. Mitzi came over this morning and said she and Arthur were up all night. It seems this lady who was killed was Arthur's first wife and he's very upset." I thought about this for a minute. "Not that he wouldn't have been upset anyway having a woman die on the front seat of his car. I know it would upset me."

Sister looked up from the foot massaging. "Debbie told me that, too. I didn't know Arthur had been married before."

"It was a teenage thing. Their folks had it annulled. But he's still shaken up, of course. It's in the paper. Poison."

"Yuck."

I handed Sister the newspaper which was still on the table and she read the notice.

"That doctor said it was her heart, Mouse. The one in the white tennis shorts."

A heart in white tennis shorts? Fighting Sister's grammar is a losing battle. So all I said was, "Well, maybe her heart was bad, too. Mitzi said she had diabetes and a lot of circulatory problems. Maybe that's why she was having trouble walking yesterday." I sat down across from Sister. "Mitzi said that now she wouldn't have to suffer."

Sister frowned and put the paper down. "She was having trouble walking because she was about to croak. And what are you saying, that someone put her out of her misery?"

I thought about this a moment. "I guess they did. I wouldn't think this was a Dr. Kevorkian thing, though. Not at the Hunan Hut and not with poison that did her the way that did. Lord, it was awful. Those convulsions."

"Well, damn," Sister said. "I'll bet Arthur *is* upset. The first one's rough. I think I was more upset when Will Alec died than I was when Philip and Roger died. No sadder, of course, but you sort of get used to it." She hesitated. "Well, maybe you don't get used to it, that's not what I meant. You just learn the drill." Another pause. "And there was already a place for them at Elmwood. That made a difference. When Will Alec died, I even had to buy a cemetery plot."

Learn the drill? "But you got a nice roomy one."

"Got the adjoining ones. Good thinking, too, Miss Smarty. When Philip tumped over in the shower, Elmwood was right there waiting for him. No problem."

I got back to the subject of Sophie Sawyer. "I don't know if this lady will be buried here or not. She lived in Chicago for years and I guess that's where her husband's buried. Her two daughters will probably want to take her back up there."

"Really? Did their mother have any money?"

"Lots, I think. Why?"

"Because that's the number one reason people get killed, except for being mad at each other. Speaking of which, what about Lisa?"

"She's asleep." I rubbed my hand over my forehead where I felt a headache lurking. "I don't have any idea what's going on. All

Lisa will say is that she doesn't want to talk about it, and that Alan doesn't love her any more."

"Another woman."

A definite twinge of pain over my right eye.

"Surely not. Let's not jump to conclusions."

"Of course it is. Alan's smack dab in the middle of bimbo territory."

"Would you care to elucidate?" I got up, took the aspirin from the cabinet, and poured a glass of water.

"He's in his thirties, successful, handsome, been married fifteen years. He's in an office surrounded by attractive women. Bimbo territory."

I chewed the aspirin thoughtfully.

Mary Alice winced. "Why don't you swallow those things like a normal person?"

"They get stuck." I held the bottle out. "You want some?"

"No thanks. You take too many of those things."

"On days like today I do," I agreed. I sat back down. "Bimbo territory?"

"Absolutely."

I usually don't put much stock in Mary Alice's theories, but this one might merit some consideration. Alan is our middle child and has always been the good, solid one. He's never had the offbeat imagination of his brother Freddie or the mischievousness of his sister Haley. He's dependable and kind and has always seemed contented with his lot. Surely he hadn't fallen for some bimbo.

"I hate the word bimbo," I said.

"Because you're still a feminist."

"Possibly."

"Then tell me this. What would you call a cute twenty-two-year-old blonde who was coming on to Fred?"

"Dead meat."

"Well, I don't think you have anything to worry about," Sister said. "She'd have to be crazy."

"Hey, y'all. Hey, Aunt Sister." Lisa stood in the doorway looking like something Muffin had dragged in.

"My God, Lisa. What have you done to your hair?" Subtlety has never been one of Mary Alice's strong suits. I cringed when I remembered this was exactly what I had said when I saw Lisa.

But Lisa seemed too tired to take offense. She ran her hand through her hair absently. "It's supposed to be a Spice Girl look. The boys said it looks like Old Spice."

"Here, honey," I said. "Sit down. What

do kids know? You want some lunch? I made some tuna fish salad. And I've got cream cheese, if you'd rather have that."

"You got any Coke?"

"Sure."

"Get me some, too," Sister said when I got up. "I had lunch at The Club and those orange rolls always make me thirsty." Then, to Lisa as she sat down, "Debbie says you and Alan have had some kind of falling out. Is he running around?"

Like Fred says, the woman has the nerve of a bad tooth. I held my breath expecting Lisa to collapse into tears or, worst-case scenario, though she has never seemed violent, bop Sister over the head with the sugar bowl and tell her it was none of her damned business. What I didn't expect was Lisa's answer.

"Yes, ma'am. Her name is Coralee Gibbons."

I breathed again but not very well. My baby boy was in trouble.

"Who is Coralee Gibbons?" I asked.

"A woman who works in his office."

Sister flashed me a triumphant look and mouthed, "Bimbo territory."

But Lisa caught the gesture. "She's not a bimbo, Aunt Sister. I wish she were."

I poured Coke and handed each of them a

glass. “Tell us about her. And are you sure?”

Lisa had begun to cry again. Sister handed her a paper napkin. Those paper napkins were coming in handy today.

“He admits it. And she’s forty-five if she’s a day. She’s got grown children and she’s not even pretty.” Lisa looked up with tears welling in her eyes. “She wears green eyeshadow and short-sleeved suits. You know, like Janet Reno.”

Sister looked puzzled. “I’ve never noticed Janet Reno wearing green eyeshadow.”

“But she wears suits like hers. One night I saw her at a party and she had on white patent-leather shoes. Can you believe that?”

“Good Lord,” Sister commiserated. “I hope she at least had on a white dress.”

“A short-sleeved navy suit. And dark red lipstick. Janet Reno.”

We were wandering away from the point here, to say the least.

“Exactly what does Alan say?” I asked, sitting back down.

“He says she’s the most intelligent woman he’s ever known.” Lisa held the paper napkin to her eyes again.

Sister gave a little snort. “Not if she wears white patent-leather shoes after five o’clock. And with a navy short-sleeved suit. Where is this woman from?"

Lisa shrugged an "I don't know" shrug.

"Listen," I said, "does Alan say he's in love with her? What does he say is going on?"

"He says he's confused."

"Probably those white patent-leather shoes. Does she have big feet? Not that it matters."

"Shut up, Sister." I rapped my knuckles on the table, a tactic I had often used at school. "Just shut up about the damned shoes."

Lisa looked up in surprise; Mary Alice frowned at me, picked up her Coke, and sipped it.

I took advantage of the momentary silence. "Have you talked to anyone about this? A marriage counselor?"

"Alan said he didn't want to."

"Men always say that."

I gave Sister a hard look.

"Well, they do. You just have to go on and make the appointment and then tell them. You ask me, you haven't got much to worry about, though. A woman named Coralee in her forties who dresses like Janet Reno and wears white patent shoes with a navy dress? No way, Lisa."

"You think so?" There was a hopeful look

on Lisa's face, the first I had seen.

"Absolutely."

I gave up. Might as well. There wasn't anything I could do about the situation, anyway. Alan and Lisa were going to have to work this out. I'd worry about it, of course, and hate this woman named Coralee Gibbons for rocking the boat. But it wasn't my boat. Of course, my grandsons were passengers. I hopped up.

"I'm going to make you a cream cheese sandwich," I told Lisa. "That'll go down easy."

"Make me one, too," Sister said. "I need something to go with the Coke."

"I thought you just had lunch."

"All I had was chicken salad and orange rolls." She turned back to Lisa. "Do you know, Betty Ethridge has a friend from somewhere up north who said she couldn't believe people from Alabama would eat chicken salad with orange rolls. Made Betty mad. She says she told her we even eat boiled possums with orange rolls. The woman probably believed her. Beats all."

"We do eat some strange stuff," Lisa said.

"Like what?"

"Boiled peanuts."

"Boiled peanuts aren't strange."

I was fixing the sandwiches and half listening to their conversation. Next door, Mitzi's car pulled into the driveway.

"Mitzi's home," I said. "I'm going to run the casserole over to her."

"Arthur's first wife died," Sister explained to Lisa.

"Mr. Phizer was married before?" Lisa was as startled as we had been.

"And the first wife was murdered. Poisoned yesterday at the Hunan Hut. We saw it all." To emphasize what we had witnessed, Sister lolled her head to one side and shook a little.

"Good Lord!" Lisa's eyes widened. "What happened?"

I thought Mary Alice's dramatics had made that clear enough.

"The police think somebody killed her, apparently." I handed each of them a sandwich. "It's real sad. She was at the Hunan Hut having lunch with Arthur."

Sister nodded. "A pretty woman. Couldn't walk very well what with the poison and circulatory problems." She took a bite of her sandwich.

"The first wife?" Lisa looked from one of us to the other. "Mrs. Phizer's okay, isn't she?"

"Mitzi's okay." I stuck the souffle back in the microwave. "Just upset."

"Who did it?" Lisa still hadn't picked up her sandwich.

"Maybe nobody, I still think it might have been the peanuts. That's what it looked like, a bad allergic reaction." I set the timer.

"Let's don't talk about this while we're eating. Mama always said not to talk about religion, politics, or murder while you're eating." Sister took another bite of her sandwich.

"Mama never said a word about murder." The microwave dinged and I took the casserole out.

Mary Alice nodded that yes, she had.

But Lisa ignored her. "Well, poison's a pretty effective way. Probably better than a gun. You remember when President Reagan was shot? The bullet bounced off a rib. That was what saved him."

Mary Alice put her sandwich down. "Coralee Gibbons, you say? That's an old-fashioned name."

It worked. Lisa changed subjects in a flash.

"I know. It sounds like someone's grandmother. She may be for all I know. God knows she's old enough."

I picked up the casserole, told them I would be back in a few minutes, and walked across the yard.

"How're you doing?" I asked when Mitzi

answered the back door.

"Okay, I guess."

She didn't look okay. She looked exhausted. I held out the casserole.

"Thanks, Patricia Anne. I haven't even thought about food. Come on in."

"I can't. Mary Alice and Lisa are here."

"Alan's Lisa?"

"There may be a little trouble in paradise."

"Oh, Patricia Anne, I'm sorry."

"They'll work it out."

"Sure they will."

"Is Arthur okay?"

"I think so. He found out that Sophie wanted to be cremated. She wants her ashes sprinkled from the observation tower at Vulcan."

"From Vulcan? Is that legal?"

"I don't know. He's trying to find out."

"Well, let me know if there's anything we can do to help."

"I will."

I walked back to my own kitchen. When I came in the door, Mary Alice was telling Lisa about Cedric, the Englishman.

"Pencil-thin mustache, pencil-thin fingers. And you know what that means."

Lisa was actually laughing. "Aunt Sister. You didn't!"

"Of course not. He even had little bitty ears." She paused. "But he was real nice. Talked a lot about Dunkirk."

"What's Dunkirk?" Lisa wanted to know.

Seven

If Fred had thought he was coming home for a quiet evening of supper and watching the Braves, he quickly found out he was wrong.

"I'm taking Woofer for his walk," I told Lisa.

"Okay." She looked up from the sofa where she was reading the new *Vanity Fair*. Muffin was stretched out beside her. "If the phone rings, I'm going to let the machine answer. It might be Alan."

And she ought to talk to him, I thought. But I didn't say anything. I put Woofer's leash on him and we walked to the corner to wait for Fred. When I saw the car, I waved him down.

"What's the matter?" he asked, as I opened the back door, shoved Woofer in, and then got in the front seat.

"Lisa's at our house, and I need to talk to you."

"What's Lisa doing here?"

"Drive and I'll tell you."

He drove. Woofer leaned his head over the seat and slobbered happily. I reached in my pocket for a Kleenex.

"We'd better go to the park," Fred said. "What's going on?"

"She and Alan are having trouble."

"What kind of trouble?"

"Woman trouble."

"Alan?" Fred looked at me in disbelief.

"That's what she says. Some woman in Alan's office named Coralee Gibbons. In her forties with grown children."

We had stopped at a four-way stop. Fred waved the man on our left to go ahead. "You were here first, buddy." Then to me, "Have you talked to Alan?"

"No. Debbie tried to call him. Lisa went to Debbie's first. But she couldn't get him and then she had to go to court so she left word for him to call us, that Lisa was at our house."

"And he hasn't called."

"Nope. And I tried to call the boys after I knew they'd be home from school and nobody answered."

Fred pulled into the five-car parking lot adjacent to the two tennis courts. This is a small neighborhood park designed mostly for senior citizens who play chess and checkers in a large gazebo fancifully called the Sunday Bandstand. The swings and slides are toddler size, guaranteeing that the seniors won't be bothered by rambunctious older children. The tennis courts and a basketball court, demanded by the tax-paying parents of former toddlers, are over on the side behind a chain link fence.

Surprisingly, for such lovely weather, the park was deserted except for two old gentlemen who sat on a bench, each smoking a pipe. I was suddenly reminded of a poem, "Old Friends." I tried to remember who wrote it and the exact words, but they escaped me. Something about sitting on a bench like bookends. The poem was sad; I remembered that. The friends were waiting. Waiting while the shadows lengthened. I shivered. I had just remembered the other news I had for Fred.

Woofer wasn't allowed in the park, so we sat on a bench beside the basketball court. The concrete was still warm, and he stretched out at our feet with a dog-sigh of contentment.

"What kind of shape is Lisa in?" Fred asked.

"Not too good."

"Doesn't sound like Alan, does it? I thought they were getting along just fine."

I agreed. I didn't mention Sister's theory of bimbo territory and the fact that Alan was smack in the middle of it.

Fred reached down to rub the gray hair

between Woofer's ears. "They're not getting a divorce are they?"

"Oh, Lord, I hope not. I don't know how far it's gone. Lisa said he wouldn't go for counseling."

"Well, damn."

The two old men got up and strolled out of the park, closing the gate behind them.

"That's not all."

Fred looked up in alarm. "The boys?"

"No. This isn't about Alan and Lisa. You know that lady that died yesterday at the Hunan Hut? I told you how Arthur was stroking her hand?"

He nodded.

"The police say she was poisoned."

"Poisoned!" Fred spoke so loudly, the two men turned to see if everything was all right, decided it was, and continued walking. "What on God's earth?"

"Mitzi came over this morning, saying the woman was Arthur's first wife and that somebody had murdered her."

"Arthur had a first wife? Our Arthur Phizer?"

"Well, it was a teenage thing and their folks had it annulled, so I'm not sure it counts."

Fred didn't say anything so I continued. "Her name was Sophie Sawyer and she was back here from Chicago because she was in bad health."

Fred still didn't say anything.

"Diabetes and circulatory problems," I added. "And her daughter lives here."

"Who did it?"

"They don't know."

The two of us sat like bookends while the shadows lengthened. From the nearby fire station we could hear a radio or TV turned to the early evening news.

"You got any more news for me?"

The tone of the question flew all over me. Hell, I was only the messenger. A messenger who had had a godawful day.

I jumped up so quickly that Woofer looked up in surprise.

"As a matter of fact, I do. If you want any damned supper, you're going to have to go to Morrison's."

"Well, hell. What's the matter with you, Patricia Anne?"

He said it to my back. I was stomping toward the car.

Just before we got home, I broke the silence. "Don't say anything about Lisa's hair."

"What's wrong with her hair?"

"It's white and sticks straight up in little bunches."

"What?"

"God's truth."

We looked at each other. At first it was a tentative smile for each of us, and then it was laughter, the oh, hell, everything's so bad it's funny laughter. The kind of laughter that keeps people married for forty years.

We pulled into our driveway and parked behind Lisa's car. Fred reached over and took my hand. "Tell you what. Let's go see if Lisa wants to go to Morrison's. If she doesn't, we can bring her something."

But Lisa wasn't there. A note, propped on the kitchen table, said, Gone to dinner with Aunt Sister. Love, Lisa.

I picked up the phone to see if there were any messages. There weren't.

"Try Alan's house again," Fred said.

I dialed and, surprisingly, Alan answered.

"Son?" I said. It came out as a question.

"Hey, Mama."

"Your papa wants to talk to you." I handed a startled Fred the phone and walked into the den.

"What's going on, Son?" I heard him ask.

I turned on the TV. The local news was on. A picture of a much younger Sophie Sawyer filled the screen. Murdered. Prominent family. I reached over and snapped it off.

In the kitchen "Un huh" seemed to be all

that Fred was saying.

I went down the hall pulling off my clothes. I turned on the shower as hot as I could stand it and stepped in, letting the water pound against me.

In a few minutes, Fred joined me.

"What did he say?" I asked, moving over to make room.

"Damn, this water's hot." Fred moved to the corner of the shower stall. "He says it's his fault. He says he's been involved with this other woman."

"Damn," I said. "Damn."

"You got that right."

"Turn around." I soaped a washrag and washed his back, kissing various and sundry spots. Then he scrubbed my back, also doing some kissing. But that was as far as it went. By the time *Wheel of Fortune* came on, we were in front of the TV in our robes eating the tuna fish salad I had made for lunch. Better than Morrison's.

Fred was asleep in his chair when Mary Alice and Lisa came rushing in.

"There are two police cars over at the Phizers'," Sister exclaimed.

"Two," Lisa repeated.

"Reckon what they're doing?" Sister disappeared into the dining room with Lisa trailing right behind.

"What's going on?" Fred came awake.

"Don't know. They say there are two police cars over at the Phizers'." I got up and followed them.

"Don't turn on the lights," Sister cautioned. She and Lisa had each claimed a side of the draperies for peeking. "Look there, Lisa. Another car."

"Three of them?" I peeked through the middle of the draperies. Sure enough, two cars were parked on the street. The one Sister was talking about pulled into the driveway.

Sister sneezed. "Damn, Mouse. These draperies are full of dust. When did you have them cleaned last?"

"Not long ago." Actually I couldn't remember it had been so long.

"They're getting out of the car," Lisa said.

We watched two policemen walk up to the Phizers' door and go in.

"Damn, something's really going on." Sister sneezed again. "They don't send three patrol cars out for nothing."

"Maybe they're fixing to arrest Mr. Phizer for murdering his first wife."

"Oh, for heaven's sake, Lisa." It popped out sharper than I meant it to.

But Lisa was too caught up in her imagination to take offense. "Or maybe it's Mrs. Phizer they're arresting."

"What's happening?" Fred was standing in the doorway.

"There are three police cars at the Phizers'," Sister said. "Come look. But don't get too close to the drapes. They're loaded with dust mites."

He came and peered over my head.

"The third one just came up," Lisa announced happily. "I think they're going to arrest one of the Phizers for poisoning that lady."

"Hmm." Fred took the scene in, nodded, and then said what every married man would say, given these circumstances. "Patricia Anne, why don't you go call Mitzi and find out what's going on?"

"Right now while the police are there?"

"Something could be wrong with one of them. They might need some help."

I felt guilty that I hadn't thought of that.

Lisa clutched the drapery. "Maybe Mrs. Phizer killed Mr. Phizer. Or vice versa."

"The rescue squad's not there. If one of them had had an accident or a heart attack or killed each other the rescue squad would be there." Mary Alice sneezed again. "Damn."

"I'll go call," I said. I went into the

kitchen and dialed Mitzi's number. The line was busy. I waited a couple of minutes and tried again. No luck.

"It's busy," I told the three in the dining room.

"The last group's leaving," Fred announced. "They sure didn't stay long." The two women, I noticed, had pulled dining room chairs over and settled down for some serious snooping. Fred, while not going quite that far, had his eye glued to the opening in the drapery.

"I'm going to go over and see what's wrong," I said. "Mitzi won't think I'm butting in."

Might as well have been talking to the wall for all the attention I got.

"There comes the second group leaving, too," Sister said. "What do you think the tall one has in his hand, Fred? A gun?"

"It's a cell phone."

Un huh. And this was the man I've heard make snide remarks about the telescope in Sister's sunroom. The sunroom that just happens to overlook all of Birmingham. As does Sister.

I let myself out of the kitchen door. Woofer, asleep in his igloo, didn't know anything was going on, bless his heart. The other dogs in the neighborhood knew, though. As did the other neighbors. Several front porch lights were on, and the Tripps, across the street, were standing on their steps, probably wondering whether or not they should be doing something to help.

I was caught in the headlights of the patrol car as the policemen pulled into the driveway to turn around. Okay. So all the neighbors now knew I had an old pink seersucker robe that had been washed to the point of transparency. Behind me, someone (I suspected it was Sister, though it may have been Fred) rapped on the dining room window. Spotlighted, I resisted the urge to lift my middle finger in a salute. Instead, I clutched the robe around me and ran up Mitzi's steps, wishing I'd taken the time to throw on some jeans and a shirt.

The door was opened by a nice-looking young policeman who said, "Hi, come on in." Beyond him, I could see Mitzi, Arthur, and another uniformed man sitting on the sofa. By the looks of the cups and plates on the coffee table, they were having a party.

"I just want to see Mrs. Phizer a minute," I said. No way I was going to join a party in this bathrobe. Not even an unusual party such as this one.

Mitzi heard me. "Come in, Patricia

Anne," she called.

"You come out here." I stepped away from the lighted door.

"What's going on?" she asked, joining me on the porch.

"What do you mean what's going on? There were three police cars here. We didn't know what had happened. I tried to call you, but your line was busy."

"I think one of the policemen was making a phone call." She pointed toward her porch swing. "You want to sit down a minute?"

"I want to know why three police cars were here." We sat down and the swing creaked. "I was scared something had happened." I pointed vaguely down the block, toward the Tripps on their steps, toward the lights, toward my dining room window. "We all were."

"Well, my goodness. I didn't think of that." Mitzi stood up and called to the Tripps. "Everything's fine. Thank you."

They waved, turned, and went inside. Porch lights down the street were turned off. Even most of the dogs quit barking. I suspected that in my dining room the chairs were being put back under the table.

"Isn't this the nicest place in the world to live?" Mitzi asked.

Well, of course it is if you're as sweet as

Mitzi Phizer and assume the neighbors are just concerned for your well-being.

She sat back down, and the two of us began to swing slightly. These porch swings on a warm September night are one of the things that make this the nicest place in the world to live.

"The first policemen came to ask Fred some questions about Sophie," she said. "They were real nice." She pointed toward the door. "They're the ones that are still here."

"What about all the others?"

"They just sort of showed up. I guess they had things to check out with each other. Fortunately, I'd just made a coconut cake. They all seemed to be hungry."

"I love your coconut cake."

"They did, too. I was going to take it down to Sophie's daughter's house tomorrow, but there's not much left." She smiled. "You remember how our mamas used to say that hoboes left marks on houses during the Depression so the ones coming along later would know where they could get food?"

"Sure. Now they use cell phones."

We creaked back and forth, our feet barely touching the floor.

"Is Arthur okay?"

"I guess so. He knew there would be some questions."

"How about Sophie's daughters?"

"Arabella, the one who was staying with her mother, is down at her sister's. Arthur says they get along like cats and dogs, but I guess she couldn't stay in the apartment." Mitzi shivered. "I know I wouldn't want to."

"Me neither."

"I hope Arthur doesn't have too much trouble with those two. He's the executor of Sophie's estate."

I yawned. The slow movement back and forth was soothing.

"I told him I didn't think it was a good idea when she asked him," Mitzi continued. "But Arthur said she was sick and worried, and it seemed like a burden off of her." Mitzi put her foot down and stopped the swing; my side angled out. "Tomorrow he's got to tell the girls their mama wanted to be cremated."

"They didn't know?"

"He says not. He says Sophie decided when she got back to Birmingham."

"What about scattering the ashes from Vulcan? Can they do it?"

"Arthur hasn't found out yet."

For the first time there was an edge to

Mitzi's voice. Which I could certainly understand. I wouldn't have much patience with Fred if he were up on Vulcan scattering his first wife's ashes. And being the executor of her estate. Though it was just the kind of thing Fred would do if he had had a first wife other than me and she had asked him to. It made me mad just thinking of it.

The two young policemen came out, thanked Mitzi for the cake, and headed toward their car. Arthur came out, too.

"Hey, Patricia Anne."

"Hey, Arthur. I was worried about you. All the police cars."

"Thanks. We're fine."

He didn't look fine. The man I was looking at looked worn and tired, a good ten years older than the man I had seen the day before at lunch.

Mitzi and I both stood up. The swing bumped gently against the back of our knees.

"Well, I've got to get home. Y'all take care." I wanted to say something about Sophie Sawyer's death, tell Arthur I was sorry for his loss. The loss of his friend? His ex-wife?

I ended up saying nothing about Sophie, but if they needed us to call. Anytime.

Well, how was I to know how quickly they

would take us up on the offer?

On the way back to my house, I was again caught in the glare of headlights, this time a pizza delivery van pulling into my own driveway.

"I think you have the wrong address," I said.

But of course he didn't. When I went to bed, Mary Alice, Lisa, and Fred were sitting at the kitchen table scarfing down an extra large, loaded with everything pizza. You'd think they hadn't had a bite of supper.

"Coconut cake?" Sister had a mouthful of pizza. "They were there for the cake?"

"All but the first group," I explained.

"I hate coconut," Sister said. "Gets bigger and bigger the more you chew it."

"Neither of my boys likes it, either," Lisa added. "Maybe it's genetic."

I expected some tears or at least a stop in chewing when Lisa said this. Instead she reached for another piece of pizza.

"Don't you want some, Mama?" she asked.

"Here, honey, have a piece." Fred pushed the box toward me.

"Don't be silly, Fred." Sister pulled the box back to the center of the table. "How can you be married to someone who's anorexic for forty years and not know it?"

That was when I went to bed.

About three o'clock, though, I was awakened by a nightmare. Somehow I had gotten my head stuck in a wooden box. The rest of my body had slid right through the box, but my head wouldn't make it. Some Jungian psychologist would love to have a dream like that to analyze.

I got up, tiptoed down the hall past the guest room, got some milk, and lay down on the den sofa. I was reading the *Vanity Fair* that Lisa had left on the coffee table when Fred came in.

"Maalox," he muttered on his way to the kitchen. In a moment he was back, wanting to know why I was up.

I told him about the dream, how scary it was, and asked if he thought it meant anything.

He pursed his lips as if he were really thinking. "It means you're getting the big head about something and your subconscious is saying you shouldn't."

Somehow I didn't think this would have been the Jungian psychologist's answer. Not if he wanted to keep his practice going.

Fred sat at the end of the sofa and propped his feet on the coffee table. I was about to say something smart aleck when I saw his feet. Fred's feet are so vulnerable looking. Pitiful, really. Pale, pale white. One little toe that he broke years ago sticking out at an angle.

"Pizza," he said, rubbing his belly. "How come things you love don't love you back?"

"I love you back. I love your feet."

"I'm glad." He rubbed my leg. "Do you think I ought to go to Atlanta and talk to Alan?"

"I don't know. It's the kids I'm worried about."

"Yeah. Me, too." He gave my leg a pat and stood up. "You coming back to bed?"

"I'm going to read a while." I caught his pajama bottom as he walked by. "Have you ever looked at another woman? Lusted in your heart?"

He grabbed his pajamas and slapped at my hand.

"The heart's not the problem."

It wasn't the answer I wanted to hear.

"But I never did anything about it."

I knew that.

"You never let me out of your sight long enough."

I swatted at his rear end with the *Vanity Fair*, and he went back to bed. I woke up several hours later with the light still on and the magazine still in my hand. In the kitchen, someone was making coffee. I could hear the first loud swooshes of the percolator.

Eight

"Sorry, Mama," Lisa said as I stuck my head into the kitchen. "I was hoping I wouldn't wake you up. What are you doing on the sofa?"

"I had a bad dream and couldn't go back to sleep. What time is it?"

"About seven-thirty. Pop hasn't left yet."

Lisa was looking much better this morning. More rested. And maybe I was getting used to the tufts of white hair. They didn't seem as startling.

"There's orange juice in the freezer," I told her and went to brush my teeth and see if Fred was going to Atlanta today.

"Been thinking about it," he said, buttoning his shirt. "But I think I'll call him and go over on the weekend. If I went today, he'd think he had to leave work."

Well, big deal. Men and their work. We were talking about a marriage here. Our grandchildren's security.

"Besides, I haven't figured out what to say to him anyway."

I'll bet he hadn't. Fred adores his two sons, and they love him, but their conversations center around work and sports. A whole weekend can be spent on a Daytona 500 with tidbits left over for the holidays.

"Just let him talk, tell you what's going on." I went into the bathroom, but not before I saw a pained expression on Fred's face. He would do his fatherly duty, but he really didn't want to know what was wrong in his son's life. He wanted to believe that Alan's life was perfect. He's not that way about Haley. Not only does he want to know what's going wrong, he wants to fix it. He's the same way with me. Some kind of macho thing I haven't totally figured out. Mary Alice calls it the Me Tarzan syndrome. The fact that Jane is perfectly capable of solving her own problems has somehow missed Tarzan. He hasn't a clue that he's being patronizing.

The window in our bathroom is high, so high that all anyone on the outside can see is our heads. Consequently, we leave the blinds open most of the time. Every morning the sun announces that Windex is needed here. Dust mites, dirty windows. I felt a couple of twinges of guilt. Twinges, not jolts. I'd get around to the cleaning when it got painful enough.

"I'm gone," Fred called.

"Get a lunch out of the freezer."

Something interesting was going on over at the Phizers'. A taxi had pulled up and a redheaded woman was getting out. The taxi driver hopped out, took a fairly sizable suitcase from the trunk, and carried it to the front porch for her. Arthur opened the front door, stepped out and hugged her, picked up the suitcase, and they disappeared inside. The taxi driver was halfway back to his cab when the woman rushed out of the house. She retrieved what looked like a purse from the back seat and then waved as the cab driver drove away. Arthur came out on the porch again, and they walked into the house, his arm around her waist.

I ran to see if I could catch Fred before he left. He was in the kitchen looking in the freezer.

"I think the redheaded woman you saw Arthur with just went in their house. I'll bet she's one of Sophie Sawyer's daughters. Did she look like she was in her late thirties?"

"I guess so. She was pretty." Fred came up with a package of macaroni and cheese. "Her hair was sort of a fuchsia red."

"Maybe she's another one of Mr. Phizer's wives." Lisa was sitting at the kitchen table pouring Frosted Flakes into a bowl.

I ignored this. "Fuchsia red?"

"Sort of mahogany but with some purple in it. Isn't that fuschia?"

Not to me, it wasn't.

"Sounds pretty," Lisa said.

"Bye, y'all. Thanks for the coffee, Lisa." Fred patted me on the behind, picked up his thermos and package of macaroni and cheese, and went out the back door.

"Pop's a lot nicer than Alan," Lisa announced. "Alan would have a fit if I handed him a package of frozen macaroni and cheese for lunch."

I ignored this, too, but I felt a twinge in my stomach. Being a good mother-in-law might cost me an ulcer. I poured a cup of coffee, put a lot of milk in it, and sat down across from Lisa. I hadn't taken my first sip when the phone rang.

"Anything going on next door this morning?" Mary Alice asked.

"As a matter of fact there is. A woman with fuchsia hair just arrived with a suitcase. I think maybe it's Sophie Sawyer's daughter."

"Fuchsia?"

"Actually it's sort of a mahogany. Fred called it fuchsia."

"Well, the murder made the front page of the *Birmingham News* today. There's a picture of Sophie, too, probably taken when she graduated from high school. I hate it when they do that." She paused. "It doesn't say anything about Arthur."

"Why should it?"

"Don't be dense, Mouse. He was the one having lunch with her when she was poisoned. The paper says it was strychnine. Isn't that rat poison?"

"For heaven's sake, Sister, I don't know. And Arthur wouldn't hurt a flea."

"You and I know that. But why do you think the police were over there last night?"

Questioning Arthur, of course. I sighed.

"Tell Lisa I'll pick her up a little before eleven. I've got a call waiting."

Not even a goodbye.

"Honey," I said to Lisa, "Aunt Sister's said to tell you she'll pick you up a little before eleven. Where are y'all going?"

"She's made an appointment at Delta Hairlines for me. She says I look more like a half-plucked chicken than a Spice Girl." She ran her hand through her hair. "She's probably right."

And Aunt Sister could say it and get away with it; she wasn't the mother-in-law. If Delta could do anything with Lisa's hair, she could turn water into wine. But, like Brer Rabbit, I just lay low, reached for the

Frosted Flakes and began to eat them like peanuts.

"And then we're going to have lunch somewhere good. Aunt Sister said to tell you you could come if you wanted to."

A lovely invitation. "Thanks, but this is the morning I tutor at the middle school."

"Alan said you were doing that. I didn't know you knew anything about math."

I shoved a fistful of Frosted Flakes into my mouth, but it didn't stop me from saying, "I can even do ratio and percent."

"That's nice."

Actually, it was nice. When I signed up to do tutoring, I had assumed it would be English. A math tutor was needed worse, though, so I took the job. And Lord, middle school math is easier to teach than English. Probably all the math teachers would argue with me about that. But it's such a relief to have one way to do it and one answer.

"Why don't you go get the paper?" I suggested. "It's probably in the shrubbery. Sister said the murder made the front page."

While Lisa was gone, I headed back to the bedroom. I'd throw on some jeans and take Woofer for a walk. By that time, it would be time to go to school. When I got back from school, Lisa would still be out with Mary

Alice. Another twinge of guilt hit me, but so did another twinge in the belly. Come to think of it, I'd been twinging all morning. I took a deep breath. Enough.

I looked over next door. Arthur's car was still in the driveway, but there was no sign of the woman with fuchsia hair. Fuchsia hair? After I dressed and was walking into the kitchen, though, there was a knock on the back door and Mitzi stuck her head in.

She looked neater than she had the day before. At least she had on clothes and shoes. But her face looked swollen, and the circles under her eyes were an olive green. They almost looked as if they had been painted on.

"I need to borrow some milk," she said.

This was startling. Mitzi never borrows anything. I'm the borrower, she the lender. This was totally out of character.

"Sure. Come in."

She stepped into the kitchen and held out a glass. "Can you let me have this much?"

"I've got plenty."

"Hi, Mrs. Phizer," Lisa said. She was sitting at the table reading the paper.

Mitzi started. "Hey, Lisa. I didn't see you over there. Are you okay?"

"I've left Alan."

"That's nice." Mitzi handed me the glass.

"I just need enough for cereal, Patricia Anne. Arabella Hardt, Sophie's younger daughter came in a while ago. She and her sister got in some kind of a big fight. Arthur says he's not surprised, that they never agree on anything."

Mitzi's hand was shaking.

"Why don't you sit down a minute," I suggested. "Let me get you a cup of coffee."

She didn't argue. "That would be nice. They can wait a few minutes." She pulled out a chair and sank down at the table. "Say you've left Alan, Lisa?"

"Yes, ma'am." Lisa folded the newspaper and placed it on the floor beside her. Sophie Sawyer's picture looked up at her. "He's been committing adultery with a woman in his office named Coralee Gibbons."

An office named Coralee Gibbons? The English teacher in me cringed.

Mitzi was quiet for a moment as if Lisa's words were just sinking in. She took the coffee I handed her and stared into it.

"Well, don't kill her," she said.

"No, ma'am. I wasn't planning on it."

I looked at the two of them. They appeared normal.

Mitzi reached for the sugar bowl and nodded toward the newspaper. "Last night after the police left our house, I realized they think I killed Sophie Sawyer."

I handed her a spoon. "Oh, Mitzi, of course they don't. Why would you think that?"

"They asked questions like where I was the day Sophie died. And the night before." She picked up her coffee. "What did they think I was going to say, out buying strychnine?" A shrug. "Actually, the night before, Sophie called and Arthur went back over there and I thought, Damn it, I'm tired of sitting here by myself. So I went to a movie."

Lisa leaned over and patted Mitzi's hand. "No way anybody would think you killed that lady, Mrs. Phizer."

Mitzi patted Lisa's hand. "Thanks, Lisa." She took a sip of coffee and pointed her head toward the newspaper. "Did you see that big article about Sophie's death?"

"I'd just started reading it." Lisa picked the paper up and handed it to Mitzi.

"Well, let me read the highlights to you. They really messed it up."

I joined them at the table as Mitzi read parts of the article aloud.

"Ha," she said a couple of times as she read, the kind of "ha" that means, "that's what *you* think."

Mitzi put the paper down in disgust.

"They didn't even get her husband's name right."

Lisa got up and put her cereal bowl in the dishwasher. "Anybody want any more coffee?"

"What was his name?" I reached for the paper.

"Milton Sawyer. He was an outstanding man, Patricia Anne, some kind of la-de-da financier. One of Ronald Reagan's advisers. The paper called him Hilton. Said she was the widow of Hilton Sawyer."

"Anybody?" Lisa asked again, holding up the coffee pot.

Mitzi and I both shook our heads no. I scanned the article. The only new information which was especially interesting was that Sophie's son-in-law, Dr. Joseph Batson, was the founder and CEO of Bellemina Health. Bellemina Health is a Birmingham based company which has hospitals all over the south specializing in drug rehabilitation, especially for adolescents. And the company is growing like kudzu.

"You didn't tell me her son-in-law was Joseph Batson," I said.

"Who's Joseph Batson?" Lisa wanted to know.

"One of the richest men in Birmingham. Started Bellemina Health," I explained.

Mitzi sighed. “It slipped my mind. Arthur says he’s a real nice guy, too. Arthur handles some of the company’s insurance. It’s a shame that Arabella hasn’t had as much luck with husbands as Sue has. Her last one ended up in prison. I think he was a hit man for the mob. Or something.”

“Really?” Lisa and I exclaimed together.

“Something like that.” Mitzi drank the last of her coffee and pushed her chair back. “I’ve got to get home. They need the milk for their cereal.”

I got the milk from the refrigerator. “Do you need more? I’ve got plenty.”

“No, just a glassful is fine. I guess I’ll have to go to the grocery today and do some big-time shopping. I don’t know how long Arabella will be with us.”

“She was staying with her mother?”

Mitzi nodded. “The whole thing was a temporary setup, a rented condo so Sophie could be near the hospital. I guess if Sophie had gotten better, she’d have bought a condo or a town house and Arabella might have gone back to Chicago.” Mitzi took the milk from my outstretched hand. “Anyway, Arabella says she can’t stay in the apartment now, that it’s too lonesome, and I can’t say that I blame her.”

“And her last husband’s in jail because

he's a hit man?" Lisa was still stuck on this bit of information.

"One of them was. I think it's the last one."

"How many has she had?"

"I'm not sure. Several." Mitzi took the glass of milk. "Thanks. I'll talk to y'all later."

"Wow," Lisa said as the door closed. "A real hit man."

I grabbed another handful of cereal, declared I had to go get dressed, and left as she picked the newspaper up again. When she started checking hit men's phone numbers, prices, and availability, I'd step in.

That morning I had three students to tutor. One-on-one is by far the best, but it isn't always possible. So in a little room off the library, Sharon Moore, Shatawna Bishop, and Shawn Crawford and I sat, trying to get negative integers straight. It was the first month of school, but I had tutored these three the year before and was well acquainted with them. The three S's are not my easiest group. Sharon couldn't be less interested. She can hardly see the plus and minus signs because of all the mascara loaded on her eyelashes that she bats at poor Shawn who tries to keep his mind on math, but who is a hormonal wreck at fourteen. Shatawna I haven't quite figured out. There is a distinct possibility that she knows all of this stuff already, is bored stiff, but will do anything to get out of the regular classroom where she is even more bored. It happens, as every teacher knows; these are the kids who'll drive you crazy. Even so, you keep hoping you'll reach them.

After a fairly unproductive forty minutes of eye batting from Sharon, squirming from Shawn, and yawns from Shatawna, I told them they could go back to class. I watched them crossing the library and noticed that as Shatawna passed by one of the computers, she hesitated and patted it lovingly.

Hmmm.

I caught her as she started down the hall.

Oh, yes, ma'am. Computers were her favorite things in the world.

Then if I sent a note to her teacher, could she come back and look something up for me?

Oh, yes, ma'am.

There was no mistaking the delight in her eyes which were a startling green against her African-American skin.

I went back into the library and got a computer pass, wishing that Bill Gates could have seen the expression on Shatawna's face. The schools of Alabama had been the first recipients of his foundation to provide computers so underprivileged children could have access to the Internet. They were for educational purposes, of course, but I told myself that Shatawna's wandering around on the Internet on my behalf would be educational.

She was back in a few minutes. "What do you want me to look up, Mrs. Hollowell?"

"A man named Milton Sawyer. He was a financier. One of Ronald Reagan's advisors."

"Why don't you just look him up in *Who's Who*?"

"Because I didn't think of it, Miss Smart Aleck." We grinned at each other. "You see what you can find and I will, too."

I couldn't remember how long Mitzi had said that Sophie had been widowed. I figured I was safe with the 1992 edition, though. I hefted it down from the shelf and looked in the index. There were two Milton Sawyers, Milton P. and Milton R., both on page 426. One look told me that Milton Price was the one I was looking for. His birth date was listed as 1928. He was still alive when this edition had been printed.

"It's Milton Price Sawyer," I told Shatawna who was happily clicking away.

"And he was born in 1928 in Rochester, Minnesota."

"Okay. That's a help."

I went back to my reading. Undergraduate degree from Yale. M.B.A. Harvard, 1953. Founding partner Sawyer and Thorpe, Investments. Served as a special advisor to President Ronald Reagan. He also, I noted, had served on the board of directors of at least a dozen companies that I recognized. Railroads, cosmetic firms, even giant entertainment entities.

"Lord, Mrs. Hollowell, there's over five hundred entries for that man," Shatawna announced. "What do you want to know about him?"

I wasn't sure. "Something about his family, maybe."

A couple of clicks and Shatawna informed me that his father had been a doctor, a professor at the Mayo Clinic. His mother, Sarah Weeks Sawyer, had been a well-known sculptor. There were two older sisters. He married Sophie Bedford Vaughn in 1954. There were three children, David (1955-1974), Susan (1957), and Arabella (1959).

"He died in 1994," she added.

I looked over her shoulder. "I didn't know they had a son."

Shatawna nodded. "Nineteen in 1974. I'll bet he was killed in Vietnam. That's so sad."

It was. It was terribly sad.

Several students had come in to use the computers. A couple seemed to be waiting.

"You want me to look up anything else for you, Mrs. Hollowell?"

"See if there's anything on Bellemina Health."

"Spell it. I'll look in Dog Pile."

"Dog Pile?"

"You just type it in and tell it to fetch."

Lord. I spelled Bellemina, and after a few clicks on the mouse, Shatawna informed me Bellemina had their own web site that was updated each day. Why didn't she print it out for me? Mrs. Quick charged for the paper but not much, and it looked like a lot of stuff. I could just take it home and read it.

That sounded good to me. Reading about it earlier had reminded me that it might be a good Birmingham based company for the investment club to put money in. I'd study up on it and be able to make an informed suggestion.

Shatawna hit the print button and pushed her chair back. "You really ought to get you a computer, Mrs. Hollowell. They're great."

"Shatawna," I asked, "what do you get if you add negative seven and negative five?"

She grinned widely. "Who cares?"

"Anyone who wants to get out of the eighth grade."

No use. The grin didn't fade.

I went to the school cafeteria salad bar and got a salad to go. At home, I fixed some iced tea and settled down in the den to eat and read about Bellemina Health. I don't know what I had expected, but it was boring. Today's big web site news was that they were opening a new facility in Jonesboro, Tennessee, which would be headed by a Dr. Cranston Jordan. Dr. Jordan's credentials, which were very impressive, followed. The only thing that really caught my eye was that this would be the forty-second Bellemina Health facility, the fifth to be opened this year. I put down my salad and got the newspaper from the kitchen table. Bellemina was trading at fifty-two dollars a share, up four for the year. Fifty-two sounded like a lot, but what did I know? Teachers aren't big investors in the stock market. Neither are the wives of husbands who own their own small businesses.

I put my salad plate in the dishwasher and went out to speak to Woofer. We had never gotten to take our walk this morning. He came out of his doghouse reluctantly.

"You need to be out in the sunshine," I told him, offering him a dog biscuit and rubbing my thumb over his gray head. "It's warm out here. Old animals need Vitamin D."

He took the treat and then dropped it on the ground, totally unlike him.

"What's the matter, boy? You okay?" I knelt beside him and looked into his eyes. They seemed bleary. He lay down beside me and I felt his nose to see if it was hot. I know that's not an accurate way to check if an animal has fever, but it's what you do instinctively. His nose felt cool and moist.

"You okay?" I asked again. He stretched out, his head on his front legs.

"No, you're not, are you?" I ran my hand down his back, and he shivered. I felt my stomach knot. He really was sick. I sat and pulled as much of him as I could onto my lap. Woofer is a blend of every breed of dog known to man. His head and chest are large, the rest of his body medium size. His legs are short, and he has a fan tail. We got him from the Humane Society when he was six weeks old, and he was listed as a mixture of Collie/Dachshund; the mental picture of that mating boggled my mind.

I was sitting there holding him when I heard the gate open.

"Hi, Mama."

I turned and saw Lisa, a very pretty Lisa with short curly ash blonde hair. Delta had turned the water into wine.

"You okay?" she asked.

"I think Woofer's sick. Come see what you think."

She came over, knelt beside us, and ran her hand over Woofer's head. "You sick, boy? You sick, Old Woofer?"

Woofer agreed that he was. He shivered again.

"I'm taking him to the vet," I said, not waiting for her opinion.

"You want me to help you?"

"I'd appreciate it. I'll sit with him on the backseat. Let me go call and make sure they can see him now." I moved Woofer and got up. "Your hair looks great."

"Thanks." Lisa ran her hand through her short curls. "Aunt Sister had a meeting she had to go to."

"Figures." I went in to make the call.

Our vet is sliding into retirement. He hasn't announced his intention, but he's spending more and more time in Destin, Florida, on the golf course or fishing. His assistant, the young woman who will probably take over his practice, is a doll. Tall, with long shiny brown hair pulled back in a pony tail and no makeup, she could have walked into any modeling agency and gotten a job. Instead, she and her helper lifted Woofer gently onto the table and she began to examine him efficiently, talking to him while she worked, a person who obviously loved her job.

Dr. Grant took Woofer's temperature and nodded. "It's high." She felt down his body, palpitated his abdomen, ran her hand down his legs, and then turned his left hind leg and examined it.

"Has something bitten him?" she asked.

"Not that I know of. He's in a fenced yard."

She leaned closer to examine the inside of Woofer's leg, high up on the fleshy part. "Looks like a bite," she said. "Charlie?"

The young man who had helped lift Woofer onto the table stuck his head around the door.

"I'm going to need some help here." Dr. Grant turned to me. "Mrs. Hollowell, would you mind waiting outside for a few minutes? We're going to have to do a little work here."

I hesitated.

Dr. Grant grinned. "Woofer's fine. I

don't want you hitting the floor."

"I'm okay," I said.

"Come on, Mama. She's right. You're white as a sheet." Lisa led me into the waiting room where a woman was sitting with a cat carrier beside her. "He's going to be fine."

"But I can't believe something bit him. He never gets out of the yard unless he's on a leash."

"Could have been a possum," the woman with the cat said. "That's what's happened to Mandy. I'm here to get the stitches out. Mandy chased this possum up a tree and he got ahold of her."

"But this is a medium-sized dog."

"Same thing. Possums are mean. Got those teeth that stick out." She held three fingers straight to her mouth to show what she meant. "Course it could have been a raccoon, but I hope not. Lots of them have been showing up with rabies."

Lisa thrust a *People* magazine into my hand. "Here, Mama. Read about the fifty most beautiful people of the year."

Dr. Grant called us in in a few minutes. "It's a bite. We're going to have to lance it and start him on antibiotics."

"Could it have been a raccoon?" I asked.

"My guess is a possum. There are actually

three breaks in the skin and they have teeth like this." She held her three middle fingers to her mouth, apparently the universal symbol for possum. "He'll be fine. He may be able to come home late tomorrow. Certainly by the next day."

"It was a possum, wasn't it?" the woman in the waiting room said as we left. "I knew it. Those things are mean when you rile them up."

We were quiet on the drive home. Lisa hadn't asked, but had simply opened the passenger door for me. I must still have looked pale.

"I'm going to call the boys," she said as soon as we walked into the house. "They should be home from school by now."

I left her in the den and went to clean up.

She was watching Oprah when I came back. She hit the mute button and said the boys were okay and sent their love. Their daddy had promised to take them to Ruby Tuesday for supper and they were pleased about that.

I sat down on the sofa. Oprah and Richard Gere were talking silently to each other. Probably about the peace and calm of Zen Buddhism. Something I could use a little of right now.

Lisa turned and looked at me. "Sam said

Alan had told them that we had some problems we had to work on."

I thought about the two children in Atlanta that I adored and how frightened they must be. Parents are children's ultimate security, regardless of the children's ages. Mary Alice and I were in our fifties when our mother had her first heart surgery, and our whole world had tilted.

"Maybe they could come over for the weekend," I suggested.

Lisa nodded. "I probably shouldn't have run off like I did."

Her sense seemed to have returned with her hair color. But what would I have done when I was that age if Fred had informed me he was involved with someone else?

"Aunt Sister says I should have given Alan a good kick in the butt."

"A lot your Aunt Sister knows. All her husbands were so old, a kick in the butt might have killed them."

Lisa smiled.

"We'll get it straightened out," I promised.

For some reason she seemed to believe me.

Nine

I cooked some spaghetti and opened a jar of Prego for supper. While Lisa and I were cleaning up, Fred walked out into the backyard and wandered around. Then Arthur came out into his yard, and the two of them stood at the fence talking.

"Arthur's trying to find out if he can throw that lady, that first wife of his, off of Vulcan," Fred said when he came in. "Her ashes, I mean. He says it's what she requested. I told him to just go up there and do it, it wasn't like he was littering."

"Of course not." Lisa swished a dishrag over the table. "I can think of a lot of places I'd rather be thrown off of, though." She paused. "The Grand Canyon, or even Stone Mountain."

"Ashes are scattered, not thrown," I said.

"Same thing," Fred said.

"Scattering sounds nicer." I dried my hands, went into the den, and picked up my smocking. I was determined it was going to be a normal evening.

And it was until a little after nine. Lisa took *The Bridges of Madison County* which she said she'd heard was just like the movie, and she'd loved the movie, especially when Meryl Streep almost opened the truck door and went with Clint Eastwood, and disappeared into the guest room. Muffin followed her. Fred turned on the ball game and went to sleep, and I switched over to a Lifetime movie of the month. It was a good one, too. Patty Duke fighting for her grandchildren. Little Patty Duke with grandchildren. Mind boggling.

I kept hoping Alan would call, but he didn't. I expected Mary Alice to call, but she must have gone out with pencil-thin Cedric again. Or somebody. I wondered about Woofer.

"Yew cain't hev 'em!" Patty said, doing battle with a southern accent. Doing a pretty good job, too. I was rooting for her.

It was at this moment that I heard screaming. I hit the mute button. Definitely someone screaming my name.

"Fred," I said, jumping up. "Something's wrong." By the time he was awake and I was headed toward the kitchen, someone was pounding on the back door.

"Patricia Anne!" I opened the door to a disheveled Mitzi who threw herself into my arms. "They've arrested Arthur!"

Fortunately, by this time Fred was there

to help me. We got her to a kitchen chair where she collapsed.

"Who arrested him?" I asked. All right, so I wasn't thinking too sharply.

"The police. They say he murdered Sophie Sawyer." Mitzi dropped her head to the table with a bang.

"Hand me a wet paper towel," I told Fred. "And a glass of water."

I lifted Mitzi's head and wiped her face. She sat like a child while I did this. There was a red spot on her forehead where she had hit the table. She was probably going to have a bruise. I handed her the water. "Drink some, Mitzi," I said.

Again, like a child, she followed instructions. "Thank you," she said politely. She wiped her face with the wet paper towel and sipped the water. Fred and I sat down and waited. It was a few minutes before she continued.

"They came a few minutes ago and arrested him. Told him all that stuff he had the rights to and put handcuffs on him." She held the paper towel to her face. "The same men who ate my coconut cake."

"But why?" Fred asked. "That doesn't make any sense. Why would they think Arthur killed her?"

"I have no idea. But we've got to do something to help him. Arthur can't spend the night in jail. You know what all happens in jail. You watch TV." Mitzi shuddered.

"I'll call Debbie," I said. "She doesn't do criminal law, but she should know about getting him out on bail."

"What's going on?" Lisa was standing in the door with *The Bridges of Madison County* clutched to her chest.

"Damn fool policemen arrested Arthur Phizer," Fred said.

Mitzi's head hit the table again, but this time there was a wet paper towel between her and the wood so the thunk wasn't as pronounced.

I dialed Debbie's number, praying that I didn't get her answering machine.

"Hello," she said. I don't think I've ever been happier to hear her voice.

"Debbie," I said, "Lord, I'm glad you're there."

"What's wrong, Aunt Pat? Is it Mama?"

"No, honey, I didn't mean to scare you. But Mitzi Phizer's here and Arthur's been arrested for murdering his first wife and we want to know what to do next. He can't spend the night in jail."

There was a moment of silence and then Debbie said, "Say what?"

I repeated the message while the three sitting at the table listened. They looked, I realized, like the three "See no evil" monkeys. Mitzi had her head down, her hands pressed to her ears. Lisa was rubbing her eyes, and Fred had his hands folded against his mouth.

"Mr. Phizer's been arrested?"

"Yes. For poisoning the lady who died at the Hunan Hut the other day."

"Joseph Batson's mother-in-law? That was Mr. Phizer's first wife?"

The three at the table were looking at me now.

"I'll tell you about that later. But we've got to get him out of jail, Debbie. Tonight."

"How come he murdered her?"

"He didn't. Just tell us what to do." I realized I was being abrupt. I added, "Please."

"Are you sure they arrested him? Didn't just take him in for questioning?"

"Mitzi said they read him his rights."

"Lord."

That didn't sound good.

"Let me think."

I waited while Debbie thought. Mitzi put her head back down on the table.

"Aunt Pat, I can't think of a thing you can do tonight. If it were a DUI or something minor, I could probably go down and get him out. But not for murder. Ask Mrs.

Phizer if she's sure they said murder."

I put my hand over the phone. "You're absolutely sure they said murder, Mitzi?"

"Just like on TV. Read him his rights and everything."

"Just like on TV. Read him his rights and everything," I repeated to Debbie.

"Lord, Aunt Pat. They may not even allow him bail. They'll have a hearing and the judge will have to decide. We might be able to get it done sometime tomorrow. The Phizers don't have a lawyer?"

I looked over at Mitzi. "Have you and Arthur got a lawyer?"

"The man who drew up our will. I think his name's Jake Mabrey."

"A man named Jake Mabrey drew up their will," I repeated to Debbie.

"I know Jake. This is out of his ballpark. Mine, too, Aunt Pat. I can recommend a couple of good criminal lawyers, though. You got something to write with?"

I got a piece of paper and a pen. "Okay."

"Sam Levine's good. But the best one in town is a woman named Peyton Phillips."

I wrote the names down.

"I can try and get the bail hearing set up. But Aunt Pat, you've got to explain to Mrs. Phizer that if this is a cut-and-dried case, they may not set bail. And even if they do, it'll be large."

"Like how large?"

"We're talking hundreds of thousands here, Aunt Pat. Maybe a million if they've got him for murder one."

My face must have registered shock. The three at the table looked anxious.

I tried to act cool. "I don't think that's possible," I said. Of course it wasn't. Mitzi and Arthur were like Fred and me. They didn't have hundreds of thousands of dollars lying around.

"He's still going to need the best lawyer he can find. Ask Mrs. Phizer if she'd like for me to call Peyton. She may not be able to do it, but if she can, she's the one they need and the sooner she's involved, the better."

"You ask her, honey. I think she's calmed down enough." I handed the phone to Mitzi.

"Debbie?" Mitzi said shakily.

"Not good," I mouthed to Fred and Lisa. I motioned toward the den. They followed me in there and I told them what Debbie had said.

"Good God," Fred said. "A million dollars? That's ridiculous."

From the kitchen we could hear Mitzi saying "Un-huh" occasionally.

"Old Arthur wouldn't hurt a soul." Fred

reached for the remote and turned the TV off. "They need to be arresting some of these fools riding down the road shooting people."

Lisa sank down on the sofa. "I park and ride the MARTA."

Fred sat in his recliner. "We need a MARTA."

"Un-huh," Mitzi said in the kitchen.

I was getting a headache. I sat on the sofa, closed my eyes, and rubbed my forehead.

"That'll give you wrinkles, Mama," Lisa informed me.

I should worry.

Mitzi came in and sat in my usual chair. She had the greenish pallor of a person who had been sick for a long time. "They can't do anything tonight," she said. "Debbie's going to call a woman she says is the best criminal lawyer in town and see what she can do." She hesitated. "She says he'll be fine tonight. They'll put him in a cell by himself."

I wondered if that were true or if Debbie had just told Mitzi that to make her feel better. I also wondered if she had told Mitzi how much the bail might be.

"Anyway, like I said, there's nothing we can do tonight. Debbie says she'll call me when she finds out what's going on."

"He'll be fine," Fred said.

Mitzi nodded. "I told Debbie to be sure they give him his blood pressure medicine in the morning. I put it in his pocket, but they might have taken it away from him."

"Where's Arabella?" I asked. At this rate, I was going to be on blood pressure medicine myself soon.

"She went down to Brookwood Mall just before the police came. She said she needed to walk some." Mitzi ran her hands through her hair. "I guess I'd better get home. She'll be back soon. I've got to call Bridget and Barbara, too."

Lisa stood up. "I'll go with you, Mrs. Phizer. You got any bourbon? I make the best toddy for the body you ever tasted."

Mitzi smiled. "I don't think I can keep anything down, Lisa."

"This toddy just spreads out through all your capillaries smooth as silk. You can feel it relaxing you." Lisa took Mitzi's hand. "Let me help."

"I think I've just gotten an offer I can't refuse." Mitzi stood up. "I'll call y'all when I hear from Debbie."

"We're right here," Fred said.

After we heard the backdoor close, he and I looked at each other.

"I think your son has lost his mind," Fred

said. "That Lisa's a prize."

"She is," I agreed, choosing to ignore the fact that Alan had suddenly become mine alone.

Mitzi's phone call came an hour later; Lisa's toddies had obviously done their relaxing bit. Mitzi informed us that Debbie had lined up Peyton Phillips, that there wasn't anything that could be done until morning, that she, Mitzi, was going to bed, that Arabella and Lisa were playing gin and Lisa knew where the backdoor key was hidden. There was a definite slur in her speech.

I thanked her for calling, assured her everything would be fine, and that we would see her in the morning.

"Mitzi's tipsy," I told Fred as I hung up. "Lisa's playing cards with Arabella."

"Good. Let's go to bed."

Which we did.

I didn't think I would go to sleep, but I did, falling quickly into a deep, dreamless sleep; a few hours later, I was awake just as quickly. None of the drowsy, half-dreaming I usually go through, but wide-awake alertness.

Had I heard something? I listened, but there was only the sound of Fred's light snoring. Maybe it had been Lisa coming in that had awakened me.

I slipped on my robe and opened the bedroom door. The hall was dark, but the guest room door was partway open. It was a night of the full moon, and even though the blinds were closed, I could see a shape in the bed. So Lisa was home.

I closed her door quietly thinking I would go to the den and read. But first I needed a drink of water.

Without turning on any lights, I walked into the kitchen. The moon was so bright through the bay window that I could see the clock. Three o'clock. I poured a glass of water, but instead of going back into the den, I opened the door and stepped out onto the deck.

Birmingham is so mountainous that many of the houses, Mary Alice's for one, have formidable decks and views. Nothing about our deck is formidable. It's simply a large wooden platform with a couple of steps on each side, and a railing around it with a bench attached. A place to have cookouts. The gas grill is there, and pots of geraniums and begonias in the summer. The year before, we had splurged and bought a wrought iron table and chairs. An old aluminum chaise with several of its strips broken was still there, though, and I lowered myself into it gently, hoping it would hold.

It was a beautiful night, unusually mild for early September. I looked up at the sky, trying to make out constellations. I can pick out the main ones, thanks to the local planetarium that has programs showing the Birmingham sky as it changes each season, but the moon was too bright to see many stars. The only sounds were from the distant interstate, and an occasional rustle or bird chirp. Mitzi's house was dark which meant she was sleeping, I hoped.

Worry descended on me. Policemen didn't come in and arrest people for murder without good reason. Not that I believed for a moment that Arthur could have killed Sophie. But they had evidence that was so strong, they believed that he had. And they must have thought he had a motive.

A light came on in the kitchen. I watched Lisa open a bottle of aspirin, pour some water. I didn't get up; I would frighten her if I opened the kitchen door. In a moment, the light went out.

Another worry.

Lisa has been my daughter-in-law for fifteen years, and we've always had a very pleasant relationship. But we've never been very close. She and Alan have always lived in Atlanta, and I was teaching and she was working and had the children. Most of the distance was my fault, though, I had to admit. Having suffered from what Sister called the mother-in-law from hell for twenty-five years, I was determined that I was not going to interfere in my children's marriages. Maybe I had gone too far in the other direction. But at least Lisa had felt free to come to us when she needed help.

The kitchen light came on again. Fred this time. He opened the back door and looked out.

"Honey, what are you doing out there? You okay?"

"Just couldn't sleep. Come out and look at the moon."

He stepped out onto the deck, the kitchen light behind him making his gray-white hair a halo.

"Sit with me," I said.

"No way that chair would hold us both." He held out his hand. "Come on back to bed. It's getting chilly out here."

I took his hand. "I love you," I said. Sometimes you suddenly realize how much.

"And I love you. We got any Maalox?"

"Always." I got up and followed him into the kitchen.

"You know what?" he said. "Let's call

Haley. It's lunchtime in Warsaw. I'll bet she's home."

She was. She was fixing up their apartment that was just two blocks from the university, not far from Old Town which really wasn't old but rebuilt, but looked old. The weather was beautiful, already feeling like fall. She couldn't wait for us to come visit. We had to get e-mail. Send her some of those Combat things. Philip liked his classes. There were wonderful restaurants. They'd tried several. And was everything all right at home?

Everything was fine, we assured her. After we hung up, we went to bed and went right to sleep.

Ten

Fred had gone to work when I woke up, and the door to the guest room was closed so I assumed Lisa was still asleep. It was a few minutes after eight so I called the vet before I poured my coffee.

"His fever's down this morning," she reported. "Can you get antibiotics down him?"

"Absolutely," I promised.

"Then there's a good chance he can go home this afternoon. Call me."

I hung up and dialed Fred's number to tell him the good news, but Karen, his secretary, said he hadn't gotten there yet. So I told her to give him the message.

"Mr. Hollowell didn't tell me Woofer's sick," she said indignantly.

"He just got sick yesterday. The vet thinks a possum bit him."

"One bit my cat," Karen said. "You could see right where those teeth went in."

I knew Karen was holding her fingers up in the universal possum sign.

"I'll tell Mr. Hollowell soon as he comes in. Possums. I swear."

I had just sat down at the table with my

first cup of coffee and the paper when there was a knock on the backdoor.

"Mrs. Hollowell?" Arabella Hardt stood there in a blue chenille bathrobe. Her dark red hair was uncombed, she had on no makeup, and she was one of the most beautiful women I had ever seen. Her eyes were golden-green, the color Mama always called tiger eyes, and her skin was pale and flawless. "I'm Arabella. Aunt Mitzi wants to know if you have any Pepto-Bismol. She's sick to her stomach this morning."

"Come in, Arabella. I'm sure I do. You want some coffee while I look?"

"No, ma'am. But thank you. Is Lisa up?"

"I think she's still asleep. Her door's closed. Sit down. I'll be back in a minute." At the rate people were consuming my medical supplies, I was going to have to make a trip to the drugstore.

When I came back, bottle in hand, Arabella was standing at the bay window, looking out.

"I like your kitchen," she said.

"Thanks. Is Mitzi very sick?"

Arabella shook her head no. "She says it's nerves and bourbon."

"She's not much of a drinker."

Arabella took the bottle. "Must not be. She didn't have that much."

"I was so sorry about your mother. I just met her once. She was lovely."

"Thank you." Arabella paused a moment as if she were going to say something else, and then said, "I'd better get this over to Aunt Mitzi."

"If she doesn't get to feeling better, call me."

"I will. Thanks."

I watched her cross the yard. There was an outside chance the color of that hair was real.

"What did Arabella want?" Lisa was standing behind me.

"Mitzi's not feeling well this morning. She came to get some Pepto-Bismol. Did you know she calls her *aunt* Mitzi?"

Lisa poured a cup of coffee. "Aunt Mitzi and Uncle Arthur. I noticed that, too. Well, I guess they are related in a way."

Not in any way I could think of, but I let it go.

"I like her," Lisa said.

"She's certainly beautiful."

"And down-to-earth." Lisa put two teaspoons of sugar in her coffee. "Have you called about Woofer?"

"He's better. We can probably get him this afternoon."

"That's great."

"And we talked to Haley last night. Actually about three o'clock this morning. She's happy as a lark."

"I knew she would be. I'll bet you she's pregnant by Christmas."

"I think she hopes so."

I was putting the clothes in the washing machine when the phone rang. Lisa answered it, talked a few minutes, and then handed it to me. "It's Aunt Sister."

"What's going on over there?" she asked. "Debbie called and said Arthur's been arrested for murder."

"God's truth. It's crazy. Have you been talking to her this morning?"

"Just hung up. I was out with Cedric last night. And Mouse, you're not going to believe what happened."

I was sure I would find out, but I asked what anyway.

"He wanted to go up to Vulcan's observation tower and I thought, Well, why not. I've lived here all my life and I've never been up there. It'll be sort of an adventure. And believe you me, it was."

"You didn't climb the stairs?" For a moment I thought the adventure had been calling 911.

"Of course not. But the elevator got stuck. We were there for about an hour. Me,

Cedric, a man from Cincinnati, and two guys from Bangladesh, stuck halfway up Vulcan."

"My Lord. Did anybody panic?"

"We weren't *falling*, Mouse. We were just sitting there. We called down and told them we were stuck and then we played poker. I had some cards in my purse. And those guys from Bangladesh, I've never seen folks who could play poker like that. No telling what they could have done if they'd spoken English. Cedric and I each lost about ten dollars and I don't know about the guy from Cincinnati, but he was losing, too. The floor sure got hard, though. I kept switching from my knees to my butt, but I'm still sore this morning."

"Are you making this up?"

"How could I make up two card sharks from Bangladesh stuck on the Vulcan elevator? Where is Bangladesh, anyway?"

"I'm not sure," I admitted. "Somewhere near India. I'm impressed they're visiting Birmingham, though."

"I think they're here for medical treatment at UAB. Maybe heart surgery. The older guy kept clutching his chest."

"But it didn't affect his poker playing."

"Not one bit. In fact, it may have been a distracting maneuver."

"It's possible." I knew I would be hearing this story for some time, so I asked what else Debbie had had to say about Arthur.

"That's what I called to tell you. She said this lawyer, who charges an arm and a leg, incidentally, has set up a bail hearing for Arthur at one o'clock."

"That's good. Is it the woman lawyer?"

"Peyton somebody. How come you didn't call last night and tell me about Arthur being arrested?"

"I tried. You were stuck in the elevator."

"That's true," Sister conceded. "How's Mitzi?"

"Not too good. A little while ago, Arabella, Sophie's daughter, came over for some Pepto-Bismol."

"I'm not surprised. I'm glad none of my husbands ever murdered anybody."

"Arthur didn't murder anybody."

"Well, I know that." A beep announced there was a call waiting. "Gotta go," Sister said. "Talk to you later."

I turned from the phone shaking my head.

"What is it?" Lisa looked up from her cereal.

I told her about Sister's adventure on the elevator. I embellished it some, clutching my chest like the man from Bangladesh, and got the laughter I was hoping for. I poured myself some coffee and sat down before I told her that Arthur's bail hearing was set for one o'clock.

"I hope Mrs. Phizer feels like going," Lisa said.

"I'll go check on her in a little while." I didn't mention the fact that the bail might be way beyond the Phizers' financial means. In fact, the lawyer charging "an arm and a leg," as Sister had described it, was a worry.

I finished putting the clothes in the washing machine, fixed a bowl of cereal, and followed Lisa out to the deck where she was sitting at the table in the September sun. It was a beautiful morning, the kind of morning that would have been perfect for a long walk with Woofer. Damn. I'd never joke again about him being a Norwegian possum hound.

I sat down across from Lisa. "You said Arabella was down-to-earth? Mitzi described her as the wild child, the one Sophie worried about."

"She sounded real sensible to me. Shaken up about her mother's death, but who wouldn't be. I mean, Lord, who expects their mother to get poisoned?"

Good question.

"Did she say anything about her sister?" I asked.

"Not really. I got the impression they're not very close."

"That's what Mitzi said." I finished my cereal and pushed the bowl back. "I looked up their father on the computer at school yesterday. He was a very outstanding man. One of Ronald Reagan's advisors."

"She didn't mention him." Lisa leaned her head back and closed her eyes. "This sun feels wonderful."

"Ummm." I closed my own eyes, stretched out and soaked up a few harmful UV rays.

"I'm glad I'm here," Lisa said. "If I'd gone home to Dalton, Mother and Daddy would have had a fit. Daddy probably would have taken a shotgun to Alan."

Knowing Lisa's mild-mannered father, I doubted this seriously, but it still caused a flutter in my stomach. "I'm glad you're here, too." I didn't condone what Alan had done, but I wanted him all in one piece. "And I'm going to take advantage of your presence. Come help me take the draperies down. Your Aunt Sister's right. They need cleaning."

"They sure do," Lisa agreed.

One excuse I have for not cleaning house more is that when I do one thing, I see something else that needs doing. That was what happened with the draperies. When we got them down, we saw how bad the windows needed washing.

Lisa pitched in and helped, and when we were finished, she volunteered to take the draperies to the cleaners. While she was gone, I hopped into the shower, put on some shorts and a tee shirt, and went next door to check on Mitzi and see if there was anything I could do to help.

"She's feeling better," Arabella reported when she came to the door. "She's still lying down, though. Come on in, Mrs. Hollowell."

"No, I'm not lying down." Mitzi was standing in the den doorway. "I'm feeling much better."

I was glad she'd told me; the woman looked like death warmed over.

"Can I get you something, Aunt Mitzi?" Arabella asked. "Some Coke?"

"Thanks, Arabella. That would be nice. Let's sit in the den, Patricia Anne."

The Phizers' house and our house have an identical floor plan. So do most of the other houses on our block since most of them were built in the 1930's. Living room, dining room, and kitchen were originally lined up down one side and two bedrooms and bath down the other. Kitchens, dens, master bedrooms, and baths have been added to most of them, but the original plan is recognizable. Most of the people who have remodeled have had the sense to keep the large front porches which, with the sidewalks, make it such a nice neighborhood.

I followed Mitzi into the den. She's a larger woman than I am, but if she didn't make it to the sofa, I was prepared to break her fall somehow.

"Lisa and I have been washing windows," I said brightly as she sat down. "I took down the dining room draperies and the windows looked awful."

Mitzi smiled and nodded.

"And Mary Alice got stuck in the elevator at Vulcan last night with four guys, two of them from Bangladesh. They played poker until the park people rescued them."

I sat across from Mitzi. "Do you know where Bangladesh is?"

"Asia somewhere?"

"It's on the Bay of Bengal. It's surrounded by India," Arabella called from the kitchen. "We went there with Daddy one time when it was part of Pakistan."

I thought about my unread stacks of *National Geographics*; I really should do better.

"In fact," Arabella came into the den and

handed Mitzi and me both a Coke, "Sue, my sister, got malaria while we were there. She and Mama and I had to come home earlier than we had planned."

I took the Coke and thanked her. "Did you travel much with your father?"

"Not as much as I would have liked to." Arabella went back to the kitchen. In a moment she was back with her own glass. "Some. Mama wasn't much of a traveler." She took a sip of her Coke. "Sue wasn't either. My brother, David, went with him a lot, though." Another sip. "David was killed in a car crash while he was in college."

"I'm so sorry," I said.

Arabella shrugged. "The irony was that Daddy was pulling all kinds of strings to keep him out of Vietnam."

"That wasn't uncommon," I said. "It was a confusing time."

"People didn't know what to do," Mitzi agreed.

"Some people did." Then abruptly, Arabella said, "I'm going to take a shower. Can I get you anything else, Aunt Mitzi?"

"I'm fine, honey. You go ahead."

"I'll see you later, Mrs. Hollowell." Arabella disappeared down the hall.

"Such a nice child," Mitzi said.

Down-to-earth and a nice child? There

had been a lot of bitterness in Arabella's voice when she talked about her family.

I changed the subject. "Have you heard from Arthur this morning?"

"The lawyer called. She said she had a long talk with him and he's okay. He was worried about me." Mitzi tried to smile. "Bless his heart."

"Are you going to feel like going to the hearing?"

"I have to go."

"Okay if I go with you?"

"I'd appreciate it. I don't even know how a bail bond hearing works. Do you?"

"Not really. I guess we'll find out, though." I kept quiet about what Debbie had said about the amount of money the bail might be. Maybe she was wrong.

"I know it's going to be a lot of money," Mitzi said as if she had read my thoughts. "Peyton Phillips has already asked me if our house is paid for. I told her it was."

I wondered if Peyton had also told her that they might not set bail. I hadn't been able to mention the possibility the night before.

"Hell, Mitzi, we'll get Arthur out. We'll get Sister to come up with the money. Lord knows she's loaded."

Mitzi actually grinned. "Mary Alice

would love your generous offer."

"She'd do it."

"She probably would, bless her heart. Let's wait and see what happens. Okay?"

And that was the way we left it.

The Birmingham library, the city hall, the museum, and the Jefferson County courthouse all face Linn Park, a lovely park with large trees and a fountain. I let Mitzi and Arabella out in front of the courthouse and drove around looking for a parking place. Fortunately, I spotted a woman unlocking a car by the side of the library. I made a totally illegal, dangerous U turn and grabbed the place. I waited a moment for a policeman to tap on the window. This area and the area around Southside near the university are the most highly patrolled in the city. But I had lucked out. I locked the car and walked across the park where a lot of people were taking advantage of the beautiful weather by eating their lunches outside. Beds of red and pink begonias were still in full bloom.

The sun was so bright, I had to wait a moment for my eyes to adjust when I entered the courthouse. I almost missed the large figure darting into the women's rest room. My sister, Mary Alice. What the hell?

"I'm here to buy Cedric a fishing license,"

she said, when I announced to her feet that I knew she was in there.

Have I ever mentioned that Sister is the worst liar in the world? She has a way of twitching her lips like a rabbit that's a dead giveaway. But you don't have to be looking at her. Her voice gets a little higher, a little sweeter.

"No, you're not. Cedric doesn't even need a fishing license if he's over sixty-five. He may not even need one anyway since he's a foreigner."

The toilet flushed and Sister sailed out of the cubicle. "Well, that's what I'm here for. He wants a fishing license. He's going up to Logan Martin Lake tomorrow."

"For the Bass Master tournament?" The tournament had been the week before.

"Yes." Sister was trying to figure out how the water turned on in the sink.

"Just pass your hand under the faucet," I said.

"I hate plumbers. They do things deliberately to confuse people." She washed her hands and reached for a paper towel. "What are you doing here?"

"I brought Mitzi down for Arthur's bond hearing."

"Well, I hope everything turns out okay." She dried her hands and threw the towel into a wastebasket. "Gotta go."

"Wouldn't want Cedric to miss those bass. Hope they aren't pencil-thin ones."

I thought it was funny; she didn't. She forged out of the room, and by the time I came out into the hall, she was heading toward the license department. I got on the elevator and punched the button for the third floor. Whatever she was there for and trying to hide would come out.

Mitzi and Arabella were sitting on a bench outside an impressive mahogany door. Standing beside them by a window were a man and woman. His head was bent toward her as she talked quietly. They both looked up as I asked what was going on.

"The lawyer's in there with the judge," Arabella said. "She told us to wait out here." She turned toward the couple. "Mrs. Hollowell, this is my sister, Sue, and her husband, Joseph Batson."

The Batsons didn't look at all like I had imagined. Sue Batson was a large, rather imposing looking woman, at least two inches taller than her husband. Pale, with dishwater blonde hair and eyes puffed from crying, she didn't look at all like her sister. Joseph Batson could have passed for one of the Smith brothers from the cough drops, except the Smith brothers were neater.

Thin, and dressed in a wrinkled white shirt and blue jeans, he had dark hair receding on the top and pulled back into a small ponytail. He also had a beard, an ample one, sprinkled with gray. He was not my idea of a multimillionaire entrepreneur.

He had a lovely smile, though, and a firm handshake. His wife, on the other hand, simply nodded at the introduction. I wondered what they were doing here, if Mitzi or Arabella had called them.

Mitzi answered my unasked question. "Sue called this morning and I told her about the hearing. They're here to testify on Arthur's behalf if they need to."

"Best guy in the world," Joseph Batson said. "Been handling our insurance for years. I can't believe they'd even think he could be involved with Sophie's death."

Sue turned and looked out of the window, her expression one of such grief that I knew just hearing the words "Sophie's death" had been like a blow.

"According to the lawyer, though," Joseph continued, "it's not going to be that kind of hearing. The judge is simply going to determine how much bail to set."

Or whether to set it. But I didn't say anything. I sat down by Mitzi and asked her how she was feeling.

"Pretty good. I'll just be glad to get Arthur home."

Arabella patted her hand. "It's all just crazy."

"We've got to bury Mama," Sue Batson said.

We all looked at her, startled. Tears were running down her face.

"We do. She can't lie there in that morgue like this. We buried Daddy the day after he died and poor David was buried the day he was killed. We just threw him in the ground."

Joseph Batson moved over and put his arm around his wife's shoulder.

Arabella clenched her hands together; the knuckles shone white. "It was what Mama and Daddy wanted, Sue. You know that." She looked at her sister. "None of us were thinking clearly at the time."

"That's for sure."

"Hush, Sue." Joseph Batson patted his wife's arm. "We're not thinking clearly now, either."

I had no idea what was going on between the sisters, but one thing was clear. Sue didn't know that her mother had asked to be cremated and to have her ashes scattered from Vulcan. I didn't envy Arthur the job of telling her.

Sue Batson reached in her purse, pulled out a tissue, and mopped her face. "I have to go to the bathroom," she announced and walked away down the hall.

"I'm sorry, Arabella," Joseph said. "She's just terribly upset."

Arabella nodded.

"I want to see Arthur," Mitzi said.

I took her hand. "We all do."

But it was about fifteen minutes later before the door opened and a pretty blonde woman stuck her head out. "Dr. Batson, could you come in a minute?"

"Sure." He looked down the hall. Sue had still not come back from the rest room.

"I'll go check on her," I said.

"Thanks." He followed the woman who I assumed was Peyton Phillips into the judge's chambers.

"I'll go see about her, Mrs. Hollowell," Arabella said.

I wasn't sure that was a good idea, but fortunately we saw Sue coming down the hall just as Arabella stood up.

"Where's Joseph?" she asked. The time in the rest room had obviously been spent with cold water and the reapplication of makeup. Sue's eyes were still puffy, but she had pulled herself together.

"He went with the lawyer," I said. I

pointed toward the door. "In there."

Sue returned to her window. Arabella announced that she would be back in a minute and walked down the hall. Mitzi stood up, stretched, and sat back down.

The next few minutes seemed endless. Arabella didn't come back, Sue stood by her window, and Mitzi and I tried to make conversation which was hopeless since every other sentence was "What do you suppose is happening in there?"

Finally, the same blonde opened the door again and asked Mitzi to come in.

She squeezed my hand as she stood up. "Tell me he's okay, Patricia Anne."

"He's okay, Mitzi."

"He really is, Mrs. Phizer," said the blonde.

I hoped that meant the judge had granted Arthur bail.

Eleven

After Mitzi left, Sue came over to sit by me. "I'm sorry, Mrs. Hollowell. You're not seeing my family at its best."

I hoped not.

"I'm so sorry about your mother," I said. "She seemed like a lovely lady."

"She was." Sue had a tissue in her hand that she was shredding. "She was the gentlest, kindest woman in the world. It's hard to grasp the fact that someone killed her. Murdered her." Pieces of tissue drifted to the floor. She reached down and picked them up.

"Joseph and I were so glad when Mother decided to come to Birmingham for treatment. We thought she would stay with us. Joseph knows all the other medical people, and he knew who should be treating her."

More tissue drifted to the floor.

"She wanted to stay near UAB, though. She never wanted to bother anybody, or be in the way. Not that she ever would have been in the way with Joseph and me."

"Do you have children, Sue?" I asked.

"A son and a daughter. They're both in

college. Zoe is at the university in Tuscaloosa, Dickie's here at UAB. He has an apartment. Zoe wanted to come right home, and Dickie spent last night with us. But there's not a thing they can do. No use their missing classes."

She should have let them do what they wanted to, I thought. Their grandmother was dead. The hell with classes. I would have had my kids home in a minute.

Sue slumped back against the bench and stretched her legs out. She was wearing a short beige linen skirt and a beige and white shirt, very simple and probably very expensive, but not flattering. It was hard not to compare her to the beautiful Arabella.

She motioned her head toward the closed door in front of us. "I hope they're letting Joseph put up Mr. Phizer's bail."

The thought had crossed my mind that that was what was happening in there, too.

"My niece said it would be a lot."

Sue shrugged. "Joseph's got it. Sometimes I worry that he's overextending."

"Don't tell me that. Mitzi and my sister and I are getting in an investment club, and I was going to recommend Bellemina Health stock."

"Oh, it's safe. That's not what I meant." She didn't elaborate on what she had meant, and I didn't ask. Arabella was walking down the hall toward us, the sun glinting through the window on her red hair. Two men passing by her almost bumped into each other as they both looked back.

"Anything?" she asked as she sat down by me.

"Nothing," I answered.

Arabella pulled a Mars Bar from her purse and peeled the paper back. "Either of you want some?"

I shook my head no; Sue ignored her. Arabella sank her teeth into the chocolate and said, "Mmmm."

Just at that moment, the door opened and Mitzi, Joseph Batson, and the small blonde woman came out. Mitzi was crying, and Joseph had his arm around her.

"It's okay," the blonde assured us. "They'll have him out in a couple of hours."

"A couple of hours?" Sue asked.

"It takes that long to process the papers." Peyton Phillips came over, introduced herself, and shook hands with Sue and me.

Arabella smiled brightly and held up a half-eaten candy bar. "Want some?"

"No thanks," said the size two Peyton, smiling just as brightly. "I had pecan pie for lunch. With whipped cream." Good for her,

I thought. She turned to Mitzi. "I'll call you late this afternoon, Mrs. Phizer, and I'll be over tonight. Okay? Don't you worry, now."

Mitzi nodded into Joseph Batson's chest.

With a small wave, Peyton headed down the hall. Arthur was in good hands.

"Five hundred thousand dollars, Patricia Anne. Can you believe it? He knew the bond was going to cost a fortune. That's what he was there for, I found out, not just to testify on Arthur's behalf. Five hundred thousand dollars, and Joseph just wrote them out a check." Mitzi sniffled into a tissue. "If he hadn't been there, there's no way I could have gotten Arthur out. I can't believe he did that for us."

"I can believe he did it for you. What I can't believe is that anybody can write a check for that amount."

"I know. It boggles the mind."

Mitzi and I were going up Twentieth Street by Vulcan on our way home. She had agreed to let Joseph and Sue bring Arthur home, which told me she was feeling terrible. Arabella had said she was going to the library and would take a cab home. So Mitzi and I were alone.

"You want me to stop by the drugstore for anything?" I asked.

"No. I think I'll go lie down a while. Is it okay if I replace your Pepto-Bismol to-morrow?"

"It's a gift."

"Gee, thanks."

"What are friends for."

Lisa was sitting on my front steps. As I turned into the driveway, she waved and came over to the car. "Everything all right?"

"He'll be home in a little while," Mitzi said.

"Oh, Mrs. Phizer, I'm so glad. That's wonderful."

"Joseph Batson wrote a check for five hundred thousand dollars, Lisa." Mitzi opened the door and got out. "Can you be-lieve that? Can you believe anybody could write a check for half a million dollars?"

"Nobody I know. Where's Arabella?"

"At the library. And I'm going to go lie down a while. Watch a little of Oprah."

"Can I get you anything?" I asked.

"I'm fine."

She didn't look fine; she looked slightly green. But I knew she wanted to be by her-self and relax.

"I've got a surprise for you, Mama," Lisa said as we started toward the back.

For a second I had a wild hope that Alan had shown up and they were going back to

Atlanta together. But when I opened the gate, there was my precious Woofer, lying in the sun, his nose between his paws. When I ran to him, he rolled over for me to scratch his belly.

"The vet called and said he could come home, so I went and got him," Lisa said. "She gave us some pills to give him."

I knelt and rubbed my cheek against his head. He smelled like the vet's office. Damn possum.

"Has he had anything to eat?" I asked.

"I gave him a couple of dog biscuits. You want me to open him a can of food?"

"You hungry, boy?"

Woofer thumped his tail.

"I'll get him a can." Lisa disappeared into the kitchen.

I sat on the grass and pulled Woofer, as much of him as I could, into my lap. The sun was warm across my shoulders and I suddenly felt very tired and sleepy.

"Here you go." Lisa was back with the food which Woofer sniffed at and refused.

I took a small amount and held it out to him in my hand. He ate it as if he were just trying to please me. I gave him several bites until he turned away.

"It'll take him a day or two to get his appetite back," Lisa said.

"Thank you for my wonderful surprise."

"You're so welcome." She sat down beside me. "What happened down at the courthouse?"

"I've never seen two sisters any more different than Sue and Arabella."

"Tell me."

So I did, sitting in the grass in the warm September sun, my Woofer stretched out beside me.

"I thought Arabella was nice," Lisa said.

"She probably is, away from her sister. They really seem to dislike each other."

"That's a shame."

"Yes, it is."

"What does the sister look like? Is she as beautiful as Arabella?"

"Nice looking, but not beautiful. She's larger and has dark blonde hair." I patted Woofer. "When Arabella wasn't around, she was very pleasant."

"Well, what about Mr. Phizer? What's the next step?"

"I have no idea. I'm assuming the police have a mighty good case or they wouldn't have arrested him."

Lisa hesitated. "You really don't think he could have done it?"

"Absolutely not."

"What about Arabella or Sue?"

"They might kill each other, but they both seem to have loved their mother dearly."

"How about the son-in-law?"

"Nice as he can be. None of them had the opportunity anyway. The woman was just sitting there having lunch and was poisoned."

"Having lunch with Mr. Phizer."

"Right. And Arthur didn't do it."

Lisa smiled and rubbed Woofer's ear. "Well, you and Aunt Sister are pretty good at figuring these things out. Looks like you've got your work cut out for you here."

God's truth.

Arthur got home around five. Lisa called to me that a Mercedes had just pulled into the Phizers' driveway and if the woman who had just gotten out was Arabella's sister, she could see what I meant.

I looked through the bare, clean dining room windows and saw Joseph and Sue Batson standing beside the car and Mitzi hugging Arthur so hard he nearly lost his balance. Sometime during the afternoon, Barbara and Bridget, the Phizers' daughters, had arrived, and they stood on the porch smiling, Bridget holding her baby, Andrew Cade. I was sure Mitzi had told both of them that she was fine and they shouldn't leave work. But I was glad to see them, and I'm sure Mitzi was, too.

Joseph and Sue stayed only a minute, and then the Phizers went inside, Arthur carrying Andrew Cade. They probably wouldn't feel much like eating, but Lisa had gone to the Piggly Wiggly earlier and picked up barbecued chicken, potato salad, and baked beans for both the Phizers and us.

There was nothing wrong with Fred's appetite, though. After he showered, we sat on the deck with Woofer stretched out beside us, and ate our supper while I told him about what had happened at the courthouse.

"A half a million dollars? He just wrote a check?"

"Close your mouth," I said and assured him that this was what had happened.

"Damn."

"We're having our first investment club meeting tomorrow," I said. "I'm going to recommend Bellemina Health stock."

"You do that, honey. Damn. A half a million dollars?"

"You sound like me." Lisa pushed her chair back. "Who wants lemon icebox pie?"

"I don't think I want that child to go back

to Alan," Fred said as she disappeared into the kitchen.

We sat on the deck talking for a long time. Lisa told us some of the things the boys had done that we had missed out on, soccer games, weekend hiking trips, the fact that Sam was becoming a computer whiz.

Atlanta isn't that far away, just a short drive, but we were missing so many milestones in our grandchildren's lives. Dammit, we had to do better.

Fred listed the stocks that the investment club should buy. Definitely AT&T and the people who made Viagra. Pharmaceuticals and communications would make us rich. Guaranteed.

"Wal-Mart's done pretty good for you," I said.

"Been worried about it ever since Sam Walton died. He knew how to run that business." And he had been the one who had told Fred to buy the stock, a plain fellow from Arkansas who had sat by Fred in the coach section of a Delta plane on his way to Atlanta, and told him he thought Wal-Mart stock was going to do pretty good.

We saw Barbara and Bridget drive away, and the lights go out at the Phizers'.

"I don't think Arabella's there," Lisa said.

"Maybe she went back to her mother's

apartment." I yawned. It had been a long day.

"Come on, boy." Fred picked Woofer up. "You need to be in your house tonight."

"Wait. He has to have his pill." Lisa went into the kitchen and was back in a moment. She reached over, pressed the sides of Woofer's mouth open and popped the pill in. It was done so expertly, he didn't seem to mind.

Fred was right. One could get used to Lisa's presence.

I think I was asleep before Fred came to bed. It's seldom that I zonk out like that. I remember wondering what Sister was up to and why I hadn't heard from her and what a cock-and-bull story that was about a fishing license for Cedric. And then I was gone.

Sometime during the night, I awoke just as easily. Strips of moonlight were slicing through the venetian blinds and across our bed; the air conditioner was humming softly.

I got up without turning on any lights and went to the bathroom. Then I tiptoed down the hall to the kitchen, suddenly hungry for some cereal.

It was an incredibly beautiful night. The air outside, I knew, would feel like cool silk. So before I poured the Cheerios, and still without turning on the lights, I slipped on some huaraches that were under the table, got the flashlight out of the junk drawer, and took several dog biscuits from the box. Woofer had disappeared inside his igloo right after supper, and I wanted to check on him.

The first touch of fall was in the air, a dryness. The weather was still hot, but not the melting hot of late August. I walked across the yard, knelt and whispered to Woofer to come out and enjoy the night.

I could hear his tail thumping, and in a minute he stuck his head out.

"You okay?" I asked.

He came all of the way out and accepted a dog biscuit. He was fine.

I patted him and started back toward the house. It was then that I saw the flickering light at the back of the Phizers' house. I stopped, puzzled. The light became a flame.

Dear God.

For a second, I couldn't think what to do first. I started toward the Phizers' but detoured into my kitchen and called 911. Then I had the presence of mind to realize I could call Mitzi quicker than I could run over there.

Arthur answered sleepily.

"Your house is on fire," I screeched.

"Y'all get out! Right now."

"What?"

"Your house. A fire. Get out!"

I raced down the hall to get my robe.

"What is it?" Lisa was standing in her door.

"A fire at the Phizers'."

Fred had gotten out of bed and was opening the blinds when I ran into the bedroom, banging my hip on the bedpost. I could see through the window that the small flicker was now a serious fire.

"My God!" He grabbed his pants and was stumbling into them as he made for the door. "I've got to go see if they're all right."

"Put on some shoes!" I felt across the bed for my robe. It hadn't occurred to me to turn on a light, but as he left, he had the presence of mind to flip the switch. I immediately saw my robe, threw it on, and ran after him.

We live three blocks from a fire station for which I was especially grateful this night. As I went out, one fire truck was already pulling into the driveway and the firemen were jumping off, yelling at each other. Another truck pulled up in front and the men ran across the yard.

But above the flashing red lights of the fire trucks was the terrible sight of flames shooting into the night sky from the back of Mitzi and Arthur's house. How could this have happened so suddenly?

Firemen were dragging hoses toward the back of the house. Water was already shooting high in the air and onto the flames which hissed and sparked. I ran toward the front of the house, dodging firemen and waterhoses and saw Fred standing with Mitzi and Arthur.

"You okay?" I was out of breath.

"Oh, Patricia Anne." Mitzi collapsed into my arms. "Oh, God, I can't believe this!"

"Are you all right?"

"We're okay," Arthur said in a shaky voice.

A fireman came running by. "Do y'all mind moving out to the sidewalk?"

We moved. A small crowd of neighbors was gathered there already, watching. I wondered what time it was.

"What caused it? Bad wiring?" someone asked.

No one answered. We stood, huddled together, watching the orange flames, helpless. The air was heavy with smoke; my eyes began to burn. Several people coughed and rubbed their eyes, but no one left.

And then, in a few minutes, from the front of the house we could no longer see fire snaking into the night sky. I hoped that was a good sign. I had seen enough fires on TV, though, to know that if it had crept into the attic, it could explode from under the eaves anywhere, everywhere. All we could do was wait.

"Where's Arabella?" I had just realized she should be there.

"I hope she's at her mother's apartment. Come here, honey." Arthur put his arms around Mitzi and pressed her face to his shoulder. "Just don't look."

"But she's not here."

To my relief, Arthur shook his head no.

"This is awful," Mitzi sobbed.

"Maybe not, honey." Arthur rubbed her shoulder. "Anyway, we're out, and we're okay, and that's the important thing." He turned to us. "The damn smoke alarm didn't go off. If you hadn't called, Patricia Anne, we'd still be in there."

Don Tripp from across the street overheard him and said, "You need more than one smoke alarm, Arthur."

"Hell, we have three, Don. None of them went off."

"Damn! You need to check those things every so often, you know."

"I do."

"Our wedding pictures, Arthur," Mitzi

sobbed. "And the girls' wedding pictures."

"They're probably fine. And the girls have copies of them." He smoothed her hair. "Why don't you let Patricia Anne take you over to her house. Make us all a big pot of coffee."

Mitzi looked up at him.

"Okay? Will you do that? There's not a thing you can do here."

"He's right, Mitzi." I said. "We can at least make everybody coffee."

"But I don't want to leave."

"Please, honey." Arthur nodded toward the house. "I think they're getting it under control, anyway."

Mitzi looked at the firemen and the hoses, the flashing lights. "You think so?"

"I do. And it's chilly out here. You go make that coffee."

She looked at me. "Patricia Anne?"

"We'll be back in a little while, Arthur." I looked around for Fred, but he had disappeared. I took Mitzi's hand and led her toward my house.

Lisa was waiting for us at the gate and holding a blanket. "I was just bringing this over," she said. She wrapped it around the shaking Mitzi and led her up the steps and into the kitchen.

"Woofer's in here, Mama," Lisa called

from the door. "I brought him in so he wouldn't get scared. Muffin's still in my bed asleep."

I swear, my son Alan had lost his mind, taking a chance on losing this girl. I stood for a moment looking over at the fire that was now just sparks, grateful that it had been no worse.

When I went inside, Mitzi was on the sofa in the den, wrapped in the blanket but still shivering.

"Lisa's making the coffee," she said, her teeth chattering. "Why on earth would I be cold? It's not cold in here."

I took her hands and rubbed them. They were like ice. Was she going into shock?

I tried to remember what the first-aid manuals said. Head down? No. That was for fainting. Lord, all those years of teaching and all those emergencies, and I couldn't think what to do. Well, getting her warm sure wouldn't hurt.

"Lie down, Mitzi," I said, "and prop your feet up on this pillow." If she got any worse, I decided, I would go and get one of the firemen. Some aspirin? That's what they say to take if you think you're having a heart attack. Wouldn't hurt.

I tucked the blanket around her and rushed into the bathroom. Mary Alice had talked me into joining a tap dancing class with her the year before and I had ended up the very first day with tendinitis. Haley had brought me a thing, God only knows what you call it, that you put in the microwave for a couple of minutes. It's flexible and holds the heat for a half hour or so. I had wrapped it around my thigh for the tendonitis, and it had felt wonderful.

I grabbed it, hurried back to the kitchen, and threw it into the microwave.

"What's that?" Lisa wanted to know.

"A thing that you heat up and put on you."

"One of those microwave heating packs?"

"I reckon." I reached in the cabinet, got two aspirin, poured some water in a glass and took them to Mitzi. I was back in the kitchen by the time the microwave dinged. Lisa was looking out of the window at the Phizers' house.

"I think it's over," she said. "They're rolling up one of the hoses."

"Good. Where's Woofer?"

"Asleep in the utility room. I'll bring Mrs. Phizer some coffee."

The heat pack smelled like freshly baked bread. It was so hot, though, I had to wrap it in a dish towel before I placed it between Mitzi and the back of the sofa.

"Lord, that feels good," she said. "I don't know why I'm so cold."

"You've been through a lot today." What time was it anyway?

Lisa came in with a coffee mug in one hand and the sugar bowl in the other. "This should warm you up, Mrs. Phizer. Put a lot of sugar in it."

"Don't sit up too fast," I warned.

"I'm okay."

She wasn't okay, but the coffee would do her good. She sat up, and I put the heat pack against her back.

She put two teaspoonfuls of sugar into the mug, stirred it, and sipped carefully.

"What time is it?" I asked Lisa.

"A little after three."

The coffee shook in Mitzi's hand. She reached over and placed it on the table. "If it hadn't been for your call, Patricia Anne, I hate to think what would have happened."

"Your smoke alarm didn't go off, Mrs. Phizer?"

"Our three smoke alarms didn't go off."

Lisa glanced around at me and frowned.

"You forgot to check the batteries?"

"Arthur said he checked them, but he must not have."

I hoped that was true. I didn't want to think of the alternative. An alternative that

Mitzi hadn't thought of yet.

The back door opened and Fred came in. The smell of smoke came in with him. "Everything's under control over there, Mitzi," he said, sticking his head into the den. "Those guys know what they're doing. Arthur said to tell you that most of the damage is at the back, and the rest of the house is okay. Smoke, of course."

Mitzi teared up. "The house isn't gone?"

"Nothing that can't be fixed, Mitzi. I promise you. The firemen are going to stay over there for a while longer to make sure. I came to get us some coffee. Arthur says he'll be here in a little while."

"Y'all can sleep in the boys' room, Mitzi." The boys' room had been my ironing and sewing room for fifteen years, but there were comfortable twin beds in there.

"I'll make up the beds," Lisa said.

"Thanks. I don't think I'll sleep much, but thanks." Mitzi wiped the tears from her face. "I can't believe three smoke alarms and not a one of them went off. Can y'all?"

"There's a police car over there, just pulled up. That's probably what they're looking into," Fred said.

Mitzi didn't need to hear this now. And, truthfully, neither did I.

"Take the coffee, Fred," I said. "There

are some Styrofoam cups in the cabinet over the refrigerator."

For once he caught on to the tone of my voice and left.

Twelve

Dawn comes slowly in September. I hadn't gone back to sleep, though Fred and Arthur had come in around four.

"You awake?" Fred whispered.

I assured him that I was.

He pulled off the pants he had on over his pajamas, got in the bed, and held me. He smelled like smoke, I probably did, too, and we lay there, our arms around each other.

"Is Arthur okay?" I asked.

"He's lying down."

I rubbed his back between his shoulder blades. In a few minutes, his breathing shallowed.

But sleep was lost for me. I watched the day beginning, first as a pale light through the blinds, a light I might be imagining, and then a definite brightness. I slipped from the bed.

"What?" Fred murmured sleepily.

"Nothing. Go back to sleep." I pulled on some jeans and a sweater, found the huaraches I had had on earlier, and slipped down the hall. There was no sound from either of the other bedrooms.

Hopefully, everyone was asleep.

I stepped onto the back porch into a perfect late summer dawn. The sun hadn't crested the horizon yet, but the sky was more blue than gray, with a pink glow toward the east. If I had come out at this time yesterday morning, I would have smelled the Carolina jasmine blooming along the fence. Today there was smoke.

A heavy dew seeped through the weave of my shoes as I went to check on Woofer. He looked up, wagged his tail, and yawned.

"Go back to sleep," I told him, just as I had told Fred.

I opened the gate and walked next door to the Phizers'. I wondered if the crape myrtle tree had suffered any damage from the fire. Mitzi's beautiful daylilies had, I saw immediately. They had been trampled by the firemen or had a heavy hose dragged over them. I lifted one of the long stems that yesterday had held a deep rust-colored flower. When I let it go, it dropped to the ground.

The crape myrtle tree had fared better. Hopefully, it was far enough away from the house that the heat hadn't done any damage. I examined one of the lower limbs. While I was looking at it, the first rays of the sun broke across the horizon. It was a perfect beginning of a September day.

And then I turned and looked at the house.

I guess I had expected to see the back wall of the house gone, but it was standing. The kitchen windows as well as the back bedroom windows were knocked out, and the kitchen door was hanging askew. But it still didn't look as bad as I had thought it would.

Mitzi had a five-legged table that had belonged to her grandmother, a funny-looking table that was a conversation piece. Could the table still be there? I walked slowly toward the house.

"Morning, Patricia Anne."

I jumped. I had been concentrating so on the damage to the house, that I hadn't seen Officer Bo Mitchell of the Birmingham Police Department as she came around the corner.

"Morning, Bo. You're out mighty early."

"No, I'm out late. I get off work at seven."

Mary Alice and I had gotten to know Bo Peep Mitchell just before Christmas when a former student of mine had gotten us involved in a murder at a Birmingham art gallery. Funny and kind, Bo has never seemed tough enough to me to be a "Dickless Tracy" as she says the women are sometimes still called at the department, not always behind their backs. She's also a very pretty woman, her skin a café au lait. The first time I had seen her, her eyes were green like my student Shatawna's, the legacy, I supposed, of a Caucasian ancestor. Later I found out she had contact lenses that she changed to suit her mood. Today her eyes were a dark brown and her hair was plaited into cornrows.

"What are you doing here?" I asked, after a hug.

"Guess I'm arresting you. You have the right to remain silent, you know."

"For what?"

"Messing around, I reckon." She held up some yellow crime tape. "They sent me out to put this up and here you are, already heading through the door."

I eyed the tape. "How come you're putting that up?"

"So folks like you won't be messing around until we can get a good look."

"You think it's arson?"

"The folks downtown must think something."

A small blonde woman in a police uniform walked around the house. Probably still in her early twenties, she looked more like a college student than a policeman.

Bo introduced us. "Patricia Anne Hollowell, Joanie Salk."

I'm sure I looked startled. Jonas Salk?

"Don't you just love it?" Bo said.

"No, Bo Peep, I don't. It drives me crazy." The young woman caught my hand in a firm handshake. "It's Joanie, Mrs. Hollowell. I tell myself my parents just weren't thinking."

I smiled at her. "It's a very nice name."

"Beats the hell out of Bo Peep," Bo grumbled. "I think my mama plain lost her mind. Here." She handed Joanie the end of the tape. "Go tie this around that drainpipe at the corner."

"They had three smoke alarms, and none of them went off," I said.

"Is that right." It wasn't a question. She already knew it.

Joanie reached the corner and the drainpipe. "Is there some special kind of way I'm supposed to tie this?"

"So it won't fall off." By this time, Bo was attaching the tape to the drain at the other corner of the house.

"You putting this in front, too?" I asked.

Bo shook her head no. "The front looks fine. It would just grab the attention of folks coming down the street."

"Should I leave some slack?" Joanie called.

Bo rolled her eyes slightly at me before

she answered, "Not much." Then she asked me, "Where are the Phizers?"

"Over at my house. I hope they're asleep. The last two days have been unbelievable for them."

Bo nodded. "Mr. Phizer the one I've seen cutting his grass in shorts and wing-tip shoes and dress socks? Not much hair on top?"

I grinned. "It's not a pretty sight. But he's such a nice man, Bo. And they've got him charged with murdering his first wife."

Joanie had rejoined us by this time.

"But you don't think he did it."

"Of course not. Arthur wouldn't swat a fly." I glanced at Bo's watch. "What time is it?"

"A little after six. Why?"

"Y'all want some coffee? Come on and I'll fix us some."

"You got any sweet rolls?"

"Always."

"But what if the dispatcher calls us?" Joanie asked.

Bo tapped the pager on her belt. "And you can run to the car every few minutes."

"Okay."

It didn't take much intuition to realize these two were not headed for the partnership longevity of a Cagney and Lacey.

The house was still quiet. I brought the coffee and sweet rolls out to the deck where Bo was sitting, her legs stretched out, her shoes off. Woofer had waked up and come to investigate the company.

"Joanie's gone to the car. She'll be back in a minute." She reached over and patted Woofer.

I put the tray on the table. "He just came home from the vet yesterday. She thinks a possum bit him."

"Lot of them around." Bo yawned, and then smiled. "Sorry."

"You tired?" I asked. Silly question.

"I hate working nights. I don't complain, though." She put a teaspoon of sugar into her coffee. "When I get to be chief, I can sleep."

"You want to be chief of police?"

"I'm going to be." Bo bit into a sweet roll and chewed. "Mmm. Good."

I sweetened my own coffee. This nice woman as chief of police?

"I know what you're thinking, but," Bo pointed to her head, "the ability's here, not dangling where most folks think."

She was right, of course.

Joanie came and joined us, helping herself to coffee and sweet rolls. "Nothing on the radio."

Bo turned to me. "Tell me about the Sawyer woman who was murdered. I know she was connected to Mr. Phizer in some way. Sort of a first wife, but not really."

They ate sweet rolls and drank coffee while I told them about Sophie Sawyer and Arthur's teenage marriage, how it had been annulled and they had each married other people and had long marriages. When I got to the daughters and mentioned that Sue Batson, Sophie's daughter, was married to Joseph Batson, Bo gave a little whistle.

"Money."

"He wrote a check for half a million dollars yesterday for Arthur's bail."

"That boggles the mind."

"I know."

"Someone in my family had money once," Joanie volunteered. "I don't remember his name but I've heard my mother talk about him."

"That's nice," Bo said.

"He raised Hereford cows down around Harpersville. Left all his money to Auburn University for cow research."

"I'm sure the family was thrilled about that," Bo replied.

But sarcasm seemed lost on Joanie Salk, just as it's lost on my sister.

"Not really. They were hoping to inherit some of it."

Nope. This was not going to be a Cagney and Lacey duo. But back to business, I said, "There wasn't any motive for Arthur to have killed Sophie Sawyer. He was very fond of her, maybe still loved her like you do your first love. She was sick, and he was trying to help her."

Joanie Salk put down her coffee cup. "Maybe she was going to leave him a lot of money and she decided not to, to change her will and leave it to somebody else and he killed her before she could."

"Right," Bo agreed. "Maybe she decided to leave it to Auburn for cow research."

This time, Joanie frowned.

Bo pushed her chair back. "We've got to go."

"Well, what about the Phizers?" I asked. "They're going to need some things out of their house. Can they go in?"

"Somebody will be over here after a while," Bo said. "Somebody from the department. They'll go in with them to get their stuff. Soon as everything's checked out they can get the insurance folks out here and do what they want to. In the meantime, it's a crime scene."

"A crime scene," Joanie Salk repeated,

patting her holster and getting up. "Joe Pepper will probably be here after while."

Bo rubbed her forehead as if she were getting a headache. "Probably. Come on, Joanie. We've got to go check out. Thanks, Patricia Anne, for the coffee."

"You're welcome. Who's Joe Pepper?"

"Arson guy."

Joanie smiled sweetly. "Thanks, Mrs. Hollowell. I just graduated from the academy last week, and everybody's being so nice."

"I'll meet you at the car in a minute, Joanie," Bo said.

"Okay." She gave a little wiggle of her fingers and opened the gate.

Bo and I wiggled back.

"Just a couple of things, Patricia Anne. Don't let the dumb blonde act fool you. She's mean as hell and twice as smart."

I grinned. "I'm glad to hear it."

"And tell your friend, Arthur Phizer, that if I were him, I wouldn't bend over. His wife might be safer not sleeping with him, too."

"What?"

"Tell him if he's smart, he'll cover his ass." Bo grabbed another sweet roll and left.

I could see the yellow crime tape next door. It glowed in the rays of the early morning sun. If the fire had been deliberately set, and the smoke alarms fixed so they wouldn't go off, then Arthur, had, indeed, better cover his ass.

But why? It had to have something to do with Sophie Sawyer's death, but what? I shivered in the warm September air.

I collected the morning paper from the driveway and went into the kitchen. I had just gotten a pound of turkey bacon out of the freezer when Lisa came in. She had on a tee shirt and shorts with Mickey and Minnie Mouse rollerblading on them and looked as if she hadn't slept much, either. She sat down at the table and groaned, "Coffee."

"The police have been next door," I said, pouring her a cup. "They put crime scene tape across the back of the Phizers' house."

"They think it's arson?"

I nodded. I handed her the cup and sat down at the table with her. "They're investigating. I expect they'll be looking at the smoke alarms, too."

"But who on God's earth would want to hurt the Phizers?"

"Maybe the same person who killed Sophie Sawyer."

"I read once," Lisa said, reaching for the cream, "that ninety-five percent of all murders are committed for money or jealousy."

"You and Aunt Sister. Well, Sue and

Joseph Batson sure didn't need Sophie's money. And Arthur's not rich, but he wouldn't stand to inherit anything if Sophie died. At least, I don't think so."

"Which leaves Arabella." Lisa stirred her coffee thoughtfully. "What do we know about her?"

"She and Sue don't get along, and she's had a couple of failed marriages. I have no idea about her financial status."

"Maybe Sue was jealous because Arabella was her mother's favorite, and she killed her mother."

"This is crazy," I said. "I don't think any of them killed anybody." I thought about the Phizers' house. "Or tried to kill anybody."

I got up and put the bacon into the microwave to defrost. Sausage, scrambled eggs, grits, and buttered biscuits were what I wanted, what we had eaten happily for years until someone figured out that cholesterol has a habit of taking up permanent residence in our arteries. One more thing to feel guilty about. I had ruined my children's blood vessels by feeding them well.

"Did your mother ever cook turnip greens with fatback?" I asked Lisa.

"Sure. Only she called it streak of lean. Best turnip greens in the world." She turned a page of the newspaper. "No telling what my arteries look like."

Well, this morning we were going to have scrambled eggs with the turkey bacon, "irregardless" as Mama used to say. We all needed some comfort food. Hell, I might even fry the eggs, sunnyside up and risk salmonella. Live dangerously. Sop the yellows on drop biscuits.

I was reaching for the flour when the phone rang. I grabbed it, hoping it hadn't wakened Mitzi and Arthur. It was time for Fred to get up, anyway.

"I'll pick you up at a quarter till ten," Sister said. "And I think I may be engaged."

"Why are you picking me up, and to whom are you engaged?"

"For the investment club. Today's the day, isn't it?"

I glanced at the bulletin board beside the refrigerator.

"Yes. Who are you marrying?"

"I didn't say I was marrying anybody. Lord, Mouse. I just said I was engaged." There was a pause. "I think." Another pause. "Anyway, I just put him on the plane to London, so it's nothing to worry about."

"Cedric?"

"Of course. Did you think it was the blind guy or one of the guys from Bangladesh? I'm on my way home from the airport now. Have you decided which stocks to recommend?"

"Bellemina Health, for one. Maybe Rubbermaid. And I need to talk to you. You wouldn't believe what all's been happening over here."

"Fred must have gotten his prescription for Viagra refilled."

"Fred doesn't need Viagra." I looked up and saw Fred standing in the doorway. "Gotta go," I said and hung up.

"Mary Alice?" he asked.

I nodded.

He sat down at the table across from a grinning Lisa.

"Morning, Pop," she said, handing him the sports section of the paper.

"Good morning, Lisa."

I made the drop biscuits to the sound of silence broken only by the occasional rustle of newspapers. Sister would have loved it.

Arthur came in as we were finishing eating. Mitzi, he said, was still asleep. He ate a biscuit, turning down the offer of an egg, and then he, Fred, and Lisa went next door to see what the damage looked like in the daylight.

"I can't believe they've put crime tape up," he said as they went out the door.

"What do they think? That somebody tried to burn us down?"

The answer was so obvious, that none of us voiced it.

I straightened up the kitchen and sat down in the den to look at the paper. There was a small paragraph in the Metro section that said insurance executive Arthur Phizer, 64, had been arrested for the murder of socialite Sophie Sawyer, 64, the mother-in-law of Dr. Joseph Batson, CEO of Bellemina Health. Phizer had been released on a $500,000 bond.

Socialite? That seemed like such an old-fashioned word. And what kind of socializing had Sophie done in Birmingham, anyway? She'd been gone for forty years and was sick when she came back. And no mention of husband or children. Just the fact that she had a rich son-in-law.

The phone rang, and I grabbed it. It was Debbie wanting to know if the Phizers were pleased with Peyton, that it had been a miracle that Peyton had taken the case as busy as she was. She had tried to call them, but their phone was out of order. Maybe I ought to report it.

I told her about the fire, the smoke alarms that didn't go off, the police tape.

"Lord, Aunt Pat." She sounded as out of

breath as I was. "Are Mr. and Mrs. Phizer okay?"

"Shaken up by everything that's happened."

"Has anybody called Peyton?"

"Not that I know of. Why would they need a lawyer for a fire?"

"If the police suspect arson, she needs to know. I'll call her. Okay?"

"Sure. By the way, your mother's engaged again."

"Cedric?"

"Yep. She just put him on a plane to London."

Debbie giggled. "That woman. Let's not order the invitations yet."

"I don't even know Cedric's last name."

"I doubt Mama does."

We hung up laughing.

Thirteen

"You go on, Mama. I'll be here when Mrs. Phizer wakes up."

I was dressed and waiting for Mary Alice, Fred had gone on to work, and Arthur had gone to talk to the insurance people. He had had no trouble getting his things from next door. The place was swarming with policemen, he said, and please tell Mitzi that the five-legged table was okay, maybe a little water damage, but nothing that couldn't be fixed.

When he left, he was dressed in a gray suit and looked nice. But no one at the insurance company was going to doubt that there had been a fire at his house. He reeked of smoke.

"I'll even go next door with her," Lisa offered. "Everything they own will have to be sent to the cleaners."

"I wonder about the upholstered furniture. A lot of it will have to be replaced because of smoke."

The back door opened and Mary Alice stuck her head in. "What in the world is going on over at the Phizers'?"

"It's a long story. I'll tell you on the way to the meeting."

"Morning, Aunt Sister," Lisa said. "Congratulations on your engagement."

"Thanks, honey. But I'm not going to rush into anything."

I swear she was serious.

I found my purse and told Lisa we would be at the Homewood Library if she needed us.

"Why would she need us?" Sister asked as I closed the back door. "Has she heard from Alan?"

"Not that I know of. He's still climbing Fool's Hill."

"Of all our children, I thought he would be the last one to do that."

"Me too," I agreed.

"You want to clue me in on that?" Sister pointed next door to the police cars and the crime tape. "Are Mitzi and Arthur okay?"

"Not exactly."

We got in the car, and in the fifteen minutes it took us to get to the Homewood Library, I had just hit the high points of everything that had happened. Sister's side of the conversation consisted of a few "Say what's?" and "Have mercies!"

"There's a lot more," I said as she pulled into a parking space.

"Well, wait until after the meeting. I don't want to miss anything."

I should worry. There's not much that Sister misses.

The Homewood library is a wonderful example of what can be done with an older building. Originally a church, it has been turned into a perfect library. The sanctuary with its vaulted ceiling and large stained glass window is now the main part of the library housing the reference department and the adult books. The children's department was once the church offices and the chapel, and the room that served as a church parlor and a place for wedding receptions and church suppers is now a medium-sized auditorium. But one of the best features is the Sunday school rooms downstairs. They are perfect for meetings and are used by the whole community.

"Don't you dare recommend condom stocks," I warned Mary Alice as we walked down the hall toward the noise of women talking.

"Why not? Shirley Gibbs, my broker, says they're better than ever since Viagra. I still think she should have come. It's dumb not to have some expert guidance."

"Well, let's see what the group is like."

The group looked as if the Sunday school

class that had met there for years had never moved out. About a dozen women ranging in age from mid-forties to, I swear, a hundred sat around drinking tea and talking. One of them sported a yellow crocheted hat.

"No condoms," I muttered to Sister. "I mean it."

"Patricia Anne and Mary Alice." Connie Harris, Mitzi's friend, rose and came to greet us. The youngest woman in the group, a pretty blonde who was giving middle age a run for its money came with her and was introduced as Joy McWain.

"We're just so glad you're joining us," Joy enthused. "Isn't this exciting? I told Connie I don't know when I've been so excited about anything. Can I get y'all some tea?"

"Thanks," I said.

"Well, y'all just find a place to sit down. I'll bring it to you." I swear the word perky had been invented for this woman.

"Unsweetened," Sister said.

Two lines appeared between perky Joy's eyes. "I think it's all sweet."

"That's fine," I said, pinching the back of Sister's arm slightly.

"Y'all come over here and sit down," Connie said. "And tell me how Mitzi is. I didn't figure she would be here this morning. I just can't believe Arthur was arrested for murder."

"Her house burned down last night." Sister settled into the chair next to the elderly woman in the crocheted hat. "Hey, how are you?" she said to her.

"Tolerable," the woman answered.

Connie clutched her chest and sank down by Sister. "Mitzi's house burned down? Oh, my Lord!"

"Just the back part," I said. Somehow it didn't sound consoling.

"Is she all right?" Connie was still clutching her chest.

"She's at my house and was still asleep when I left," I explained. "I hope she's okay."

"But what happened?"

"Someone tried to kill them," Sister informed her.

"What?" Connie clutched tighter.

"Here you are, ladies." Joy McWain handed us two large red plastic cups that were already sweating and a couple of paper napkins. "You all right, Mrs. Harris?"

Connie nodded.

"Someone tried to kill me once," Crocheted Hat said.

Perky Joy smiled. "Now, Miss Bessie, you know better than that."

"Got the scar to prove it. Here, missy, I'll

show you." The woman started to unbutton her blouse.

"That's okay, Miss Bessie," Joy said. "We believe you."

"What happened?" Sister asked. "Did they shoot you or what?"

"Stuck me in the gut with a knife. Right down on Twentieth Street and me just going in the dentist's office for a root canal." She sniffed. "Said, 'Hand me your purse, old woman.' I said, 'Like hell I will,' and he pulls out this knife."

Sister was intrigued. "What did you do?"

"Shot him. I'd have been all right if he hadn't fallen frontward. Looks like he'd have gone backwards."

"Wow," Sister said.

Connie Harris fanned herself with a paper napkin while Crocheted Hat informed us that she hoped we'd invest in condoms, and did we know which company made the best ones? Was it true some were fruit flavored?

"My God," Connie muttered, fanning harder.

Any reply Sister would have made, and I'm sure there would have been one, was cut off by Joy McWain clapping her hands for attention.

"Welcome, everybody. Let's go around and introduce ourselves," she said. "Mr.

Alcorn Jones, the president of First Financial Trust, is going to come help us get started today, but he's going to be a few minutes late." She pointed to the woman sitting next to the refreshment table who said her name was Mary Beatty and she was a happy wife, the mother of five, the grandmother of twelve, and a good old Southern Baptist.

Sister leaned around Connie and whispered, "Are we supposed to say all that?"

I whispered back, "Just say you're rich and just got engaged."

"What about you? You don't have anything to say."

Too bad Connie was in the way. "I'll say I'm your sister."

After everybody had introduced herself (Sister had just given her name as had Crocheted Hat, Bessie McCoy), Joy said we should give our club a name.

The titles suggested ranged from Serendipity to Stocky Ladies. Joy wrote all the suggestions down on a chalkboard. Connie Harris, who had recovered some, came up with the name Pennies from Heaven, which a lot of the women liked. Bessie McCoy suggested Homewood Heifers. ("We're hoping for a bull market, but we're heifers, and we're meeting at the Homewood Library.")

Sister said she liked that name, but she and Bessie were a minority of two. The majority finally voted on The Birmingham Ladies' Investment Club, the recommendation of Mary Beatty, the happily married mother of many.

"Stinks," Bessie McCoy said, scratching her head through her crocheted hat.

While we were having this discussion, a man in a dark suit had come into the room and had sat down in a chair near the door. In his sixties, he had a George Hamilton tan that made the white fringe of hair around his bald head look like a halo. He was either courting melanoma on a regular basis or stopping by Rich's cosmetic counter for self-tanning lotions every other day. My bet was on the latter.

Name decided on, though some of the women grumbled that it lacked originality, Joy introduced Alcorn Jones whose smile was as white as his hair. I made myself a mental note to try tanning lotion again. I had tried it years ago and ended up a streaked orange. And itching.

Sister, I noticed, who was wearing her *H.M.S. Pinafore* outfit today, had snapped to attention at Alcorn Jones's appearance. I wondered how far across the Atlantic Cedric was by now. The point of no return?

Fare thee well, Cedric.

"Good morning, ladies." Alcorn Jones's voice was deep and warm. "And thank you, Joy, for inviting me to the organizational meeting of the Birmingham Ladies' Investment Club. You are embarking on a financial voyage that will be both educational and lucrative."

The word lucrative got our attention, as did his next words, "Now, I'm going to help you get organized." He paused. "You're going to need to take notes."

There was a scrambling in purses for pens and something to write on. This man meant business.

"First of all," he said, "organize yourselves as a partnership. It's easier, and that way each person is responsible for keeping up with her own taxable income."

I wrote "Partnership, each own tax" in my little spiral notebook.

"You're going to need at least four officers, a senior partner, a junior partner, a recording partner, and a financial partner, the person who will actually buy and sell the stocks."

I scribbled this down, as did every other woman in the room. I glanced over at Sister. Every other woman but Mary Alice was taking notes. She was sitting there calmly taking the silver foil off of a Hershey's Kiss.

"Connie," I whispered, "switch places with me."

Still writing, Connie moved into my chair so I could sit next to Sister.

"How come you're not writing this down?" I asked.

"Because you are. Both of us don't need to."

I could feel my blood pressure rushing up like the red line in a thermometer. Some day, maybe some day soon, this woman was going to cause me to have a stroke.

"Each member should be responsible for following at least one stock," Alcorn Jones said.

I wrote down "Each — one stock." "Start writing," I hissed at Sister. "Right this minute."

Miss Chocolate Breath leaned over and whispered in my ear, "All he's doing is repeating word for word what's in the Beardstown Ladies' book on investment clubs. Shirley Gibbs gave me a copy of it to study."

I gave her a hard look. "You don't study."

"Okay, but you just listen. Now he's going to tell us about the initial investment and the monthly contribution."

Which he did. I wrote it down anyway. In

fact, I took notes for almost half an hour.

"And a final word of advice," Alcorn Jones said, "I recommend that your portfolios be well balanced. You should have stocks in at least five fields, technology — including communications such as computers — health, pharmaceuticals, proven retailers, and entertainment such as Disney."

"Write that down," Sister told me. "I don't remember that being in the book."

"The Southern Baptists are boycotting Disney," Mary Beatty informed him.

"Hey!" Bessie McCoy spoke so loudly, we all jumped. "This club's about making money, not morals."

Alcorn Jones smiled easily at both women. "These are the things you ladies will have to work out."

"Well, there are some things I won't compromise on," Mary Beatty said. "I'm laying that on the table right now."

I figured Bessie McCoy had something in her purse to lay on the table that might change Mary's mind.

The bank president glanced at his Rolex and declared that he was late for a meeting, and to feel free to call on him at any time, that his bank would handle our stock at a discount rate. With that, he disappeared through the door so quickly, I wouldn't have been surprised to see a puff of smoke.

"Hey." Sister turned to Connie and me. "This club's going to be fun."

"It's almost lunchtime," perky Joy said. "How about the same time, next week. It'll give us time to think about what Mr. Jones said, and we'll make some definite decisions then. Okay?"

Okay.

"I think you ought to be the financial partner, Mouse. You should have told them you tutor in math."

"Wash your mouth out with soap." The lack of sleep from the night before was catching up with me. I was fighting to keep my eyes open as we drove through Homewood.

"I'm hungry. Here," Sister handed me the phone. "Call and see how many people are at your house and we'll stop and get lunch for everybody."

I dialed sleepily, and Debbie answered the phone.

"Hey, honey," I said. "What are you doing there?"

"Brought you an e-mail from Haley. Lisa's been catching me up on all that's been going on. I can't believe it."

"None of us can."

"Is that Debbie?" Sister asked.

I nodded.

"Ask her if my grandson is up to Chinese food today."

"Your mama and I are on the way home. We're going to bring lunch and she wants to know if you feel like Chinese. Who all's there?"

"Lisa and Mrs. Phizer and me. And I'm feeling pretty good today."

"Ask the others if it's okay."

"Chinese okay?" I heard Debbie asking. In a moment she told me, "Anything."

"We'll see you in a few minutes then." I hung up the phone. "They said anything. Just three of them."

"We can stop at the Hunan Hut and get some stuff from the buffet."

Which we did. It was a mistake, though. The whole time I was putting food onto the Styrofoam plates, I had the eerie feeling that if I turned around fast enough I would see Sophie and Arthur sitting in the corner booth and he would be stroking her hand. Or I would see them walking across the parking lot, her leaning against him, him lifting her into the car. Damn, damn.

"I'm glad to get out of there," I said as we made for the car, both carrying sacks.

"Couldn't you just see Sophie and Arthur in there?"

"No, but I saw Alcorn Jones with a girl young enough to be his granddaughter."

"Really?"

"Yeah." She sounded angry. "Him and his fake tan and capped teeth."

This was so unlike Mary Alice that I should have noticed, but I was still caught up in the Sophie-Arthur memories. And I was looking forward to getting the e-mail from Haley. I know I worry too much about her, but Lord, she's a long way from home.

When we came through the gate, we saw that Arabella Hardt had joined the group. She was sitting on the steps petting Woofer and moved over to let us by. The others were sitting at the table. Mitzi, I noticed, looked better; there was some color in her cheeks and her eyes were brighter. Arabella was the one who looked sick today. In fact, she looked as if she had been crying all night. Dark glasses hid her eyes, but not all of the puffiness. She had on some old denim shorts and a stained shirt that the Goodwill would have refused.

"Hey, Mama. Aunt Sister." Lisa jumped up, gave me a hug, and took the sack of food I was carrying. "Ummm, this smells wonderful."

Debbie took Mary Alice's sack. "We'll put this out on the kitchen table," she said. "We'll call you when it's ready."

I sat in the chair that Lisa had vacated.

"I'm feeling better," Mitzi said. "How did the meeting go?"

"Interesting."

Mary Alice sat down. "Do you know a woman named Bessie McCoy, Mitzi?"

"Did she have on a crocheted hat?"

"Yep."

"She always wears that hat. She got scalped when she was a child."

"Scalped? Like with a tomahawk?"

Mitzi shrugged. "I'm not sure how it happened; I never asked. But she's an artist. I'm surprised you don't know her. Her stuff's in all the banks. The kind of stuff you can't tell if it's upside-down or not. Why?"

"I think she's going to keep the meetings interesting." Sister gestured to Arabella. "Come join us, Arabella. You okay?"

Arabella stood up, came over, and said she was okay but had better be moseying along, that she had a lot to do.

"Stay for lunch," I said. "We brought plenty."

Arabella shook her head. "I just came by to check on Aunt Mitzi."

"One egg roll?" Sister asked.

"Don't think it would stay down. But thanks. I'll see y'all later."

Mitzi got up and followed her to the gate where they had a quiet conversation.

"She just found out her mother wants to be cremated," Mitzi explained when she came back. "I think the reality of her death is just sinking in."

"Poor child," Sister said. "I know what that's like, what with losing all my husbands so suddenly. It took days for it to sink in."

"Maybe Cedric will outlast you," I said.

She looked at me, puzzled.

"Cedric, the man to whom you have plighted your troth."

"My troth isn't plighted. Good Lord, Mouse." She thought for a minute. "What's a plighted troth, anyway? It sounds like a gum disease."

"Are you engaged, Mary Alice?" Mitzi asked.

"Sort of."

"Well, congratulations. Who to?"

"An Englishman named Cedric."

I knew she didn't remember his last name.

Fortunately, Mitzi didn't ask. She sat down and held out a key.

"I promised that I would go pick out an outfit for Sophie. That's really why Arabella came over here. She says she can't go in the apartment."

"I thought she spent the night there last night," I said.

"She says she couldn't. She ended up staying with a friend."

Debbie opened the back door. "Lunch is on the table."

"Patricia Anne?"

I knew what Mitzi was going to ask.

"Sure. I'll go with you."

"I'll go with you, too," Sister said. "You don't want to pick out anything too pretty." She pushed her chair back. "Come on. I'm starving."

Fourteen

The University of Alabama's medical center in Birmingham is an amazing group of hospitals. My children were born at University Hospital which, with the dental school, was at that time the whole university facility. Now there's a hospital for, as Fred says, "whatever ails you." Cataracts? The eye hospital. Heart? Cancer? Diabetes? Psychological problems? There's a hospital for you. Are you a veteran? A child? You get the picture. In fact, UAB, its hospitals and clinics are now the financial backbone of Birmingham, taking the place held so long by the steel mills.

And patients and their families have to have places to stay, particularly those who are here for extended treatment. So around the perimeter of the medical complex, residential motels, hotels, and condominiums have sprung up. Sophie was living in one of the latter, a ten-story building of very elegant apartments. Most of them are occupied by permanent residents who work at the medical center, but some of them are for lease, for a pretty penny, I'm sure. Especially Sophie's apartment which was one of four on the tenth floor.

Mitzi unlocked the door and we stepped into one of the loveliest rooms I had ever seen. Simply furnished, it was done in beige and white. A white carpet, beige and white plaid sofa, beige and white striped chairs. A few accents of turquoise in a pillow, a lamp, a geometric wall hanging. The walls were white, the draperies that covered the sliding door to the balcony the same beige and white stripe of the chairs. The dining and kitchen area angled off to one side and were set aside from the main room by two white columns.

"Oh, this is beautiful," Mitzi said. "Look at this, y'all."

We were looking and admiring. It was even lovelier when Mitzi opened the draperies and we were greeted by a view of the distant mountains and their many shades of late summer green. On the balcony were a chaise and a small table with two ice cream chairs. This, I suspected, was where Sophie had spent much of her time, probably even eating her meals there.

"I'll bet Bill Bodiford decorated this," Sister said. "He tried to put some of those wire chairs on my porch. I told him he had to be kidding. I like the colors, though."

The apartment was designed for maximum privacy with the two bedrooms and baths on opposite sides of the great room. Sophie's was the first one we walked into, and it was a mess. Drawers had been opened and not closed. In the lovely white bathroom, several cigarettes floated in the turquoise toilet.

"Damn," Mitzi said. "You'd think the police would leave it in better shape than this."

On the front wall of the bedroom was a window with vertical blinds. Sophie could lie here, I realized, and see the setting sun. Its rays were already striping the white carpet. There was also a sliding door that opened to the balcony.

Mitzi opened the closet's doors and a light came on, illuminating the contents.

"She didn't have many clothes," Sister remarked. "I thought she had money."

"She came here because she was sick," I reminded her. "She wouldn't need many clothes just to go to the hospital for treatment."

"She was at the Hunan Hut with Arthur."

I gave her a dirty look which she ignored.

But Mitzi wasn't upset. "You're right. There's not much here to choose from." She began to separate the outfits. "Tell me what you think."

I didn't want to say what I was thinking, that whatever we picked out was going to go up in smoke. "How about that gray suit?"

Mitzi took down a light gray suit and looked at it. "It's real expensive, y'all. Look." She showed us Sophie's name embroidered on the back of the lapel. "It was made for her."

Suddenly, Mitzi began to cry. I took the suit away from her and said, "This will do fine, Mitzi." Dammit, that Arabella shouldn't have asked Mitzi to do this.

"It's an old suit, anyway," Mary Alice added. "Look at the width of those lapels."

"It's just so sad that her life had to end this way." Mitzi stepped into the bathroom, got some toilet paper, and wiped her eyes while I held the gray suit.

"Look at those lapels," Sister repeated. "This one needs to go."

"Well," Mitzi said, blowing her nose. "This isn't solving anything."

"I guess not," I agreed.

Mitzi rolled off some more toilet paper, stepped back into the bedroom, and took a deep breath. "You're right. The gray suit's fine. Now what about shoes and underwear?"

"For what?" Sister asked.

"Because you can't get into heaven

without underwear." I aimed a slight kick at her but missed.

I laid the suit across a chair while Mitzi opened one of the drawers that lingerie was spilling out of.

"Oh, my," she said.

"What?" I walked over and looked at a drawer brimming with silk: silk camisoles, silk panties, silk bras.

"Isn't this beautiful?" Mitzi picked up a peach-colored camisole with a single rose embroidered on the front.

I felt the material. "You couldn't throw it in the washing machine, Mitzi."

Mitzi looked up and actually smiled. "That's true. Cotton Jockeys are hard to beat."

Sister gave up on us, walked over to the nightstand, and opened the drawer.

"Get out of there," I said when I realized what she was doing.

"I'm just looking."

"For what?"

"Look at this." She came over with a silver framed picture of a young Sophie, a man, and three teenage children. It had been taken on the deck of a boat. The family, dressed in shorts and swimsuits smiled into the camera. The boy, who must be David, was already taller than his father.

Tan and handsome, he stood with an arm draped casually around each of his sisters' shoulders, while his parents stood slightly away from the threesome, their arms around each other's waist.

"They were a beautiful family, weren't they?" Mitzi had come to stand beside us.

I nodded. "Arabella said her brother was killed in a car accident?"

"In college. There were three boys in the car. Two were killed. The other boy was hurt, terribly, but survived."

"Were drugs or alcohol involved? Sue said they buried him the same day. She sounded like her parents were trying to cover something up."

"Maybe, though who knows? Milton Sawyer was on the way up in the political world and if his son were on drugs and responsible for the death and injury of two others, it might have hurt his career. But I doubt that was it. I've always thought they couldn't bear the thought of an autopsy on David's body. He was the family's shining star." She paused. "I know that Sue never has believed David was on drugs. She says he was Mr. Clean, always."

"And Arabella?"

"It's one of the bones of contention between them." Mitzi took the picture and looked at it. "They both adored him, but Arabella never thought he was perfect."

"Not many people are."

"None that I know of," Sister said.

"Sophie called Arthur the night David was killed. Arthur cried like a baby. Said he'd never heard such pain."

"So you'd known about Sophie all along?" I asked.

"Oh, sure. They stayed in touch. I've known that Arthur's always loved a seventeen-year-old Sophie, Patricia Anne. But he's loved me at every age."

"I'll put this back where I got it," Sister said, reaching for the picture.

Damned if I didn't have to go in the bathroom and get some toilet paper to mop my eyes.

"I don't see a hang-up bag here. We should have brought one." Mitzi was back at the closet.

"Maybe there's one in the other bedroom. I'll go look," I said. "If there's not, we can just use a plastic bag from the kitchen."

I crossed the great room and entered Arabella's bedroom. It was a duplicate of her mother's except everything was in place; this room hadn't been trashed like the other bedroom had. The bed was covered by a turquoise and white checked bedspread and the drawers were closed. There were no family pictures, no books or magazines lying about, nothing personal.

Mary Alice had followed me. "It's neat in here. And where's her stuff?"

In the closet, a couple of skirts, blouses, and pants were lined up neatly. I opened the chest of drawers and saw the same order, several pairs of panties, bras, camisoles stacked neatly. I walked into the bathroom and opened the drawers. No cosmetics, lotions, creams.

"Nothing in the nightstand," Sister reported.

I walked back into the bedroom. "Mitzi," I called, "Come here."

"What?" She stuck her head in the door.

"Look at this room. I don't believe Arabella's been staying here."

"Well, she hasn't for the last couple of days."

"No, I mean at all. This room hasn't been lived in. There's not even anything in the bathroom drawers."

"There sure isn't." Sister walked out of the bathroom. "And she's a redhead. She'd need a lot of stuff for her skin." She held up a shirt she had taken from the closet. "Did y'all know Land's End has started carrying larger sizes?"

"Is that a large size?" I asked. "Arabella's probably a size six."

"No. But it's from Land's End. I got a couple of their bathing suits."

"Arabella brought a bunch of stuff to our house," Mitzi said. "Maybe everything she had here in Birmingham."

"Well, there's not even a lipstick here," Sister said.

"I don't get it." Mitzi walked into the bathroom. "She was supposed to be living here and taking care of her mother. But you're right, Mary Alice. The towels in here haven't even been touched."

"I don't think the clothes have either," I said. "It's like they were just put there for show."

Mitzi came back into the bedroom, sat on the bed, and ran her hand over the turquoise and white bedspread. "But why would she lie about it? She said this was where she was staying, remember? She came to our house because she said she couldn't bear to come back here."

"Well," Sister said, "there are a few clothes here in the dresser. I guess she could have stayed some nights. The bar of soap in the shower has never been wet, though. Did y'all notice that?"

I hadn't. Mary Alice had been more

observant than I had.

"And nothing smells like Shalimar," Mitzi added.

Now *that* I had noticed.

"She hadn't been in our house five minutes until everything smelled like Shalimar."

"I wonder where she was last night," I said.

"With a friend, she said." Mitzi sniffed. "Definitely no Shalimar in here."

"Where is she now?"

"Same friend, I guess. Somebody on Southside. Arthur has the phone number."

"You don't know who the friend is?"

Mitzi shook her head. "No. But she visited her grandparents here when she was growing up and got to know a lot of people."

"She's a good-looking girl," Sister said. "I'll bet her visits made quite a splash."

"She had a beautiful mother."

For the first time there was bitterness in Mitzi's voice. She realized it and said, "I'm sorry, y'all. But I never thought Sophie would be a problem for Arthur and me. I mean, Lord, it was almost fifty years ago. And here he is, arrested for her murder, someone tries to burn our house down, for God only knows what reason, and on top of that, he's responsible for seeing that she's cremated and her estate is settled. Damn." She stood up. "Did you see a bag in that closet?"

"No. I'll see if there's a garbage bag." I went into the kitchen and looked in the small pantry. Mitzi and Mary Alice followed me.

"Here's one," I said. I slit a hole in the top of the bag and Mitzi slid the hanger through it and pulled the plastic down over the suit. Trying to keep the outfit from wrinkling I guess. God knows why. Shoes and underwear went into a Piggly Wiggly sack.

"I suppose that's it." Mitzi walked back into the great room and laid the suit over a chair. I thought she was going to close the draperies, but instead, she slid the glass doors open and stepped onto the balcony. Sunlight angled across it.

"Look at that view."

We looked. It was the same view Mary Alice has from her house on the top of Red Mountain, except she looks down on this building.

"Maybe we should sell our house and buy something like this apartment." Mitzi was leaning too far over the railing to suit me.

"Hmmm."

To my relief, she turned and sat on one of the ice cream chairs. I pulled out the other one and sat down, too. Mary Alice sat in the chaise, though it would have been interesting to see her in one of the chairs.

"You wouldn't have a place for your flowers." I didn't mention the fact that penthouses were sky high in more ways than one.

"That's true." She drummed her fingers against the table. "And I wouldn't have you for a neighbor."

"That's for sure."

The three of us were quiet for a few minutes, watching the late afternoon traffic increase.

Mitzi sighed. "They think the poison was in the artificial sweetener Sophie put in her tea at the restaurant."

"Which doesn't mean Arthur gave it to her," I said. "Some crazy could have left a packet on the table."

"But there's more. A lot more. Sophie left a note saying that she had asked Arthur to help her die."

"What?"

"That's what it said." Mitzi went on sounding as if she were quoting, " 'To whom it may concern: I, Sophie V. Sawyer, have requested that my beloved friend Arthur Phizer assist in my suicide when the time comes. He understands that it is my wish to die while I am still relatively pain-free and of sound mind. He is not to be held responsible in any way since this is my choice. I trust that my family will understand. I love them with all my heart.' "

"I can't believe that! Where did they find it?"

"Sophie mailed it to her doctor. He got it the day after she died and called the police."

"But Mitzi," Sister said, "strychnine at the Hunan Hut isn't a logical assisted suicide."

"Which Arthur says she never asked him to do, anyway. Help her die. Maybe she had planned on asking him if she became terminally ill. I don't know." She stood up. "We've got to go before the traffic gets any heavier."

We followed her through the apartment, full of questions.

"What do her daughters think about what's happened?" Sister asked.

"They believe Arthur. They've seen the note, and they probably think their mother did ask him to help her die, but they don't believe he did it."

"But the police do."

"Obviously."

Just as we reached the door, we heard a key in the lock and it opened. We jumped back, startled. A petite redheaded young woman stood there, apparently as startled as we were.

Mitzi recovered her composure first. "May we help you?" she asked.

"I'm Zoe Batson," the girl said. "This is my grandmother's apartment."

"I'm Mitzi Phizer, Zoe, and these are my friends Mrs. Hollowell and Mrs. Crane."

Zoe could have been her aunt Arabella's child. She had the same dark red hair (fuschia, Fred would have called it), the same fair skin. And she was beautiful.

"Oh, Mrs. Phizer, of course." She rewarded all of us with a bright smile. "It's so nice to meet you."

She didn't question our presence in the apartment, but I felt compelled to explain the sacks in our hands. Clothes for her grandmother's funeral. (Okay, so funeral wasn't the right word, but what was?) Her aunt Arabella had sent us.

"That's what I'm here for, too," she said. "Mama sent me to get Grandmama some clothes."

"You want to see what we picked out?" Mitzi asked.

"Sure."

"We got her gray suit." We walked back to the sofa and Mitzi pulled the bag up so she could see.

Zoe fingered the material slowly. "Wool and silk." She took the bag off. "Look at those lapels. What would you say? 1965?"

The three of us who had been wearing suits in 1965 had no idea.

"I know it's old," Mary Alice said.

"It's so beautiful. A classic." Zoe picked the suit up and held it against her. "Let's get something else. My whole class will have a fit over this when they see it."

"Your class?" I asked.

"I'm a style major at the university. Fashion. Design," she added when the three of us looked blank.

Zoe herself was wearing ragged jeans and a blue denim shirt. So much for style.

She put the suit down and looked into the sack. "Not Ferragamo shoes, y'all. No way." She pulled out the gray pumps. "And a size five. Umm. My size."

"Tell you what, Zoe," Mitzi said. "Why don't you just go on and pick something out? I'm sure it will be fine with Arabella."

Zoe nodded. "She and Mama should have gotten together on this, not put you to this trouble." She picked up the suit again. "I was thinking a nightgown and peignoir might be nice."

"They're all silk," Mary Alice said.

Zoe looked pained.

"You know, I really like that child," Sister said. We were waiting for the elevator. "So pleasant and sensible. Makes you have hope for the future."

"And they said the South wouldn't rise again." I punched the button again. Someone on the fourth floor was holding the door open.

"I hope she's still as pleasant when she finds out about her grandmother's will," Mitzi said. And while we were waiting for the elevator, she dropped another little bombshell, the fact that Sophie hadn't made Arthur an ordinary executor. He was to serve in a trustee capacity.

"What?" I asked. "What does that mean?"

"It means he's in charge of her estate. He'll run it just like Sophie did. It means her heirs, which includes the two Batson children, won't be able to get their hands on the estate all at once. It'll continue just as Sophie had it set up with them getting what amounts to a very generous allowance and dividends. Arthur says he knows she did it because of Arabella, that Sophie knew she didn't have any money sense and was trying to protect her." Mitzi shrugged. "The police caught on to that right away, too. If Arthur were dishonest, he could help himself to the money."

"Which is how much?" It was none of my business, but, damn, I felt like I'd been hit over the head here.

"A lot. Maybe as much as twenty or thirty million."

"Good Lord!" I couldn't imagine that many zeros.

Sister whistled.

The elevator door opened and we stepped in. By the time we reached the lobby, it had dawned on me that Arthur's being the trustee of Sophie's estate might well be why Mitzi and Arthur had nearly been cremated before Sophie.

"I know what you're thinking," Mitzi said. "Arabella wasn't here where she said she was, and she can't get all of her inheritance at one time as long as Arthur is the trustee."

"That's right."

"Well, the police questioned her. They said she had an airtight alibi. Personally, I don't even think they should have questioned her."

Well, somebody had tried to do the Phizers in.

By this time we had reached Mitzi's car. I crawled in the back seat and we all buckled up. But Mitzi hesitated before she started the car, the key in the ignition.

"You know who the police really think started the fire? Arthur."

We both looked at her, startled. "What?" we asked at the same time.

"God's truth. They think he did it so it would look like somebody was trying to get rid of him. So he could claim it was the same person who did Sophie in."

"That's crazy, Mitzi," Sister said.

"Tell me about it." She started the car and waited a moment until she could ease into the traffic which is always heavy around the medical center.

We drove over the mountain, past Vulcan's bare behind mooning us in the late afternoon sun, and into our neighborhood which looked deceptively peaceful.

Mary Alice announced that she couldn't stay for supper, that her writing class was having a spring equinox party.

"You mean a fall equinox party."

"Nope. Spring. It's too cold to have it in March. Who wants to go skinny dipping and howl at the moon when it's forty degrees?"

I hoped she was kidding, but knowing my sister, I wasn't at all sure.

"Y'all have a good time," Mitzi said.

"Planning on it." She backed her Jaguar out and hauled.

The smell of pot roast greeted Mitzi and me when we opened the back door. Bless that Lisa. She was sitting in the den reading and informed us that we had dozens of messages, that she had written them down. Actually there were five of them, four for Mitzi (Arthur had called twice) and one for me.

"Mr. Phizer said to call as soon as you got in," Lisa said.

"Go ahead," I told Mitzi. A glance at my message told me there was nothing urgent, just Joy McWain of the investment club.

"I'll call from the bedroom," Mitzi said.

"Is she okay?" Lisa asked after Mitzi left.

"A hell of a lot better than I would be." I sat down, pulled off my shoes, and told her about the apartment as well as what Mitzi had told me about Arthur.

Like me, Lisa was startled. "And Mrs. Sawyer mailed the note to her doctor?"

I nodded. "Saying Arthur was going to help her commit suicide, and that he shouldn't be held responsible."

"And she thought that would get him off? Sophie Sawyer didn't know much about Alabama law, did she?"

"Or any other state's law. You can't just go around saying 'So-and-so's going to kill me, but it's all right, I asked him to.' And she wasn't even terminally ill."

Lisa shook her head. "And she made him a trustee of her estate, not a regular executor? Lord, the woman practically reserved him a cell in Kilby prison."

"The last thing she would have wanted to do, I'm sure." I leaned back in my chair. "That roast smells wonderful. Thank you."

"You're welcome. I figured you'd be tired when you got in."

"I am." I closed my eyes and said my mantra. Immediately, I felt myself relaxing. Years ago, Sister dragged me to a Transcendental Meditation class. We were to carry fruit and flowers which Sister forgot, so I had to give her one of my bananas and a zinnia. We were chanted over and then taken into separate rooms where we were given our mantras. We were also told never to tell anyone our mantra.

Sister told me hers on the way home; mine is still a secret. And works. She claims they gave her a bad mantra because all she had was the one banana I gave her that was so old fruit flies followed her into the room.

So I was slipping into a relaxation mode when Mitzi came back into the den and said the insurance company had an apartment on Valley Avenue where she and Arthur could stay while their house was being fixed, and Arthur wanted her to meet him over there.

"Come back here for supper," Lisa said.

"We will. We may want to spend the night again."

"Of course. You know you're welcome here for as long as you want," I said. I sat up and stretched. "I need to go take Woofer for his walk."

"I've already taken him," Lisa said.

"Then I'll just go check on him."

I walked out with Mitzi. The pot roast smelled great, Woofer was fine, and I should have been very grateful. But the time was fast approaching for Lisa to head back to Atlanta and, as Sister so delicately put it, kick butt.

As I went back in, I remembered the e-mail from Haley that I hadn't read.

Nothing new. She was very happy. Let her know if Muffin was getting along okay. And make it several packages of those Combat roach bait things. Mail them as soon as possible. Lord. The roaches of Warsaw had met their match.

Fifteen

Arthur and Mitzi came back for supper. The apartment, they said, was fine. Hopefully, they wouldn't have to stay there very long. The contractor had promised to start on their house the next day.

Fred and I glanced at each other. We remembered what it had been like adding on the breakfast room and the bay window. Maybe Mitzi and Arthur would have better luck, though. Lord knows, they were due some.

I had filled Fred in on what Mitzi had told me about Arthur's problems.

"Damn," he said. "Doesn't sound good."

But in spite of our worry, we had a pleasant evening, deliberately avoiding the subject of Sophie Sawyer. Lisa's supper was delicious, and after we ate, Fred and Arthur watched the Braves and Mitzi, Lisa, and I played gin.

I had forgotten to return Joy McWain's call, but she called me again around nine. My name had been suggested as the financial partner of the investment club (and I knew good and well who had suggested it) and would I be willing to have my name brought up for consideration at the next meeting.

I promised her I would think about it and get back to her. I wasn't sure I wanted to take on the responsibility. On the other hand, it would be interesting.

We all went to bed early. I fell asleep immediately and deeply and was dreaming of Sister howling at the moon when I awakened enough to realize the noise was real. Woofer wasn't barking, but making a strange, howling noise.

"Fred," I said, grabbing for my robe. "Something's wrong with Woofer."

"Choo," he said, which was followed by a snore.

I hurried down the dark hall, through the den and into the kitchen. No one but me seemed to have been awakened by the sounds. I reached up to turn on the back lights and that's when I saw the light in the Phizers' house. Someone was over there with a flashlight. Someone walking through their dining room, hesitatingly, turning the light out. No, I realized. There was still a glow. They had moved into the hall.

I opened the kitchen door quietly and stepped onto the back porch. Woofer ambled up the steps to greet me.

"Who is it, boy?" I whispered. "Is that what you're fussing about?"

The flashlight next door slid across the inside of the burned kitchen.

"Come on, sweetie." I pulled Woofer into the house, picked up the phone, and called 911.

"Mrs. Hollowell," the 911 operator said. "Is that you again? What's going on tonight?"

Damn.

I told her.

So much for the quiet, sleeping neighborhood and the moonlit late summer night. In about three minutes, two police cars, sirens blaring, came screeching to a halt in front of the Phizers'. All of the lights in all of the houses came on, including ours. Fred, Lisa, Mitzi, and Arthur came staggering out of their beds, and Woofer decided to howl again.

"What's going on?" Arthur, I noticed, slept in his boxers.

"Somebody's going through your house."

"Our house?"

"I called 911."

"The police are in our house?" Mitzi sounded confused. "Is it another fire?"

"No, it was somebody with a flashlight. I saw them."

Woofer leaned his head back and howled.

"Hush, Woofer." Lisa patted his head.

"You called 911?" Fred went to the window and looked out. "Turn the lights out. I can't see what's going on."

"I'm going to go find out." Arthur opened the back door and started out.

"Not without your pants, Arthur." Mitzi stopped him. "Go put on some clothes."

Fred realized he just had on pajamas and rushed down the hall behind Arthur.

"Woofer was howling," I explained to Mitzi and Lisa, "and I got up to see about him and saw somebody with a flashlight going through your house."

"A burglar," Lisa said. "I've heard of burglars looking in the paper for fires and finding out that way which houses aren't occupied. They do it when people are at funerals, too. That's why you never want to put the address of the person who died in the paper."

"Oh, my." Mitzi clutched her robe together. "I wonder what they got."

"Nothing," I said, crossing my fingers.

"The silver and my good pearls are still in the fire safe in the hall closet. I should have gotten them out yesterday, shouldn't I?"

"Probably," Lisa agreed. "Professional burglars can open up a little safe in a minute."

She was my daughter-in-law. I couldn't give her the elbow punch or the slight kick like I can my sister. So I suggested that we go out in the backyard and see what was happening.

As we stepped outside, Joanie Salk, Bo Mitchell's partner, was coming up the steps.

"Mrs. Hollowell, you're the one who called 911 again?" She was out of breath.

I nodded. The queen of the 911 system. "There was somebody over there going through the house with a flashlight."

Arthur and Fred came rushing out nearly knocking Joanie down.

"Wait a minute, y'all," she called. But they dashed through the gate. She sighed. "They really shouldn't go over there."

"I don't think they noticed you were a policeman," I said.

"I don't guess it matters." She took a small spiral notebook from her pocket. "Can I ask you a few questions?"

"Sure. But I don't know anything. Just that somebody was over there."

"We know that. She's still there. Says her name's Arabella Hardt and you know her, that she's been staying there."

"Arabella?" I think all three of us said it at the same time.

"You know her?"

"Of course we do," Mitzi said.

"You're Mrs. Phizer?" Joanie asked.

Mitzi nodded. "And she did spend a night or two with us. But I can't imagine what she would be doing over there tonight."

"She says she came back for some of her things."

I looked through the window at the kitchen clock. "At two-thirty in the morning?"

Joanie Salk shrugged. "Y'all wait here a minute. I'll go see what's going on."

"Well, damn," Mitzi said. "Arabella."

The September night was cool. I suggested that we go back inside.

"What kind of things could she have come back for?" Lisa asked as we sat down at the kitchen table. "Clothes?"

"I suppose," Mitzi said. "They'll smell like smoke, though."

"Whatever she's after, why didn't she wait until morning?" I asked. "What kind of sense does it make to go into a house that's been damaged by fire in the middle of the night? Plus, she knew the police had it cordoned off."

"Maybe she's been drinking," Lisa suggested.

"I guess it's possible," Mitzi said. She put her head down on the table. "Lord, I'm tired."

"Why don't you go back to bed?" I said. "Now that you know it was Arabella and not a burglar. There's not a thing you can do."

Mitzi looked up. "Do you think they'll arrest her?"

"No. Arthur will vouch for her. It'll all be ironed out in the morning."

"Then I think I will." Mitzi pushed her chair back. "I swear I think those Sawyers are going to do me in."

"Not if you don't let them. You want some milk?"

"I just want to sleep." Pretty, sparkly Mitzi looked like an old, old woman.

Lisa and I looked at each other after Mitzi left.

"What do you think?" she whispered.

I shrugged. I had just thought of something. "You remember when Arabella first came?"

Lisa nodded. "She was in a cab. She had a bunch of stuff."

"I wonder how she got here tonight."

"Maybe she's rented a car."

"Probably." It was reasonable. In fact, if she and her mother had been here for some time, they should already have had a car. So why had Arabella arrived in a taxi the first time? And there hadn't been a car there when I had come home and found her sitting on our back steps. Curiouser and curiouser.

I got up and got each of us a glass of milk. We were sitting at the table playing two-hand bridge when Fred came in.

"That damn fool Arabella Hardt," he said.

"What did they do to her?" I asked.

"Not a thing. She was crying. Said she had to get some clothes to wear to her mother's funeral. The police were all but apologizing to her."

"Where is she now? And where's Arthur?"

"He's gone to take her home." Fred picked up my milk and finished it.

"Back to her mother's apartment?"

"Hell, Patricia Anne, I don't know. Come on, let's go back to bed."

"How come Arthur's taking her? Didn't she have a car?"

"Because she was drunk as a skunk. That's why." Fred put the empty glass in the sink.

"Poor thing." Lisa gathered up the cards.

"Poor thing, my butt," Fred said. "I'm going to bed. Are y'all coming or are you going to stay up all night? We've got to start getting some sleep around here."

"Lisa," I asked, "are you familiar with the word curmudgeon?"

"Does it mean grumpy old man?"
"You got it."
"Not funny," the old curmudgeon said. We turned out the light and followed him down the hall, grinning.

There was a mass exodus from the house the next morning which surprised me. I woke to the sound of Fred taking a shower and got up to put on some coffee. When I walked into the kitchen, Lisa and Alan were sitting at the table. I caught my breath. A dozen red roses were in a vase on the counter.
"Hey, Mama," he said, getting up to hug me.
"Hey, sweetheart." This man is a foot taller than I am and weighs a hundred pounds more, but he's my baby. I patted him on the back. "I'll come back in a few minutes. Give you time to talk."
"We've been talking for a couple of hours, Mama," Lisa said. "I never went back to sleep last night, and I came back to get some more milk, and there was Alan standing at the door. Nearly scared me to death."
"Well, are you hungry? You want me to fix you some breakfast?"
Alan pulled out a chair for me. "Sit down, Mama. We've had some cereal."

He sat down, too, and leaned forward. "I couldn't sleep last night, either. All I could think of was what a fool I'd been acting. So I woke the boys up and told them I was coming to Birmingham to apologize to Lisa and the rest of you and ask if their mother would come back. I apologized to them, too."

"I'm going home, Mama," Lisa said. "We've got a lot of things to work out, but we've got fifteen years of our lives invested in this marriage, and we've made two wonderful children together. And I told Alan that, by damn, we aren't going to throw it away, that we're going to get some help."

"That's wonderful." I felt like a weight had been lifted from me.

"I'm going to go get my stuff together," Lisa said.

"You need some help?" Alan asked.

Lisa shook her head no. "You sit here and talk to your mama."

"She's a wonderful girl, son," I said as Lisa disappeared down the hall.

"I know."

I got up and poured each of us a cup of coffee. The roses on the counter were catching the early morning sun. "Where did you get the flowers in the middle of the night?"

He looked sheepish. "The Winn-Dixie. I figured it wouldn't hurt." He took the coffee. "How's Haley?"

I was telling him about Warsaw's roach problem when his father walked in.

"Well," Fred said. "About time."

The two of them hugged and beat each other on the back.

"I apologize, Papa."

Alan was beginning to sound like one of the steps of AA.

"It's that sweet girl in yonder who deserves your apology," Fred said. "They just don't come any better than Lisa."

"I know that, Papa."

I left them and went down the hall to the guest bedroom where Lisa was closing her suitcase.

"You okay?" I asked.

"I will be." She looked at me. "Won't I?"

"You will be."

She hugged me. "Thank you for everything."

And then they were gone, and the house seemed empty. Lisa had become such an integral part of our lives so quickly, maybe helping to fill the gap left by Haley. Who knows.

"You think they can work it out?" Fred asked as he came back into the kitchen. He had walked out to the car with Alan. "I told him to act like he's got some sense."

Good fatherly advice.

"They'll work it out." I poured him some apple juice and stuck two waffles in the toaster. Then I went out to give Woofer his breakfast and tell him he was a good dog.

The Phizers left just as quickly. They came in with their suitcases packed while I was putting the sheets from Lisa's bed in the washing machine.

"We're gone," Mitzi announced. "I'll call you as soon as I know what our phone number is. And we'll be over every day seeing about the house, I'm sure."

"Don't you want some coffee? Something to eat?"

"We had some earlier with Lisa and Alan. She told us she was going home. I'm so glad, Patricia Anne."

What a busy household this had been early this morning while I slept.

"Was Arabella okay?" I asked Arthur.

"She'd been drinking. But yes, she was okay. I took her back to her mother's apartment. She was embarrassed to have caused so much commotion."

Mitzi and I glanced at each other. She had apparently not told Arthur of our suspicions about Arabella not living there.

Mitzi hugged me. "Thanks for everything. I told Lisa I'd keep my fingers crossed for her and Alan."

"We all will. You call me, now."

A hug from Arthur and they, too, were gone. I had my house back, and it seemed strange. Strange and good. Maybe we could get some sleep.

I started the washing machine, went into the den, turned on *The Price Is Right,* and picked up my smocking. Muffin climbed into my lap. Life, for a few minutes, seemed normal.

The phone rang. Mary Alice. She was stopping by Subway. Did Lisa and I want chicken salad sandwiches for lunch?

"I do. Lisa's gone. Alan came for her, full of apologies."

Yes. Life was getting back to normal. Whatever that is.

"And did you howl at the moon?" I asked her later as I was pouring tea and after we had agreed that it was wonderful that Lisa and Alan had gone home to face their problems which, hopefully could be resolved okay.

"Of course. Even wrote a haiku about it. We all did. You want to hear it?"

"Sure."

She reached in her purse, pulled out a

notebook and read:

"We howl at the moon.
The sun crosses the equator
and heads back this way."

"That's lovely," I said. It really was. I wasn't about to tell her that every English teacher in the world automatically counts syllables when haikus are read and that she had one too many in the second line.

"There's another one."

I put the tea on the table and sat down. "Okay."

"Dew falls on the grass
I wonder what I've stepped in
in the cow pasture."

She looked up and giggled. "Everybody liked that one."

"I can understand why. So the party was in a pasture?"

"Lord, yes. We all sat on the ground. My behind's so sore today you wouldn't believe. And I'd totally forgotten we were supposed to bring some kind of back-to-nature food to eat, so I stopped by Hardee's and got a big box of fried chicken. That was the main thing everybody ate. The kudzu quiche somebody brought was pretty good, though." She bit into her Subway.

"Kudzu quiche?"

"Tasted about like spinach. Now, tell me about Mitzi and Arthur's apartment."

I not only told her what I knew about the apartment, I told her about Arabella's visit during the night and that I was never going to call 911 again, that the woman recognized my voice.

"How's Arthur doing?"

"Seems to be doing pretty good. Do you know what happens now that he's out on bail? Did Debbie tell you?"

"They have an arraignment in a couple of weeks."

"What's that?"

"Debbie says Peyton and Arthur go before the judge and the judge tells him what he's been charged with and asks him if he has a lawyer."

"But he already knows that."

"That's the way it works."

I couldn't argue with that.

While we were eating, a car pulled into the Phizers' driveway. Two men in suits got out and walked around the back. Woofer barked happily. He was feeling better.

"Did Joy McWain call you?" Mary Alice asked.

I nodded. "I told her I'd think about it. I'll do it if you'll help me."

Sister put her sandwich down and looked straight at me. "I don't think I can, Mouse."

"Why?"

"Because they're set on Alcorn Jones's bank doing the actual investing for them and on him advising them."

"What's wrong with that?"

"You don't remember skinny Al Jones that I went to high school with?"

"No. Should I?"

"Probably not. I never talked about him after the accident." Mary Alice held out her sandwich and examined it as if she were looking for something.

I was intrigued. If I hadn't known Sister better, I would have sworn she was blushing. "What accident?"

"I think I lost my virginity to him."

"Accidentally?"

"Yes, Miss Goody Two-Shoes, accidentally. We were parked up on Ruffner Mountain on the road that leads to the fire tower, and we were in the backseat of his '48 Ford just fooling around, and he hadn't put the brakes on good, I guess. Anyway, the car rolled a couple of feet and hit a tree. Just bumped it, really. Didn't do any damage to the car."

"But you lost your virginity when the car hit." I took a big sip of tea, trying to picture this.

"I said I *think* I did."

I spit tea all over my sandwich.

"Well, good Lord, Mouse, it's not that funny." Sister got up and rolled a couple of paper towels off the holder. "Besides, he told everybody at school." She handed me the towels which I laughed into. "I've never forgiven him. I guarantee you."

I sobbed into the paper towel. "Poor Alcorn," I managed to say.

"Poor Alcorn, my foot. He's the reason I didn't get to be Homecoming queen. I'm sure of it. Bragging about it. Ruining my reputation."

"Oh, God." I laughed harder.

In a minute, I heard Mary Alice giggle. "Well, I guess it was a little bit funny."

I nodded.

"Anyway, you see why I don't want to have anything to do with him. He's not a gentleman." Mary Alice picked up her sandwich and began to eat again.

And I knew I couldn't deal with him either. I could just imagine trying to talk investment club business with him and all the time seeing that car bump the tree. I'd have to call Joy and tell her to forget my being the financial partner.

Eventually I calmed down, took the soggy top off of my sandwich and got up to get a fork. The two men at the Phizers' were down on their hands and knees looking under the house.

"What do you think those men are doing?" I asked. "You think they're insurance adjusters?"

Mary Alice stood up and looked. "Probably. Or detectives. Looks like they wouldn't have worn good suits, though."

We watched them for a minute. One of them was pointing at something; the other nodded.

"Where did the fire start?" Sister asked.

"Under the back bedroom, I understand. And spread to the kitchen."

"Gasoline?"

"I guess. The batteries were gone from all of the smoke alarms."

"And they think Arthur killed Sophie Sawyer and then set fire to his house as a diversion? Fun and games."

"Well, you heard Mitzi." Then I remembered what Bo Mitchell had said about Arthur's watching his rear. "No. I think they believe somebody else is involved." I told Sister what Bo had said.

The men next door got up and brushed

off their knees. One of them took a cell phone from his pocket and was talking to someone as he walked toward my house. In a moment the front doorbell rang.

"Mrs. Hollowell?" He was a small man with very black hair and olive skin. "I'm Joe Pepper. Arson. Do you mind if I ask you a few questions?"

Of course I didn't mind. I invited him into the living room. It took Sister all of a minute to join us.

I introduced them and the first thing she asked was if he was a sergeant.

"No ma'am. Why?"

"It would be fun to be Sergeant Pepper."

The man was too young for the Beatles. I could tell he didn't have any idea what she was talking about. He smiled politely, though, and got out the usual spiral notebook.

Yes, I was checking on my dog who had been sick, probably bitten by a possum. No, I hadn't seen anybody at the Phizers'. All I saw was a glow and then a flame and I called 911 and then the Phizers and told them to get out.

"Anything else?"

The firemen were there in about two minutes which was great. They smashed some flowers, but all in all, did a good job.

"We stood on the sidewalk and watched," I added. "Then the Phizers came home with us."

"Was it gasoline?" Sister asked.

"Some sort of flammable substance." Joe Pepper closed his notebook. I noticed he hadn't written anything. I obviously was not a font of information.

"Thanks, ladies," he said. "I may be back in touch, Mrs. Hollowell."

"He seemed nice but you sure didn't have much to tell him," Sister said as we went back to the kitchen.

I got a package of cookies from the cabinet and put them on the table. "You want your tea freshened?"

She nodded yes.

"How much did you have to pay Peyton Phillips?" I asked.

"What?"

"Peyton Phillips. Her retainer. Your own daughter said Peyton charges a fortune, but Mitzi hasn't mentioned any charges. You weren't buying Cedric a fishing license." I poured her tea. "How is he, by the way?"

"Fine. He called this morning."

"What's his last name?"

"Hawkins. Why?"

"Mary Alice Tate Sullivan Nachman Crane Hawkins."

Sister helped herself to several cookies. "I may not take his name. Or maybe I'll hyphenate the Tate and Hawkins. That's real English. Mary Alice Tate-Hawkins."

She looked too pleased at the idea. It was time for a subject change. "Have you been thinking about any stocks to suggest next week? You are going, aren't you?"

"Of course I am. I'm going to suggest AmSouth Bank. Tick Al Jones off. I've heard they're about to buy his bank out."

"I'm sure that will upset him."

"I hope so. Him and his Ruffner Mountain." She reached for another cookie. "Just couldn't keep his mouth shut."

Among other things.

Sixteen

The next few days were fairly uneventful. The good late summer weather hung on with no heat waves, something we dread in Birmingham in September, especially if there's no rain. September and October are always dry, and we depend on the occasional thunderstorms to see us through. This year was perfect, the late afternoon rains rolling in on time.

Woofer was feeling well; we resumed our walks. Lisa called and said she and Alan were going for counseling and they were taking the boys white water rafting on the Nantahala in a couple of weeks. One morning the doorbell rang, and the florist handed me a beautiful azalea topiary from Alan. I took this as a sign he was feeling properly remorseful.

E-mails were coming in regularly from Haley. I even sent her one when I went to tutor. Shatawna, delighted to get out of class for a few minutes, showed me how. "It's *so* easy, Mrs. Hollowell." And it was. I started shopping for a computer.

The Gateway store was down the street

from Bonnie Blue's shop, so I dropped in on her and we went to lunch. She asked about "what's-his-name" and Mary Alice. She'd heard they were engaged. Cedric, I assured her, was fading like the Cheshire Cat's grin.

There was no work going on over at the Phizers'. Big surprise. But Mitzi had stopped by and told me that she, Arthur, Arabella, Sue, Joseph, and the two grandchildren had scattered Sophie's ashes off of Vulcan, that she thought it would be nice like in *The Bridges of Madison County* when the ashes blew gently into the river by the bridge. But they must not have done as good a job of cremating Sophie as they had Francesca.

"It wasn't all ashes, Patricia Anne. Plus, some of it blew back on us. Sue fainted."

"They don't get much experience here cremating."

"True. Looks like they'd have done a better job, though. They're advertised in the Yellow Pages."

She and Arthur were okay, though, getting settled. And they had gotten all their clothes from the cleaners. And they had put the stuff from the fire safe into their safety-deposit-box. Arabella had admitted that she had not been staying with Sophie all the time, but had been staying with a friend close by so she could check on her frequently.

"A man, I assume," Mitzi said. "She didn't volunteer any names."

"But why would she have lied about it?"

"Didn't want us to think she was neglecting Sophie, I guess."

That didn't make a grain of sense, but not much about the Sawyer family had.

Things seemed so peaceful that first part of September, it surprised me to look out of the kitchen window and see the Phizers' charred kitchen, to remember that Arthur was out on bail, charged with murder.

I used the time well, though. I studied the *Beardstown Ladies' Common Sense Investment Guide*, watched the stock market analysts on TV, and bought several *Wall Street Journals*. I even requested and received the annual report for Bellemina Health. I'd told Joy McWain that I wouldn't be the financial partner, but that wouldn't stop me from doing my homework. And Bellemina Health was the way to go.

When Mary Alice picked me up for the next meeting, she was wearing what looked suspiciously like a bullfighter's outfit: black pants that fit her lower legs tightly, a white shirt, and a red cape. I was pretty sure I knew who the bull was.

"Nice outfit," I lied. "Did you get it at Bonnie Blue's?"

She shook her head no. "Bought it on one of those TV shopping networks. This woman who used to be on *The Young and the Restless* designed it. I tell you they're all into that now. I think that's one of the stocks we ought to buy. They're making fortunes selling stuff on TV."

"Buy shopping network stock? I thought you were going to recommend AmSouth."

"Changed my mind. That was just to bug Al Jones."

When we got to the meeting, Miss Bessie, the lady who had been scalped, had saved us seats and waved to us. Today she was wearing a pink crocheted hat. Alcorn Jones was at a table by the door, pouring himself some coffee. Sister swished by him on her ballet slippers. Torro!

If the bull saw the red flag, he ignored it.

We got a lot done that day. The partners were chosen, a committee was appointed to write the partnership agreement, and those who were ready suggested stocks. Carnival Cruise Lines was mentioned as a possibility because Kathie Lee was their spokesperson and Cody had been conceived on a Carnival Cruise. And, bless her heart, Kathie Lee had held up her head through all of her troubles.

"She's a real Christian," the Baptist lady said.

"Any of the cruise lines would be a good investment," Alcorn Jones agreed. "They're certainly popular. Most of them aren't American companies, though. I think Carnival is Liberian."

A lady in a purple suit spoke up. "That's the truth. I went on a cruise and most of the crew didn't speak English. I don't remember if it was Carnival or not. The food was great, though."

"What about Wal-Mart?" another lady said. "Kathie Lee does Wal-Mart, too."

Miss Bessie spoke up. "I like Kathie Lee, but I don't like that Gelman. He's too full of himself."

"Regis is nice. And so is Joy," someone added.

Everyone agreed that was so.

When my turn came and I recommended Bellemina Health, Alcorn Jones was enthusiastic. He would have mentioned it if I hadn't. Nowhere but up. Great buy. Locally headquartered, too.

Mary Alice recommended AmSouth Bank; Alcorn Jones looked pained. Torro!

"I don't know about that Bellemina Health stock," Miss Bessie informed me later. She, Sister, and I were doing some serious eating at a restaurant in Homewood where you could get two vegetables, meat, cornbread, and tea for $4.99. "I've known that Joseph Batson all his life. His family lived next door to us when he was growing up. Mean as a snake. I wouldn't let my kids play with him."

"What did he do?" Mary Alice dipped a piece of country fried steak into her mashed potatoes, swished it around, and lifted it, coated, to her mouth. Her eyes widened. "Lord, that's good."

"Beat up on them. He was just spoiled rotten. Change of life baby." Miss Bessie followed Mary Alice's example with the mashed potatoes, but held the fork in the air, potatoes dangling precariously, while she said, "Never thought he'd amount to a hill of beans. Just shows." She put the food in her mouth and chewed thoughtfully. "Helped to marry that rich Sawyer girl from Chicago."

"What do you know about his family?" I asked.

"His mama and papa or his wife and children?"

"Any of them." I explained about Arthur and how he was mixed up with the Batsons.

Miss Bessie nodded. "Been reading about that in the paper."

"Well, Arthur Phizer didn't kill Sophie Sawyer," I said. "You can take my word for that. He was set up."

"By one of those Batsons, probably." Mary Alice motioned for the waitress to pour us some more tea. And did they have peach cobbler today?

"I wouldn't be surprised," Miss Bessie said after the waitress left. "That Joseph was spoiled rotten."

"We were at Sophie's apartment the other day getting her some clothes when Zoe showed up," I said. "She seems nice."

"That's what I hear." Miss Bessie sipped her tea. "Her brother's spent more time in his daddy's hospitals than he has at home, though."

"On drugs?"

"Alcohol. Something. I remember when old Mrs. Batson was sick and in a nursing home," Miss Bessie frowned, "must have been six or seven years ago. Anyway. I went to visit her, and all she could talk about was how worried she was about Dickie. And he couldn't have been more than thirteen or fourteen at the time. Bless her heart."

Mary Alice pushed back her already empty plate. "His other grandmother would have known it, too, then. That would be a good reason not to hand money over to him.

I'd love to read that will."

"But he's already swimming in money," I said.

"I doubt that," Miss Bessie said. "Joseph Batson's made such a success out of Bellemina because he's got the first dollar he ever made." She pushed her empty plate aside, too. "Of course, Dickie and Zoe will have it someday." She burped slightly and patted her chest. "From both sides."

But what if Dickie had wanted it right now? He wouldn't have known that Sophie had made Arthur the trustee of the estate. He would have assumed that with Sophie gone, the money would be theirs.

But then I was back to one of the essential problems. They knew their grandmother wasn't well. All they had to do was wait a while.

Unless. I took a mouthful of broccoli and chewed thoughtfully. Okay, Dickie was on drugs. He could have gone to his grandmother for some quick money. She refused, and he decided to hurry her death along. Then he found out Arthur stood between him and his inheritance. Get rid of Arthur. Set his house on fire. But could Dickie have planted the poison some way? The odds were against it.

"Is your sister on one of those chew-your-food-fifty-times diets?" Miss Bessie asked Mary Alice.

"She has an eating disorder," Sister said.

I swallowed quickly. "I do not. I was just thinking."

"She does, too. She's anorexic." Sister waved to the waitress. "Y'all want ice cream on your cobbler?"

We did.

The next day the peaceful week was over. Somebody shot Arthur Phizer in the butt.

I had just come in from walking Woofer when the phone rang. It was Bridget Phizer, saying that her father was in the emergency room at UAB, that he had been shot as he was leaving his apartment.

"Oh God, Bridget," I said. "How bad is it, and who did it?"

"We don't know, Mrs. Hollowell. Somebody shot him in the back. That's all I know. But I've got the baby here. Could you come get him and keep him for a while?"

Of course I would. I didn't even stop to change clothes.

Mitzi, Bridget, and Barbara were sitting in a corner of the emergency waiting room when I rushed in. Bridget was holding Andrew Cade and they all seemed to be in better shape than I had thought they would be.

"Here's Mrs. Hollowell, Mama," Bridget said to Mitzi who was reading a *People* magazine.

Mitzi looked up. "Oh, Patricia Anne." Barbara moved over and I sat by Mitzi and took her hand.

"What happened?"

"He went out the front door and I didn't even hear the shot. The man in the next apartment did, though, and went running out."

"Is he conscious?"

"I'm sure they gave him a local. They're sewing him up."

"He's going to have trouble sitting for a few days," Barbara said.

Relief flooded me. "He's shot in the behind?" I turned to Bridget. "You scared me half to death when you said he was shot in the back."

"I'm sorry. Mama wasn't specific about the location when she called me."

"I didn't know," Mitzi said. "He had on his gray suit and he was yelling."

"The neighbor banged on Mama's door and called 911," Barbara said.

Shot in the butt. Damn. Bo Peep was right. He should have covered his ass.

"Did he see who did it?"

Bridget answered this time. "No. They're

in the corner apartment. Whoever did it stepped around the corner as Daddy came out, shot him from behind, and ran back." Andrew Cade lifted his plump hand to her mouth; she kissed it and spoke around it. "The police don't think it was robbery. One of those damn Sawyers, if you ask me, and I told them so, too."

"Mrs. Phizer?"

We all looked up at the young nurse who stood before us.

"Mr. Phizer's all fixed up, but the police would like to talk to you. They're with him back in the emergency room."

"Was it bad?" Mitzi's voice shook.

The nurse shook her head no. "Right across the cheeks. Both sides. We sewed him up so neat, he can still wear his bikini Speedo."

The idea of Arthur in a Speedo bikini was more mind-boggling than the gunshot.

"You want us to go with you, Mama?" Bridget asked. "I want to make sure the police know it was one of those Sawyers who did it. It's been nothing but trouble since they showed up."

"I'll keep Andrew Cade," I volunteered.

Bridget handed the baby to me, and the three of them followed the nurse down the hall. Andrew Cade's face puckered up as he saw his mother leaving.

"She'll be back in a minute, sweetheart," I said. I reached in my purse and handed him my car keys to play with. My key ring is a small plastic cylinder filled with clear liquid. In the liquid are suspended hundreds of tiny colored stars that swish from one end to the other when it's moved. Much like a snow dome. Andrew Cade was immediately fascinated.

There is no place in the world much worse than an emergency room waiting room and, believe me, I am not into suffering. I jiggled Andrew Cade on my knees (this child was getting heavy) and glued my eyes to one of the three TVs bolted high on the wall. Regis and Kathie Lee were on which reminded me of the investment club, which reminded me of Miss Bessie, which reminded me of what she had told us about Dickie Batson.

"Mama," Andrew Cade said.

"She'll be back in a minute, darling."

Maybe it was Dickie who had shot Arthur this morning. It was possible. And it could have been Dickie who had set the Phizers' house on fire. He might have been willing to wait for his grandmother's death (or maybe he hadn't), but Arthur could control Dickie's inheritance for a long time.

"Hey, I thought you might be here."

I looked up and saw Bo Mitchell.

"Are you the only policeman in Birmingham? I thought you were working nights."

"Just the busiest. I'm on days for a while now. Started this week." She sat down beside me. Andrew Cade held out his arms to her and she took him. "Hey, you sweetie. What's your name?"

"His name's Andrew Cade. He's the Phizers' grandson."

"I figured. They say back in the emergency room that Mr. Phizer didn't follow my advice."

"Nope. Both cheeks. Hell, Bo. When are y'all going to do something? Somebody tries to burn him up and now shoots him. And y'all still have him arrested for murder."

"The wheels of justice do creak along." Bo turned the key chain so the stars would pour up through the liquid. Andrew Cade laughed.

"It was one of the Batson-Sawyer crew, Bo. You know that. Probably Dick Batson, the grandson."

"He's a doll," she said. For a moment I thought she was talking about Andrew Cade until she said, "We're well acquainted with him."

"Anything serious?"

"Patricia Anne, you got any idea how much money Bellemina pours into the Birmingham economy?"

"Enough to lessen the seriousness of something?"

"You got it." She ran her hand through Andrew Cade's blonde curls. "Baby doll, you grow up good now," she told him.

"Where's Joanie?"

"Gone to get a Coke up at the cafeteria. Wouldn't use the vending machine. Thinks they'll say, 'Oh, no, Miss Police Lady, you're protecting us. We're not taking your money.' "

"And they won't?"

"Lord, no." Bo smiled. "That girl's got some learning to do."

"Have you talked to Arthur? I assume that's why you're here. Somebody else is back there now questioning him."

"I left. Wasn't doing any good. He didn't know anything. Just walked out of his apartment and whoomp, got it in the butt." Bo looked up. "Here comes Joanie."

Joanie Salk was carrying a huge paper cup, a straw stuck through the plastic top.

"How much?" Bo asked.

Joanie's face pinkened. "A dollar eighty-five."

"Un huh." Bo stood up and handed Andrew Cade to me. "Gotta go catch the bad guys."

"Well, I told you which one you'd better look at."

"We'll do it. Say goodbye to Mrs. Hollowell, Joanie."

"Bye, Mrs. Hollowell."

I watched them walk toward the door, Joanie offering Bo a straw, Bo laughing.

Barbara and Bridget were back in a few minutes. Bridget took Andrew Cade from me and hugged him.

"They're asking Mama and Daddy all sorts of things," she said. "You'd think Mama was the one shot him."

"He can go home in a little while, can't he?"

"Soon as the police get through and Mama can check him out."

"I've got to get back to work," Barbara said. "Now that I know Daddy's all right."

"Well, why don't I take Andrew Cade home with me, Bridget," I suggested. "You can stay with your mother and drive them home."

"You sure?"

"Absolutely. I'd love to have him."

"Well, if you're sure, that would be great." She reached beside the chair.

"Here's his diaper bag, and there's a bottle and a couple of cans of formula in it. If you've got any apple sauce, or just mash up some English peas."

"We'll be fine." It wasn't the time to remind her I'd been there several times. Andrew Cade was her first.

"I'll go get his car seat then and meet you out front." Bridget and Barbara walked out together.

"This is it," I heard Barbara say. "Enough."

I hoped so.

Seventeen

Andrew Cade went to sleep on the way home. I carried him into the house still strapped in his car seat and put him on the floor in the den. If I went to sleep with my neck in that position, I would never be able to turn it again. But he was sleeping peacefully. I went in the bedroom to call Fred and to check my phone messages.

There was only one message, Sister saying she had found me a computer, cheap. That sounded good, though Sister and I don't always agree on the meaning of "cheap."

Fred answered the phone on the first ring. "Metal Fab."

"Honey," I said, "somebody shot Arthur Phizer."

"Arthur? Arthur's dead?"

"No, honey. He's shot in the butt." I should have told him that first.

"Well, Lord, Patricia Anne. What happened?"

I told him what I knew and that Arthur was probably on his way home. "Both cheeks," I added.

"You think I should go over there?"

"No. He's fine. Bridget's there with Mitzi, and I have Andrew Cade here. His daddy's in Atlanta."

"Well, damn." There was silence for a moment. I could hear the sounds of the shop in the background, men talking, the rattle of the crane. Then Fred added, "You'd think Arthur would be the last person in the world anybody would want to shoot."

"Or burn up."

Another silence. Then, "Both cheeks?"

I could swear I heard a snicker. Then, "Skinny as Arthur is, they had to take good aim."

"The nurse said they stitched him up so good, he'll still be able to wear his Speedo bikini."

A definite snicker. "God forbid."

"Hey, this is serious," I reminded him.

"I know it is, hon. Call me if you hear anything. Lord. Both cheeks."

I tried to return Mary Alice's call, but Tiffany, the Magic Maid, answered. Sister was at a meeting.

I tiptoed back through the den. Andrew Cade was still sound asleep in his car seat. I checked the pantry; there was applesauce and a can of English peas. We were in business.

The morning was catching up with me. I fixed myself a Coke, got a bag of pretzels and the morning paper, and sat down at the kitchen table. But I couldn't concentrate on the paper.

What I had reminded Fred of was true. This was serious business. So Arthur had been shot in the butt. Pure luck. Whoever was doing the shooting hadn't been fooling around. Regardless of what Fred had said about their aim, they weren't trying to scare Arthur, not with a gun. They had meant to kill him. And it had to have something to do with Sophie, with the fact that he was the trustee of her estate. Which boiled down to the Batson-Sawyers, of course. The only problem being that there were five of them.

I shook some of the pretzels onto the newspaper. I ate a few of them and drank some of the Coke. Then I took nine of the pretzels and laid them out in a pattern. This is the old schoolteacher in me. I know what visual aids can do in helping to solve a puzzle.

At the top, I placed two sets of two. Sophie and Milton and Mitzi and Arthur. The only connection was between Sophie and Arthur. Mitzi wasn't jealous of Sophie. Well, maybe a little bit (I remembered the drawer of silk lingerie), but would never harm her. Arthur would come out well financially if Sophie were dead, he had given her the poison-laced sweetener, and there was the note Sophie had sent her doctor saying she was asking Arthur to help her die. Didn't look good. But there was also the fact that there had been two attempts on Arthur's life.

I lined up five pretzels below the two pairs. Joseph, Sue, Dickie, and Zoe Batson, and Arabella Hardt. I knew in my bones, as Mama always said, that the murderer was here on this row.

There was a tap on the back door and Debbie stuck her head in. I held my finger to my lips to silence her.

"What?" she whispered, coming into the kitchen.

"Andrew Cade's in the den asleep."

Debbie looked in at the sleeping baby. "He's about to break his neck."

"He's fine. Get you a Coke and sit down."

"I had a doctor's appointment, but he's delivering a baby. So I came to take you to lunch. What's Andrew Cade doing here?"

"I went to University Hospital to get him. Arthur Phizer's going to be okay, but somebody shot him this morning. In the butt," I added quickly.

"You're kidding. Somebody shot Mr.

Phizer?" Debbie pulled out a chair and sat down.

I pointed to the line of pretzels. "One of these people."

Debbie is thoroughly acquainted with my need for visual aids. "Which one?" she asked.

"That's what I'm trying to figure out. It's one of the four Batsons or Arabella."

"Which one is which?"

This is one of my niece's most endearing qualities, her ability to immediately mesh her imagination with mine.

I pointed to each pretzel in turn. "Joseph, Sue, Dickie, Zoe, Arabella."

Debbie placed another pretzel in the line. "Arabella's boyfriend. The person she's been staying with that nobody knows anything about. He'd be very much involved, especially if their relationship is serious."

"True."

"Wait a minute, Aunt Pat." Debbie got up and fixed herself a Coke. She held up the bottle. "You want some more?"

I shook my head no.

She came back to the table, took a handful of pretzels, and began to eat them. "Let's start with the easiest ones, the ones least likely to be involved."

"Okay. Arabella's boyfriend. It's possible,

but unlikely. We're just speculating that she has one."

Debbie agreed.

"And Zoe, the granddaughter. She's cute as she can be. She came by her grandmother's apartment the other day to get some clothes to cremate Sophie in. We were there doing the same thing." I smiled, remembering. "She nearly had a fit when she saw we had picked out some Ferragamo shoes and a suit she said was a classic."

"Sounds like a good Southern girl."

"Studying style at the university."

I pushed that pretzel aside.

"And Joseph Batson." That pretzel went to the side. "He's a multimillionaire, the head of a huge, growing company. There's no reason why he would have done it."

"So that leaves Arabella, Sue, and Dickie." Debbie munched pretzels thoughtfully.

"Dickie has a history of drugs, is probably still on them, and won't be able to get his hands on his part of his grandmother's estate. Which he wouldn't have known at the time of her death."

"What about Arabella and Sue?"

"I don't want to think that either of them could have killed their mother. They both seemed to have loved her."

"Hmmm." Debbie reached for more pretzels. "They grew up in Chicago, right?"

I nodded. "With their brother David who was killed in an automobile wreck while he was in college. Mitzi described him as the shining star of the family."

"I wonder where Sue and Joseph Batson met."

"Here, I suppose. I'm sure Sophie brought her children here to visit relatives. Why?"

"Just thinking. And Arabella's been married a couple of times?"

"Two or three." I touched the Arabella pretzel. "She's the one who Mitzi says is the spendthrift. She's the reason that Sophie made Arthur the trustee of the estate, so Arabella wouldn't run through her inheritance."

"How could a person run through millions of dollars?"

I shrugged. It boggled my mind.

"And eventually she's going to inherit it."

I agreed. "But maybe Sophie thought she would have grown up by then."

"Aunt Pat, the woman's forty years old."

True. But if that wasn't the reason, why had Sophie shielded her estate behind Arthur?

"Would Peyton Phillips know anything

about the family?"

Debbie shook her head no. "I doubt it. All she did was get Mr. Phizer out on bail and I think Joseph Batson volunteered to post it. I'll call her and see."

There was a whimper from the den. Debbie and I both jumped up. Andrew Cade was looking around, puzzled at finding himself in a strange place.

"Hey, you precious thing." Debbie picked him up and hugged him. "It's okay, sweet boy." She looked at me over his blonde curls and smiled. "It's going to be different having a baby boy. We've told the twins, but they don't seem too excited."

I smiled back. "I'll get him a diaper," I said, "and fix his lunch."

"You want a dry diaper, sweetheart? And something to eat?" Debbie cooed.

It was an hour or so before we got back to the pretzels. Debbie said she didn't have a client until three, so we made Andrew Cade a playpen of sorts by turning the dining room chairs on their sides. He sat in the enclosure beating happily on some pans with a spoon and eating Cheerios. Every now and then he would pull himself up and peer over the back of a chair at us.

"He's going to be walking soon," Debbie said. "How old is he? Nine months old?"

I nodded. "And he said Mama plain as anything at the hospital." I glanced at the clock. Bridget should be by soon to pick him up.

I had fixed tomato sandwiches for lunch. The pretzel family was still in place in the middle of the table. Now Debbie reached over and removed the Sue Batson pretzel.

"It's Dickie or Arabella," she said.

"The money?"

"The money."

I grinned. "You missed your calling. You should have been a cop."

"Nope."

"The money?"

"The money."

Andrew Cade banged his agreement.

Debbie put one pretzel down. "Arabella."

"I don't want to believe that, Debbie."

Debbie put the pretzel down. "I don't either."

Andrew Cade began to fuss, and Debbie picked him up. "Aunt Pat, what if Mr. Phizer really did it, really killed Mrs. Sawyer because he loved her. There could be two things going on here, you know. He killed Mrs. Sawyer and now someone's after him."

Once more, I saw Arthur stroking Sophie's hand, saw him lifting her legs into the car. No. Surely not.

But Debbie was already shaking her head. "No. Mr. Phizer wouldn't do that."

Bridget came for Andrew Cade around two o'clock. Her daddy was pretty comfortable. They'd given him a pain pill before they sent him home. Arabella Hardt and Joseph Batson had shown up at the apartment; they'd heard about Arthur on the noon news.

"Mama should have told them to go away." Bridget picked up a sleeping Andrew Cade from a pallet I'd made for him on the floor. "I know she's just worn out with everything that's happened. But you know Mama."

"Dr. Batson paid your daddy's bail, Bridget."

"He could well afford to."

I handed Bridget the diaper bag. "Andrew Cade's been an angel."

She nodded. "He's the best baby in the world." She started out of the door and turned. "It's all about Mrs. Sawyer's will, isn't it? The fact that Daddy's the trustee."

"I'm sure it is. The police will find out."

"I hope it's while Daddy's still alive." She sounded bitter.

I hoped so, too. I waved as she went

through the gate. Then I went back inside, called Fred and told him to go by Morrison's Cafeteria and pick up supper, anything as long as he included egg custard pie. I took Woofer for a long, slow walk, and by the time I got back and took a shower, I was feeling better. By the time Fred came in with corned beef and cabbage, I was feeling much better.

After supper, I tried to call Sister again. I got her answering machine so I hung up and called Debbie. One of the two-year-olds, either Fay or May, answered the phone.

"Oh?"

"Fay? Is that you?"

"Oh?"

"May? Hey, darling, it's Aunt Pat."

"Oh? Pat?"

Fortunately, Debbie took the phone. I could hear the twin fussing about it. "Go see Daddy," Debbie said. Those were nice words to hear from the newly married Debbie though Mary Alice insists that Henry really is the twin's natural father. He contributed to the sperm bank at UAB, Debbie was impregnated there, therefore the twins must be his. Forget the odds.

"Hey, honey, it's me," I said.

"Hey, Aunt Pat. I was fixing to call you. I just talked to Peyton and she asked me about Mr. Phizer. Have you heard from him tonight?"

"Bridget came by to pick up Andrew Cade about two. She said he was okay. She said Arabella Hardt and Joseph Batson came by the apartment."

"Well, I can't believe the Batson boy did this, can you? He's got everything in the world going for him, and he gets mixed up on drugs and now I guess they've got him for attempted murder."

"What?" The shock in my voice must have alerted her.

"You didn't know? They arrested Dickie Batson about an hour ago for attempted murder. He's the one who shot Mr. Phizer and Peyton says they think he's the one who set the house on fire, too."

I thought of the line of pretzels. Why should I be surprised?

"And killed his grandmother?"

"Who knows? Peyton says she'd left him millions in her will, millions he thought he'd get as soon as his grandmother died."

"Well, I'll be damned." I let this information sink in. "How did they catch him?"

"Some woman who lives in the apartments was taking out her garbage and saw Dickie's car in the alley. She described it exactly and even remembered most of the tag number. She called the police when she heard about the shooting. Peyton says when they went to Dickie's apartment, they found the gun. Not real smart."

"And there doesn't seem to be any doubt about it?" I was already thinking about what this news was going to do to his parents, especially his mother.

"Doesn't sound like it."

"So Arthur's off the hook?"

"Probably not yet. All they've got the Batson boy for right now is shooting Mr. Phizer." There were some scuffling sounds in the background and then wails. "Wait a minute, Aunt Pat."

So it had boiled down to money after all. Dickie had probably killed his grandmother for his inheritance and tried to kill Arthur because he could hold the inheritance up.

Not a good advertisement for his father's teenage drug rehab hospitals.

"Sorry, Aunt Pat. Both of the girls wanted the same doll." Debbie sounded out of breath. "I got so busy telling you about Dickie Batson, that I didn't ask why you called."

"Believe it or not, I called to see if you'd heard anything from Peyton."

"Well, I answered that, didn't I?"

"You sure did. Where's your mother tonight? I tried to call her."

"One of her meetings. The museum, I think. Maybe the botanical gardens. How's the investment club going?"

"Fine. I recommended Bellemina Health. I wonder what Dickie's arrest will do to it."

"Probably nothing. They have a good track record. People will sympathize with the Batsons."

"Well, I sure do." I was about to tell her goodbye when I remembered something else I had called for. "Debbie, if a will's been probated, can anyone read it?"

"Sure, Aunt Pat. After they're admitted into probate, they're on file in probate court on the first floor of the courthouse. Why?"

"Just being nosy, actually. I thought I'd like to read Sophie Sawyer's will. Now that we know Dickie may be responsible, though, I don't guess it matters."

"I'm sure it's interesting reading. I can't imagine having that kind of money."

"I'm not sure I'd want to." After I hung up, I went in to tell Fred the news. He was deep into the ballgame.

"Figures," he said. "Screwed up kid. Hope his daddy doesn't get him out of it." He looked around me at the TV.

It flew all over me. He could have asked some questions, shown some concern.

"Fred Hollowell," I said. "I've been married to you for forty years, and I don't like you."

"Sure you do."

The dishtowel I had in my hand didn't do a bit of harm when I popped him with it, though it did surprise him.

Well, Lisa would want to know. I got my grandson, Sam, who informed me that his mother and daddy were out on the patio talking.

"They don't want us to hear what they're saying so they have the door pulled shut. Wait a minute, Grandma, and I'll get her."

"Never mind, honey. Just tell her it was probably Dickie Batson who did it. Okay?"

"Did what?"

"Your mama will know."

"Okay. I'll tell her. Dickie Batson."

I hung up the phone, walked into the den, and picked up my smocking.

"Lisa and Alan are talking, Fred."

"That's good, honey."

"But they're on the patio with the door closed so the boys can't hear what they're saying."

"That's real good."

I thought about it for a minute. He was right.

Eighteen

Arthur was feeling better the next afternoon when I called, but was mean as a snake, according to Mitzi.

"It hurts him to walk and to sit down. I got him one of those hemorrhoid doughnuts to sit on, but it doesn't help a bit. You wouldn't think everything would be that connected, would you."

Made sense to me. I told her we would wait until the next day to come see him. She admitted that would probably be best.

"And don't think about bringing flowers. The house is full. Joseph and Sue Batson have emptied out a couple of florist shops."

"Maybe it made them feel better."

"I don't know. They're both furious with the police. They believe Dickie didn't do it."

"But I thought somebody saw him."

"Described the car and part of the tag number. But Dickie swears he was asleep at his apartment when it happened." She paused. "Of course he says he was alone so he doesn't have an alibi, and they found the gun there that had just been shot."

"What do you think?"

"I hope he's telling the truth. I don't see how that's possible, but I hope he didn't do it."

Sweet Mitzi. If someone had shot Fred, I'd have been mad as a hornet's nest.

"And what about the arson? Do the police think he did that, too?"

"He's not charged with it, but they're investigating it. If he did, I'm telling you, Patricia Anne, I hope he ends up under the jail."

So much for Mitzi's bid for sainthood.

"Where is Dickie now?" I asked.

"Out on bail, just like Arthur is. Has it ever occurred to you, Patricia Anne, how many people we meet on the street who are out on bail?"

Truthfully, no.

I had turned on CNBC's stock report to see if Dickie's arrest had done anything to Bellemina Health, but of course it hadn't. It was too large a company for the CEO's son's crimes to affect it. In fact, as Debbie had predicted, the stock had edged up slightly. The alphabet scrolling across the bottom of the screen made me dizzy and I turned it off.

I should vacuum. I should get out my winter clothes and begin to decide what I needed to take to Poland for our Christmas trip and if I needed to buy some new warmer ones. I should register for one of the computer classes that Samford University was offering for the fall. The brochure had just come. By December, I could be proficient in Windows 98, Word, e-mail. You name it. Cyberspace would be mine.

Instead, I picked up the latest Patricia Cornwell novel that I had found at the library a few days before. In a few minutes I was knee deep in blood in the autopsy room with Dr. Kay Scarpetta. An entrance wound? Of course. Probably caused by a .38. We needed to look for the casing, out there in the leaves by Arthur's apartment. The police overlook things like that.

"Your mouth's open." Sister was standing beside my chair.

"It is not." I picked up the book which had slipped to the floor. "I was just resting my eyes."

"Well, wake up. I've got news to tell you." She sat on the sofa.

"I'm awake," I insisted.

"You sure? Because this is important."

"I'm awake, dammit." I considered throwing the book.

"I had lunch today with Al Jones at The Club."

Why did this not surprise me?

"I had that wonderful seafood au gratin. Lord that stuff's good. And he had a small steak."

My hands tightened on the book. "Is this the important news?"

"Of course not, though I know you're surprised that I had lunch with Al, given the way I feel about him."

"You mean the fact that he's not a gentleman."

"Well, he's grown up, Mouse."

In fifty years I should hope so.

"Anyway, we got to talking about Dickie Batson shooting Arthur and how sad it was, and I said I wondered if he'd killed his grandmother, and Al said that he figured when he heard about Sophie's death that it might be Joseph Batson who killed her, that Sophie and her son-in-law were not on the best of terms to say the least. In fact, I believe his words were 'they had the hot hates for each other.' "

I really was awake now. "Why? Did he say why?"

Mary Alice hugged a sofa pillow. "You remember somebody saying there were two other boys in the car when Sophie's son David was killed?"

"Yes. One of them died."

"Joseph Batson was the one who didn't."

"Really? He was the third boy?"

"Banged up pretty bad, but recovered completely. Al says Sophie never forgave him."

"For living?"

"Probably. David and the other boy were dead. But there's more. They were all apparently high as kites on something like LSD. Sophie and Milton always believed Joseph Batson was the supplier, and yet he was the one who lived."

"He was into dealing drugs?"

"He'd had several run-ins with the police. And he was a poor kid from the south in a fancy prep school who always seemed to have money."

"Well, my Lord. That's pretty circumstantial, isn't it?" But my mind was racing. If he had been responsible for the drugs that caused the death of two of his friends, and had had to live with that knowledge, then his founding Bellemina Health certainly made sense. He wouldn't want it to happen to others. And, yet, it looked as if he had failed with his own son.

"How does Alcorn Jones know all this?" I asked.

"He handled Sophie's parents' estate. Sophie's mother told everybody. He said he thought she'd have a stroke when Sue married Joseph."

"I'll bet she did. I doubt it made Sophie and Milton very happy either."

"Well, Sue must have believed Joseph was innocent."

"And married a man her family hated."

"For heaven's sake, Mouse. It happens all the time. The Capulets hated Romeo. Or the Montagues. Whichever. But the kids loved each other."

"Sue's no Juliet." I got up, went in the kitchen and fixed us both a Coke. "And where did he get the money to start Bellemina Health? From Sue?" I was thinking there might be more than love involved here.

I handed Sister her glass. She drank about half of it in one gulp. "That seafood made me thirsty." She burped slightly and then added, "Nope. He got it from the Sawyers, Sophie and Milton."

"Who hated his guts."

"Well, it turned out to be a good investment. Al says the Bellemina stock is probably the most valuable asset in Sophie's estate now."

I frowned, trying to figure this out. "But you don't set someone up in business who you hate. Who you think killed your son."

"He was their son-in-law by then. And the business was to fight drugs." Mary Alice finished her Coke and put the glass on the table. "And, like Al says, he's sure Milton Sawyer recognized Joseph Batson's business acumen."

"Got a lot of acumen, huh?"

"Loaded with it. Look at what he's done with Bellemina."

I sipped my Coke thoughtfully. "And Sophie Sawyer owned a lot of Bellemina stock?"

"A huge amount, according to Al. He's on the board of directors, incidentally. I guess it will go to her kids now. So Joseph and Sue will end up owning no telling how much of the company."

"But Arthur Phizer has control of that stock now as long as he's Sophie's executor. Trustee. Whatever."

"True." Sister wiped the coffee table with her paper napkin. "How is he?"

"Can't walk or sit. Mean as can be, Mitzi says. And Dickie's out on bail."

"Do you think there's any chance it was Dickie who killed his grandmother? Al said he thinks it's possible."

"Lord only knows. The police must not think so. They still have Arthur charged with it. And Joseph and Sue Batson are swearing that Dickie didn't shoot Arthur. He says he was at his apartment asleep and they believe him."

"You want to believe your kids, Mouse. We all believed Ray when he told us he wasn't raising marijuana in the Bankhead National Forest."

This escapade, the only trouble any of our kids has gotten into, was indirectly the reason Mary Alice's son ended up with a dive boat in Bora Bora.

"True," I agreed. I stirred the ice in my glass with my finger. There were so many things that didn't add up here, though, with the Sawyer-Batson story Mary Alice was relating. The Sawyers set up their son-in-law in business, yet they thought he was responsible for their adored son's death. Hated him. Sue married the man her parents hated, but why hadn't she felt like they did? She, also, had adored her brother. I thought of her outburst in the courthouse. "Buried the same day." And then there was the beautiful Arabella, here to take care of her sick mother, but not staying with her. Arabella and Sue who couldn't get along with each other. And Dickie. Was he so unbalanced, so needful, that he had tried to kill Arthur Phizer?

"What are you thinking about?" Mary Alice asked.

"I'm thinking it would be interesting to read Sophie Sawyer's will."

"Can we do that?"

"Debbie says that once they're admitted into probate, anyone has access to them. Probate court is on the first floor of the courthouse."

"It'll just be a bunch of all that lawyer talk. What do you think we'll find?"

"I don't know. For starters, I'd like to know how much Bellemina Health stock Sophie owned and what she did with it. She's not listed in the annual report as one of the major stockholders, but Mitzi said she was."

"And so did Al." Sister looked at her watch. "Think you'll have time to do that and still get what's-his-name's supper on the table early enough?"

This time I did throw the book. Missed, but threw it.

The probate court where the records were on file reminded me of a McDonald's. You put in your order at a counter, stand aside and wait, and then when your order is handed to you, you take it to a table. They didn't have the quick service down though. There were only a couple of other people in the room, but we had to wait fifteen minutes before Sophie Sawyer's will was brought out.

"Heavy," the clerk said, bumping it down on the counter. "What all did she leave? Half the state of Alabama?"

"A bunch of happy lawyers," Sister said.

"God's truth." The woman giggled.

Sister carried the will to a table and we sat down in heavy wooden chairs that were surprisingly comfortable, the kind that have indentations for your behind. Arthur needed these chairs. The only problem was that I'm so short, I could have used his doughnut.

"What are we looking for?" Sister asked, opening the thick binder.

"I'm not sure. I'd like to know how much Bellemina Health stock she had and who she left it to."

Sister looked at the first page and then pushed the binder my way. "Help yourself. There are enough whereofs and heretofores here to choke a horse."

I saw what she meant.

"I don't know what good it's going to do anyway. Suppose we find out she left her stock to Arabella? Or to both the girls? So what? It's none of our business, Mouse."

I looked up in surprise. "You're actually saying something isn't your business? You? The Mouth of the South?"

"Well, this is giving me the creeps. It's like looking in someone's underwear drawer."

"You should know. I never know whether my scarves are in my dresser or around your neck."

"Scarves don't count. You need a box for them in your closet anyway so they won't get wrinkled."

I unlatched the binder and handed her part of the will. "Look for Bellemina."

"Nothing but wherefores," she grumbled. But she started reading.

So did I. The section I was reading consisted of real estate which was to be sold and divided equally between Sue and Arabella. A house in Chicago, an apartment in New York, a farm in Kentucky, a townhouse in London. It was amazing. There were also several bequests to people I didn't know, plus a million dollars each for Dickie and Zoe for their education.

"This woman makes you look one step from the poorhouse," I told Sister.

"One giant step."

In a few minutes, she poked me. "Here it is. Bellemina. She left it all to the University of Alabama Health Foundation."

"You're kidding. How much did she have?"

"Over eight million shares."

I'm sure my mouth flew open. "You're lying."

"It's right here." She handed me the page and I read that the eight million, two hundred fifty thousand, one hundred forty-eight shares of Common Stock of Bellemina Health held in trust at Columbia Federal Bank of Chicago was to be devised to the Board of Trustees of the University of Alabama Health Foundation.

"My Lord! Let me write this down," I said. "I think it's over fifty percent of the company. It had to have been listed on the annual report. Probably under some blind trust."

"You mean visually impaired trust?"

"Shut up."

I was fumbling in my purse for a pen and something to write on. "You said she had the hot hates for Joseph Batson. Well, this proves it." I found the pen and an envelope and wrote down the numbers. "She lets him work for years to build the company and then gives it away to his competition."

I studied what I had written down. "I'll be damned. Do you realize that this stock is worth thirty something dollars a share? Round it off at eight million shares and you've got over two hundred and forty million dollars." I looked at Sister. "That's a quarter of a billion dollars, isn't it?"

"You're the math teacher."

"I can't count that high."

Mary Alice took the page back and studied it. "A blind trust wouldn't mean diddly. If someone owned this much of a company, the other large shareholders would find out who it was. You can bet on that. The only thing it would do is keep her name out of the annual report."

"And they would logically expect Joseph and Sue to inherit half of Sophie's shares."

"Joseph and Sue would expect it, too."

I rubbed my forehead. I was getting a headache. "What if they found out what she had done? What if she told them?"

"They'd be mad as hell."

"Mad enough to kill her?"

"Could be." Sister tapped her nails against the table. One of them popped off and landed on the will. An acrylic drop of blood. "Damn."

"Hello, ladies. What a surprise."

We looked up at Peyton Phillips, blonde hair in a French braid, not a wrinkle in her emerald green linen suit.

"What brings you here?" she asked.

I kicked Mary Alice. I didn't want this woman to think we were being nosy, which of course we were.

"Genealogy research," I lied, covering the will with my arms.

Sister kicked me back. Her kick was harder. "How are you, Peyton?"

"Fine. Have you heard from Mr. Phizer today?"

"He's uncomfortable but okay."

"I'm so glad."

"Do you think the police will drop the charges against him now?" I asked.

"I'm working on it. They think Dickie's anger was strictly directed toward Mr. Phizer, though, not his grandmother. And they think they have enough evidence against Mr. Phizer." She shrugged. "When they think they have a case sewed up, they quit investigating." A bright smile. "But I'm still trying. Y'all take care now." She gave a small wave and walked over to the counter.

"Maybe we should have told her about the will," I said to Sister.

"Mouse, look at that woman."

I looked at the perfect hair, the perfect suit, the perfect smile. "Hey, you paid her retainer."

"You're right. Let her work for it."

We are not nice people. So what.

"Beady eyes. You could see the Batson

boy had beady eyes in the newspaper pictures." Mary Alice was eating supper with Fred and me. Fred had taken Woofer for his walk while I fixed corn salad and turkey sandwiches. The sky had become slightly overcast, but it was still warm enough to sit on the deck.

Fred was sufficiently amazed at our news about the will. I had looked at the annual report as soon as I got home and saw that Columbia Federal Bank held fifty-one percent of Bellemina Health in estates and trusts. I know so little about stock, that I hadn't thought anything about it when I had first read it. And even if I had, estates and trusts sounded like more than one person.

"I wonder why it hasn't been in the financial news in the paper?" Sister asked.

I put the salad on the table. "Arthur's not the kind to make an announcement. He did well to even get the will probated with all that's been going on."

Mary Alice and Fred reached for the salad at the same time. Fred won.

"You know," he said, helping his plate generously, "executors of estates get something like five percent for settling things. Arthur's going to come out with a bunch of money."

"Enough to warrant being shot in the butt

and having his house burned?" Sister asked.

"Well, just on the Bellemina stock that's worth two hundred fifty million, if he gets five percent it's —" Fred looked at me.

"Twelve million, five hundred thousand." I nearly dropped the salad that I had taken from Fred and was handing to Sister. Arthur and Mitzi with multiple millions of dollars?

"They'll be rich as you, Mary Alice," Fred said.

"Of course they won't." Sister helped herself to the corn salad. "But I'm pleased for them. Especially if Arthur doesn't have to go to the electric chair."

"And this money is one more reason the police would think he did it," I said.

Fred bit into a sandwich and chewed thoughtfully. "I wonder when that will was written. Did y'all notice by any chance?"

Sister surprised me by saying, "I did. It was written a couple of days before Sophie died. At least the part making Arthur the executor was. It was on a separate page at the front with all sorts of legal words. But I remember thinking she changed her mind right before she died."

"Do you remember who did it?"

"You mean which lawyer? Let me think. Somebody with a bird name." Sister took a bite of salad, chewed, and swallowed. "Swan? Parrot?" She shook her head no. "Y'all help me. Name some bird names."

"Robin? Wren? Heron?"

"No. I'll think of it in a minute."

"What I was wondering," Fred said, "is who the executor was before Arthur. That person got knocked out of a bunch of money."

"Probably a bank," I said.

"Wing."

We both looked at Sister.

"John Wing. That was his name."

Fred grunted. "That's not a bird name."

I put down my fork. "I wonder if Debbie knows him. It probably was a bank like I said, but if it were an individual, they might be mad enough to kill Sophie."

"I'll call her and see if she can find out." Sister reached for the salad bowl again. "I told you, Mouse. It's money folks get killed for."

"And you're the only one in our family who has any."

"I love you too," she said.

Nineteen

"My butt hurts like hell." Arthur waddled in and sat on his inner tube, wincing. "I'm running a little fever and they've got me on antibiotics."

"He's fine," Mitzi assured us.

"Like hell."

It was Friday night and Fred and I had gone over to see Arthur. Mitzi was right about the flowers. The place was full of them.

"There were more than this," Mitzi said when I admired them. "We've shared them with the neighbors on both sides of us."

Fred gets jolly when confronted with sick friends. "Looking good, buddy," he said to Arthur. For a second I thought he was going to give him the manly punch on the arm.

So did Arthur; he cringed, and the inner tube squealed. "I look like hell and feel like hell. That damn Dickie Batson."

"He'll pay for it, darling," Mitzi soothed him.

"Hope they cut his balls off."

The flowers obviously hadn't helped.

We stayed only a few minutes. I had

hoped to ask Arthur who had been the executor of Sophie's will before she had appointed him. I also wanted to know if he had read it and realized how rich he was going to be. Instead, we wished him well and left, each of us carrying a pot of lilies which Mitzi had shut up in the bathroom because they smelled so strong.

"He looks rough," Fred said. "I can't believe everything that's happened to that old fellow."

"I can't believe how rich he's going to be. Do you think he even realizes it?"

A car pulled up as we were walking toward the street. Peyton Phillips stepped out dressed in a blue sequined dress slit up the front. The top was cut so low, there wasn't much of Peyton left to the imagination. And there was a lot of Peyton. Saline, I'd bet my bottom dollar. But, dammit, it looked good.

"Hello, you two," she said. "How's Mr. Phizer?"

"Fine." Fred was doing a good job of peering over the lilies.

"He's running a fever," I informed her.

"Oh, I'm sorry. Well, I'm on my way to the Mall Ball and I thought I'd stop by and say hello. Does he feel like company?"

The Mall Ball is an annual fund-raising

event sponsored by the Civiettes, a group of young women who do a lot of, as the name says, civic and charity work.

"He'll be pleased to see you," Fred said.

I glared at him as Peyton gave a little wave and went up the walk. "Well, he will," he said.

"Much as that woman's getting paid, she ought to find out what really happened to Sophie and get Arthur out of trouble."

"The police are working on it, honey."

"Bo Mitchell and Joanie Salk? Sergeant Pepper? Ha."

"They do it all on computers nowadays, anyway. They caught Dickie Batson, didn't they?"

"Tripped over him probably. And his parents swear he didn't do it."

"Doesn't seem to be much doubt about it. The smoking gun."

I grinned at him. "What have you been reading?"

We drove down Valley Avenue. The spotlights were doing their number on Vulcan's behind which reminded me of Arthur's problem.

"You know," I mused, looking up at the statue, "there's something real obvious we're missing here."

"Not on Vulcan."

"No, there's nothing that's not obvious about Vulcan. I mean about the relationship between Sophie and Arthur. Why would she come back after almost fifty years and make him the trustee of her estate? That doesn't make sense, does it?"

"She trusted him."

"And she didn't trust any of her family?"

"Well, she had good reason not to trust somebody. That's for sure."

"And that good reason ought to be obvious."

"The police will find out, honey."

Ha.

The next morning, Fred had to go in to work a while on a special steel order.

"Want to get in the shower with me?" he invited, rubbing the three or four hairs on his chest.

Jane declined Tarzan's offer and sent him on his way with a peanut butter and banana sandwich.

Soon after he left, a truck pulled into the Phizers' driveway. Several workmen piled out. And then a second truck. Something was actually going to be done over there. And on a Saturday.

I pulled on some jeans and a tee shirt, collected Woofer, and waved at the workmen as I went by. They were sitting on the back of the second truck drinking coffee from McDonald's cups. They waved back.

When we got back from our walk, they were gone. I didn't see them again for three days. There was a message to call Sister, though. Which I did. Henry had made a chicken potpie the night before and Debbie had called to see if we wanted the leftovers for lunch. One does not turn down Henry Lamont's food, not even the leftovers. I told her I'd be there at noon.

"Bring a salad," she said.

I called Mitzi. Arthur was feeling better; he didn't have any fever this morning. I was missing Haley, and considered calling her, but it was early evening in Warsaw and she and Philip were probably out.

"I miss your mama," I told Muffin who was sitting on the kitchen table taking a bath. "Don't you?"

She quit licking her paw for a moment and looked at me. I took that for a yes.

I needed to stay busy, do something mindless. So I cleaned out the refrigerator.

"You smell like ammonia," Mary Alice greeted me when I presented myself for lunch and handed her the Piggly Wiggly salad.

"I wore rubber gloves." I sniffed my

hands and arms. "I've been cleaning out the refrigerator."

"Well, come put some lemon hand cream on. Debbie's here."

"I saw her car. Are the twins here?"

"No. They're with Richardena. Debbie brought the potpie." Richardena is the children's nanny, one of the best things to ever come Debbie's way. Mary Alice had been leery of Richardena because she had shot her abusive, womanizing husband.

"She just fixed him so he won't run around anymore," Debbie explained.

The jury, the majority of which had been women, not only found Richardena innocent, they congratulated her. And Richardena, the kindest and gentlest of women, is now the twins' much-beloved nanny.

Debbie was sitting at the kitchen counter scratching Bubba Cat under the chin. Bubba, who sleeps on a heating pad on the counter, summer and winter, had his head lifted in bliss. One hind leg was twitching. Our animals do lead good lives.

"Hey, Aunt Pat," she said. "Guess what. Henry and I are celebrating our sixth-month anniversary tomorrow."

"And no one thought it would last." I took the cream that Sister handed me and rubbed it on my hands and arms. It did smell good.

"Debbie's got some news for you," Sister said, taking the potpie from the microwave. "She knows John Wing; she called him."

"Who?" I was still thinking about Henry and Debbie.

"The man who changed Sophie Sawyer's will. The one who made Arthur the trustee of the estate. You're not going to believe who the first executor was."

"Who?"

"Peyton Phillips," Debbie said.

"Arthur's lawyer?"

Debbie quit petting the cat, got up, and washed her hands. "I didn't know she did anything but criminal work. Surprised me. Not that she couldn't do it if she wanted to." Debbie reached for a paper towel. "And from what Mama says, it certainly would have been lucrative."

"Multimillionaire lucrative," I agreed. Peyton Phillips. I'll be damned. "We saw her last night when we went to see Arthur. She was on her way to the Mall Ball, all dressed up."

"I figure she's the one who killed Sophie. Just think how mad it must have made her to lose out on all that money." Sister reached up and got three plates from the cabinet. "Y'all come help yourselves."

"I doubt it, Mama," Debbie said, helping herself to potpie and salad. "What I'd like to know is why Mrs. Sawyer changed the will."

"She saw Arthur Phizer again and realized she'd always loved him." Sister held up her hand. "Wait a minute." She got a couple of bottles of salad dressing from the refrigerator. "The ranch is fat-free. It's pretty good."

We sat at the kitchen table; Bubba turned so he could watch us.

"Just think," Debbie said, "out of all the lawyers in Birmingham, I recommended Peyton Phillips to represent Arthur. I can't believe she didn't tell me that he had replaced her as executor of Mrs. Sawyer's estate."

"She charged a fortune, too," Sister said.

"I guess it's not unethical, but it looks like she would have mentioned it. I wouldn't think she'd feel very kindly toward him."

Sister waved her fork. "This is what happened. Peyton finds out that Sophie has changed her will. She's furious. She goes to confront her. They argue. Peyton poisons her."

"Sophie was having lunch with Arthur at the Hunan Hut," I reminded Sister.

"And she's got nothing to gain from it,

Mama," Debbie added. "If she kills Mrs. Sawyer, the will with Mr. Phizer as the executor goes on the records. As long as Mrs. Sawyer is alive, there's a chance that she might change her mind and give it back to Peyton."

I tasted the chicken potpie. Henry had done it again. "Lord, this is good." I chewed thoughtfully.

There was something we were missing here. Given the whole Sawyer-Batson clan, there were probably a whole lot of things we were missing. But something was nagging at me, just as it had the night before. Some piece of the puzzle.

"What do you know about Peyton, Debbie?" I asked.

"Mainly her reputation as a good criminal lawyer. She got her law degree at the university a few years before I did, but I've met her at social gatherings. The Birmingham women lawyers have a group that meets for lunch or dinner once a month. It used to be fairly small but not anymore."

"Married? Children?"

"I think she might have been married for a while when she was in her early twenties. No children."

I realized what had been bothering me in this whole scenario.

"Debbie, you were wondering why Sophie Sawyer removed Peyton as her executor. Why would she ever have made her the executor to start with?"

Sister handed Bubba a piece of chicken which he sniffed at. "Because her girls don't get along with each other and she hated Joseph Batson."

"But Sophie lived in Chicago. And we're not talking penny ante stuff here. Wouldn't it have been logical to have a bank or an officer of a bank handle it up there? It doesn't make sense that she would come to Birmingham and choose a young lawyer she didn't know to be the executor of her estate. You don't just pick a name out of the yellow pages for something like that."

Debbie nodded her head. "You're right, Aunt Pat."

"Good thinking, Mouse."

I am a sixty-one-year-old woman who still falls apart when my sister says something nice about me. I wonder if it's too late for counseling.

Sister waved her fork again. "This is the way it is. Peyton Phillips and Arabella Hardt are lesbian lovers and Peyton blackmailed Sophie into making her the trustee, said she would tell about their relationship."

Debbie grinned. "Mama, you couldn't

blackmail anybody with that. Not nowadays."

"I guess not. But it's an interesting thought. Anybody want some more potpie?"

We all did. Fortunately, Henry had made a lot.

"I'll tell you what, Mama," Debbie said. "I'll see what I can find out about Peyton's background, see if there's any connection to the Sawyers."

I started in on my second helping of potpie. Sister's lesbian remark had gotten me thinking. I didn't care what the relationship might be, but was it possible that the friend that Arabella was staying with was Peyton Phillips? I tried to remember the day at the courthouse when Peyton had come to get Arthur out on bail. She had introduced herself to me. I remembered that. And Arabella had asked her if she wanted some candy and Peyton had answered with a put-down remark. But had they seemed to know each other? I couldn't remember. Well, if Arabella were at Peyton's, it shouldn't be too hard to find out.

I settled down and enjoyed my lunch. Not even Bubba's meowing for more chicken bothered me.

As it turned out, Fred worked all day. I

was watching the six o'clock news when the kitchen door opened, he got a beer from the refrigerator, and came into the den.

"Rough day?" I asked.

"Trouble getting the stuff from the lab." He sat in his recliner and took a long swig of beer. "What's been happening here?"

"We found out that Peyton Phillips, Arthur's lawyer that we saw last night, used to be the executor of Sophie Sawyer's will. Up until a couple of weeks ago in fact."

"Boy, she missed out on a lot of money, didn't she."

"Maybe enough to kill for."

"Not that cute girl."

Oh, the power of saline.

"You hungry?" I asked.

"A little bit."

"There's all kinds of sandwich stuff in the refrigerator. Help yourself."

The phone rang and I answered it.

"I've got news," Debbie said. "I called Joe Wing back and he said Peyton Phillips was recently named to the board of directors of Bellemina Health, and he thinks that's what made Mrs. Sawyer so mad at her."

"But that doesn't make sense. Sophie was the largest stockholder and had trusted Peyton enough to make her her executor."

"I don't know, Aunt Pat. Doesn't make

sense to me either. But I'll see what else I can find out. And I've been thinking. Mr. Phizer definitely needs another lawyer."

"True."

We said goodbye and I hung up the phone. Fred came back in with a sandwich and another beer.

"Who was that?" he asked.

"Debbie. Tomorrow's her sixth month anniversary."

"Good. Did we hear from Haley?"

"Not today."

"From Alan and Lisa?"

"No."

"That's good, isn't it?"

Of course it was.

Twenty

Fred and I went out for brunch the next day. I was sure he sensed that I was cross with him, for no particular reason; therefore the invitation. And I don't like to be cross with him; therefore the acceptance. I have to admit I'm sure there's a lot about me that drives him crazy, too. So we dressed up and went to the Mountain Brook Inn feeling slightly celebratory.

We were seated by a window, and I was having a last cup of coffee while Fred finished his key lime pie, when I saw Joseph Batson walking across the courtyard and toward the parking lot.

"There's Joseph Batson," I mentioned to Fred.

He rolled his eyes. "I hope he had the key lime pie. It's delicious."

About two minutes later, just time for Joseph to drive off, Peyton Phillips crossed the courtyard.

"Look, Fred," I said.

He looked. "Well, I'll be damned."

"What do you want to bet that they're not coming from the restaurant?"

"Well now, you don't know that, honey."

"You're right." I nudged his leg significantly with the toe of my shoe.

"Yes, sir?" The waiter thought Fred's sudden movement backwards was a signal for him.

Fred pointed toward his cup. "Coffee?"

The waiter obliged. While he was pouring the coffee, Arabella Hardt walked across the courtyard and headed for the parking lot.

Fred smiled sweetly. "Reckon who else is here?"

"I'll bet Sue Batson isn't." And she wasn't. But the three we had seen were interesting.

I called Mary Alice as soon as I got home. Miracle of miracles, she answered the phone. "You're not going to believe this," I said, and told her about Joseph Batson, Peyton, and Arabella.

"Wow," she said. "Fred took you out to brunch?"

"Yes, Fred took me out to brunch, Miss Smarty Pants. And I saw those three sneaking out."

"You think they'd been menage-a-troising all night?"

"Maybe."

"Right where everybody in town would recognize them."

"Don't be so damn smart. They were up to something."

"I agree." Sister's voice was suddenly serious. "You know Bessie McCoy?"

"Of course. The one who got scalped."

"I don't think she really got scalped, Mouse. I think she's just plain bald, but scalping sounds like more fun."

"Doesn't sound like fun to me."

"Well anyway, she says Peyton Phillips was engaged to David Sawyer, Sophie's son that got killed. That was how Sophie knew her so well."

"Really? He was only nineteen when he died."

"Says he got her out of the cage in some go-go place on Twentieth Street. That sounds like something a nineteen-year-old boy would do."

"Peyton? In a cage?"

"Well, it could have been on a pole. Bessie wasn't sure whether she was dancing or stripping."

"You're lying."

"Am not. Bessie says it's *My Fair Lady* to a T. The Sawyers even paid for her to go to college after David died. Turned her into a lady. Well, a lawyer, anyway."

"Why?"

"Well, they could afford it, Lord knows,

and I guess they felt sorry for her." She paused. "Have you heard from Arthur today?"

I hadn't; I needed to call.

"What are you doing this afternoon?" I asked.

"Taking Fay and May to the zoo."

"But you hate the zoo."

"I'm taking Richardena, too. She loves it."

"And you'll wait for them at the restaurant."

"It works out fine that way. They have the best nachos in town."

It figured.

"Well, can you cut it short and let's go to the library?"

"What for?"

"Being nosy. Look, Sister. The Sawyers send Peyton to law school. Sophie makes her the trustee of her estate. The Sawyers set Joseph Batson up in business, making sure they retain over fifty percent of it, and just before she's murdered, Sophie removes Peyton as the trustee. Now why?"

"You think you're going to find the answers at the library?"

"I'm thinking I'd like to see what we can find out about David Sawyer and the wreck that killed him."

"Okay, I'll just take the twins to look at the monkeys and go on one train ride."

Okay. Nosy time.

I had thought it would be like looking for a needle in a haystack, but finding the story about the wreck turned out to be amazingly easy.

"What year?" Mary Alice asked.

"Nineteen seventy-four. But I'm not sure where it happened. Probably Chicago."

"He'll be in the *Chicago Tribune* obits, anyway. They're alphabetized for the year."

One click. David had died on June 3, 1974.

Another click and we had the June 4, 1974 *Chicago Tribune*. The story was on the front page under the headline WRECK CLAIMS LIVES OF TWO. The story must have been written as the news came in. It stated simply that David Vaughn Sawyer and Jerome Wesley Hinds were killed late the night before when their car crashed into a tree on Abingdon Road. A third man, Joseph Batson, had been transported to a hospital, but his injuries were not considered life-threatening. David Sawyer was the son of noted financier Milton Sawyer.

"Let's look at the next day," I suggested.

The three men had just left a fraternity

party. The driver, David Sawyer, traveling at excessive speed, had lost control of the car and hit a tree. Funeral services had already been held for Sawyer. The services for Hinds would be at Martin's Funeral Parlor at three o'clock this afternoon.

"They leave a fraternity party, slam into a tree, and no mention is made of alcohol or drugs?" Sister clicked off the page. "Hard to believe."

"They wouldn't have wanted to embarrass the Sawyers."

"Boy, things have changed. Let's see if there's anything else."

There was. Two men who had seen the wreck and stopped to help had reported that they had helped a girl out of the car. She had appeared uninjured. Joseph Batson, the survivor, had said, however, that the three men were the only occupants of the car, that the girl was not with them, but had also stopped to help.

I looked up. "Peyton?"

Sister nodded. "Or Arabella or maybe even Sue."

"Or it really could have been someone who stopped to help."

"True."

I tapped the desk in disgust. "So we've learned a lot."

"We probably have. We just don't know what it is." Sister turned off the machine. "Let's go get some frozen yogurt."

The TCBY shop was crowded since the movie next door had just let out. We found a table back in the corner by the rest room doors, a noisy place. It wasn't conducive to talking, so we waited until we were back in the car.

"I've been thinking," Sister said. "What if it really was Arabella in that car? What if she was the one driving it?"

"Then Joseph Batson could have blackmailed the hell out of the Sawyers."

"But did he?" She swung onto the Red Mountain Expressway.

"They set him up in business, sure, but he married Sue."

"Maybe she was his ace in the hole."

"Possible. I still think Peyton's the secret, though. Why did Sophie suddenly remove her as trustee?"

"You think Arthur might know?"

"Of course. Damn. Why didn't I think of that?"

"Because you're not a very good detective, Patricia Anne."

"You mean my lawyer, Peyton Phillips, is the same one that was handling Sophie's estate?" Arthur looked much better, sitting up straighter on his doughnut. "Hell, yes, I know why Sophie got rid of her. Her name was Peyton Hinds on the will, though."

Hinds. The boy killed with David Sawyer's name was Hinds.

"Sophie thought she was too buddy-buddy with Joseph Batson. Got herself put on the board of directors of Bellemina Health. Sophie decided she didn't want her handling the estate, that she might not do right by Arabella and Sue. She was as worried about Sue as she was Arabella. Never trusted Joseph."

"Did you tell the police this?" Sister asked.

"I told him to," Mitzi said. "But he didn't think it was important."

"Arthur, do you know how much money you're talking about here?" I asked.

"Quite a bit, I imagine." Arthur reached for a glass of water. "That's not why I agreed to do it though, Patricia Anne."

"Well, I know that, Arthur. But it could have been a reason for Peyton Phillips to kill Sophie. What do you know about her anyway? Was she engaged to David Sawyer?"

"Might have been, but I doubt it. I remember Sophie told me the Hinds boy who was killed when David was had a sister. She didn't say anything about her being engaged to David, though, and I can't even remember now why she mentioned it."

"Maybe she said the girl was dancing in a go-go club on Twentieth Street."

Arthur actually laughed, wincing in pain. "Commuting from Chicago? Hell, Patricia Anne. That's funny."

Mary Alice and I looked at each other. So much for Miss Crocheted Hat's information. Well, she'd gotten some stuff right.

Mitzi took the glass away from him before he spilled the water. "Arthur, I think there's a whole lot of stuff you need to tell the police."

"I told them I didn't kill Sophie."

"They may need some more help."

"Hmmm. So Peyton Hinds is Peyton Phillips and she's my lawyer. Damn. I'm on my way to the electric chair."

"The Yellow Mama," Mitzi agreed. "Arthur, it's time you started helping yourself."

"I just didn't think it was important."

"Arthur, your brains are located where you got shot," Sister said.

He frowned.

"What about Arabella, Arthur?" I told them about seeing Joseph, Peyton, and

Arabella at the Mountain Brook Inn.

"Arabella's staying there. I forgot to tell you," Mitzi said. "She said she was staying with a friend because she didn't want us to worry about her being alone."

A forty-year-old woman? Nice of her.

"And you think Joseph and Peyton were there visiting her?" Sister asked.

Arthur nodded. "Might have been there to see her. Or it might have just been a coincidence."

"Yellow Mama," Sister mouthed to me.

I pointed to my rear end and mouthed back, "Pain."

"Arthur," I tried again, "is it possible that Arabella was in the car when David was killed?"

"Not that I know of. Why? What makes you think that?"

"We just looked the wreck up in the library. The story mentioned that there might have been a girl in the car."

"No. It was just the three boys. All of them drunk or on something. David was driving."

Mitzi startled us by saying, "Arthur, I'm not so sure. Arabella doesn't drive, says it scares her to death."

"It scares me to death, too, Mitzi." Arthur switched from one cheek to the other.

"Doesn't mean a thing. In fact, I know it was the three boys. Sophie had a picture someone took of them as they left the party. Sent it to her with a sympathy card."

"You saw it?" Mary Alice asked.

"No, but she told me about it."

Mitzi frowned. "And she still had it?"

"I suppose."

"And no girl was in it?"

"I told you I never saw it." Arthur shifted his weight again. He suddenly looked startled. "You know what? Sophie told me she kept a packet of pictures and letters hidden behind the access door in her closet. I'd totally forgotten about it."

"What kind of door?" Sister asked.

"That little trap-door thing at the bottom of closets that back up to bathrooms. You know, so plumbers can get to the pipes. She said she was telling me in case anything happened to her." He slapped the arm of his chair. "Damn, I can't believe I forgot that."

"I never knew what those doors were for," Sister said. "Did you, Patricia Anne?"

I nodded that I did.

"Why would she keep them hidden?" Mitzi asked. "If she kept them hidden, they must be important."

"I doubt it."

Mitzi rolled her eyes at us. "I'm going to

go find out, Arthur. Damn it, I don't want to be a rich widow."

"Rich is fine. Widowed depends on who the husband is," Sister said. We were waiting in the Jaguar outside Mitzi's apartment.

"I think Mitzi wants to keep Arthur."

"I guess Debbie will have to recommend another lawyer then."

"She meant well."

Sister turned the rearview mirror and put on some lipstick.

"It was Peyton's fault," I said. "She should have told Debbie she was already involved in the case."

"Involved like poisoning Sophie Sawyer, maybe."

"But how could she have done it? She wasn't even there."

"Good question."

Mitzi came out of her apartment and got in the backseat. "Thanks for going with me, y'all. I swear sometimes I think that man's got room temperature I.Q. He says if there's anything there that will hurt Sue or Arabella, he doesn't want the police to see it. I told him I'd decide. I'm fed up with this stuff, I'm telling you. Imagine having to change Arthur's bandages twice a day."

Yikes. Mary Alice took off for Sophie's apartment.

Twenty-one

The apartment looked exactly the same as it had the last time we were there, of course. No one was staying there. One lone philodendron that I hadn't noticed before was wilting on the counter. I poured some water on it. Maybe I would take it home.

"I declare I love these colors," Mary Alice said as Mitzi opened the draperies. "I'm definitely going to have a decorator come look at them."

"Y'all wait a minute," Mitzi said. "I don't know if I'll need something to open this trapdoor with or not."

We followed Mitzi into the bedroom, watched her open the closet door and get down on her knees.

"I wonder what's in there," I said. "This is sort of like when Geraldo Rivera opened Al Capone's vault. Remember that?"

"I don't know, but it's a dumb place to hide something." Mitzi's voice was muffled by clothes. "I'm going to need a screwdriver. Maybe a kitchen knife will do."

I went to the kitchen and came back with a knife. In a moment we heard a pop as the door came loose. There was the sound of paper being ripped, and then Mitzi came backing out, a medium-sized manila envelope in her hand.

"Here it is." She stood up and brushed off her knees.

We walked back into the living room.

"You don't have to show it to us," Sister lied. "But I think you ought to see right away what's in it."

I gave Sister a hard look. Truth to tell, I wanted to see whatever it was.

"Oh, I'm planning on it." Mitzi sat down on the beige and white sofa and flicked back the metal clasps. She reached in and pulled out what seemed to be several pictures with a piece of paper around them.

Mitzi opened the paper. "It's a letter to Sophie."

"What does it say?" Sister asked. So much for not wanting to know.

"It says, Dear Mr. and Mrs. Sawyer, I can only imagine how grieved you must be at David's death. These pictures were taken as he was leaving the party. I hope it will console you some to see how happy he was that night. He was a wonderful person and will be missed by us all. Sincerely, Ralph Addison."

Mitzi looked at the pictures and then

handed them to us. Each showed a smiling young man waving from the passenger side of a convertible. In one, all you could see was that the driver had long, red hair. In a second one, she too, was turned toward the camera. Arabella. In a third, taken as they drove away, the two passengers in the back seat were turned and waving, but you couldn't make out their features.

"Oh, my," I said.

There were tears in Mitzi's eyes. "And Sophie couldn't throw them away. They were the last pictures she had of her son."

We heard the door open and looked up as Sue Batson came in.

"Hi," Sue said. "What are y'all doing here?"

We were caught red-handed is what we were doing there.

"Arthur sent us to get these." Mitzi handed the picture she was still holding to Sue.

Sue smiled. "What is this?" Then, "The pictures. Where did you find them?"

"Behind the trapdoor in the closet," Mitzi said.

Sue nodded as if everybody hid stuff behind trapdoors in closets. Then she reached over, took the picture Sister was holding, and sat down on the arm of the sofa to look at it. "I told Joseph that Mama would still have these."

This was not the reaction I had expected. Here was proof that her sister had been driving the car when two people, including her brother, were killed, and she seemed calm.

She studied the picture. "Wasn't he beautiful?"

I looked at the picture I was holding. David Sawyer had, indeed, been a beautiful young man.

"Of course he was beautiful." We all jumped. None of us had realized that Arabella had come into the room. She walked over to Sue and took the pictures.

"It was an accident, Arabella," Sue said. "A horrible accident."

"An accident that Mama and Daddy covered up. Let everybody think that David was driving. And I let them."

"Mama and Papa were trying to protect you." Sue said this quietly. "Just as Joseph was trying to protect you and me both."

"Bull. He was covering his own tail. Tell her about the drugs, Arabella." Peyton Phillips had come into the room unnoticed by any of us. "The ones that sweet Joseph was selling everyone."

"Shit," Sister muttered. "What kind of a tea party is this?"

Peyton yanked the pictures from Arabella. "Good. Thanks, girls. And, Mitzi, tell Arthur I appreciate him telling me where you were."

Mitzi shook her head. "Biddy brains."

"The pictures won't do you any good, Peyton," Sue said. "I'm going to the police with them. They've caused enough damage. Joseph told me about the blackmail. He told me everything."

"Fine. Then I'll have to tell the police how your darling sister killed your mother."

"You're lying."

"A little strychnine in some sugar substitute. Voila."

"But it was Arthur's sweetener," Mitzi said.

"And intended for him." A sigh. "We all make mistakes. His was being generous with his sugar." Peyton smiled. "Ask Arabella if she didn't slip several packets of sweetener into his pocket the day before Sophie died. The day when she and Arthur had lunch together." She turned to Mitzi. "Your husbands's got more lives than a cat."

Sue looked sick, as if she might faint any minute. "Our mother's death was an accident?"

"Sue." Arabella sank down on the sofa,

crying. "You know I would never hurt Mama."

Sue recoiled. "Just Arthur. Oh, Arabella."

Arabella cried harder. "No, I didn't. I don't know what she's talking about."

"Well," Peyton said, "you couldn't have him the trustee of all that money now, could you, Arabella? But I suppose that'll be between you and the police. Too bad Sophie wanted sweet tea. And too bad, Sue, about Dickie. But I guess he takes after his father."

Peyton gave a wave and turned to leave. As she took her first step, Sister's foot shot out, and Peyton fell over it, hitting her head on the coffee table. She lay sprawled on the carpet, not moving.

There was shocked silence in the room.

"Is she dead?" Sister gasped, when Peyton didn't move. "Don't let her be dead."

A moan assured us.

"No, but she's bleeding all over the white carpet," I said.

"I'll get a towel." Mitzi ran into the bathroom.

Guess who called 911.

"Well, do, Jesus."

"I know. By the time the paramedics and

police got there, Peyton was ready to sing like a bird. Could have been because of the scarf Sue Batson was tightening around her neck. None of us stopped her. We all knew it was just a tourniquet to stop the bleeding." I smiled at the remembrance of plump Sue sitting on Peyton screaming, "You tell the truth about my son, you scumbag!" So much for riling up a mother.

Bo Mitchell, Joanie Salk, and I were sitting at my kitchen table drinking coffee the next morning.

"I'm sorry I missed all those going-ons," Bo added. "I've seen that Peyton Phillips sashaying around down at the station. Big Gucci purse."

Joanie poured Coffee-mate into her cup. "Is that the kind with the G's on it? I saw some of them at Kmart."

"Right." Bo took the Coffee-mate from Joanie. "And then what, Patricia Anne?"

I told them the rest of the story. A real Paul Harvey I am.

"Turned out it was all Peyton. Joseph Batson wasn't involved, and I'm so glad. Peyton blackmailed him with the pictures to get on his board of directors. He didn't want Sue hurt by them, and he wasn't sure that Arabella couldn't still be charged with vehicular homicide."

"And his mother-in-law thought he was having an affair with Peyton?"

"Well, she never completely trusted him. After all, she knew he was the one who supplied the drugs the night of the car accident."

Bo sipped her coffee. "I know Peyton tried to kill Mr. Phizer because she thought Mrs. Sawyer would make her the executor again. But one thing I don't understand. How come she tried to have him killed twice more?"

I pushed the sweetrolls her way. "First of all, she simply hated him for being appointed executor. And she may have thought he would figure it out, remember how he got the sweetener and put two and two together. She was perfectly safe; Mitzi says he's got room temperature I.Q., but Peyton didn't know that."

"I'll bet she did a jig when Debbie called her to see if she would take Arthur's case."

"It made it simpler for her, that's for sure."

Joanie reached over and got one of the sweetrolls. "Well, I want to know how Peyton Phillips got the poison to Mr. Phizer."

"Simple since she's a criminal lawyer."

"Diabolical, you ask me." Bo handed Joanie a napkin. "Wipe the icing off your chin."

"She found out Arabella was meeting Arthur for lunch at Shakey's. One of her clients is a waitress there. She gave her a couple of packets of sweetener and told her to refill his tea and hand him the packets. The woman has already admitted it. She didn't know it was strychnine, of course."

"And Mr. Phizer took the sweetener?"

Bo Peep grinned. "Joanie, I'll show you Mr. Phizer cutting the grass someday. Finish your story, Patricia Anne."

"He used regular sugar, but he stuck the sweetener in his jacket pocket because he says it was the kind Sophie used."

"Where was Arabella?"

"She says she must have been in the rest room, that she doesn't remember anything about it."

"You believe her?"

"I want to. I guess y'all are going to have to figure that out. Mary Alice and I keep having to do all your work."

"And feed us sweet rolls to boot." Bo reached for another one. "How would you get strychnine in a packet of sweetener, anyway? And wouldn't it be heavier?"

"A hypodermic needle, probably," Joanie said. "And it wouldn't be much heavier. Not enough to notice."

Bo frowned. "I'll bet she thought the

Hunan Hut had awful tea."

"You probably wouldn't notice if you'd been eating that peanut stuff."

"And one of Peyton's clients shot Mr. Phizer?" Joanie asked.

"A very inept one, thank God. The same one who removed the smoke alarm batteries and set the fire. They've located him, too. I don't know who called with the information about Dickie's car. Another client, I'm sure. One of the perks of being a criminal lawyer, apparently." I got up and poured us some more coffee. "I hope the Phizers stay next door. Arthur says he's going to invest most of the money back in Bellemina Health. He feels bad about so much of Sophie's estate going to Joseph's competitor. It's too bad those folks didn't talk more."

Bo motioned toward the Phizers' house where carpenters were working like ants. "Looks like they're planning on coming back."

"You know," I said, "it's really romantic when you think about it. First loves reunited. Sophie's trust in Arthur. Her being poisoned and dying in his arms. Like a Greek tragedy."

"Joanie," Bo said. "Don't you eat any more of Patricia Anne's sweet rolls."

Twenty-two

Which brings us to why Mary Alice hit Alcorn Jones over the head and landed us in jail, something I still haven't told Haley, even though I now have a computer, not the cheap one Sister found me, but a nice one, and we're e-mailing like crazy. Her roach problem is better and she's made us reservations at the Warsaw Holiday Inn for two weeks at Christmas. They even have CNN.

It was several weeks before Mitzi got to attend one of the investment club meetings. She had a lot to do, seeing about the repairs on the house and the new glassed in back porch they were building on.

"Arthur's healed," she said. "But if he mooned anybody, it would look like a smiley face."

We were driving by Vulcan at the time which, I suppose, made her think of it.

"Get a picture," Mary Alice recommended.

Mitzi giggled. "I already have."

"What's the latest on Joseph Batson and Arabella?" I asked.

"Lord, what a mess. Sophie, bless her heart, trusted Peyton completely for years.

It was Joseph she didn't trust. Big mistake."

"But she removed Peyton as her executor when she thought she was having an affair with Joseph."

Mitzi shrugged. "I don't think it would ever have occurred to her that Peyton might be blackmailing Joseph."

"With the pictures." Mary Alice turned onto Oxmoor Road. "How did Peyton get those pictures anyway?"

"Sophie showed them to her one day. Peyton didn't actually have copies, but Joseph and Arabella didn't know that."

"Why would Sophie do that?" Mary Alice slammed on her brakes and shot a bird at a man who suddenly pulled out from a parking space in an ancient yellow Cadillac. "Watch where you're going, fool!"

"I have an idea that she wanted Peyton to understand why Arabella was so emotionally fragile, why she needed someone to look after her," Mitzi said after she caught her breath. "And Joseph and Arabella were protecting Sophie because she was sick. Neither of them realized how far Peyton would go, of course."

"Is Arabella okay?" I asked. "Did she ever say why she was lying about where she was staying?"

"She didn't want her mother to know the

extent of her drinking problem. Or us either. I think it's a relief for her that the truth is finally out, and she's getting some help. Sue's being a Rock of Gibraltar for both Arabella and Joseph now that she knows all that happened."

"You don't think she suspected?" I asked.

"Probably. But that was part of the problem. She was left out."

"Debbie says that neither Joseph nor Arabella will have to face charges."

"They won't because of the statute of limitations. Just as well. They've all suffered enough."

"Well, thank God I know all about my family," Mary Alice said. "What gets families in trouble is when they don't tell each other everything."

I swear she was serious.

Mitzi leaned forward. "Changing the subject, y'all. Tell me about Alcorn Jones. Do you recommend him, Mary Alice?"

Sister was flustered. "For what?"

"As a financial advisor. He's called us several times and says he's your advisor. We're going to need some help."

"Al Jones said he was my financial advisor?"

"Isn't he?"

"No. A woman named Shirley Gibbs handles most of my finances."

"Well, he's recommending that we invest in a real estate development that his bank is backing."

"I thought Arthur was putting most of the money back in Bellemina Health," I said.

"He is. Bellemina's going to be fine. It's just a shame Sophie never got to know Joseph better." Mitzi paused, thinking. "And we're setting Hank up in his own advertising company so he and Bridget won't have to move to Atlanta. But there's so much money left."

What a worry.

"I'll look into it," Sister promised.

And she did. It took her about two minutes to find out that almost every woman in the investment club had received an offer from Alcorn to handle their private finances.

"Peddling some real estate." Miss Bessie pushed a red crocheted hat up from her forehead. "Damn. This thing's ten sizes too big." She turned for us to see. "You think it looks tacky?"

We both shook our heads no.

"Anyway," she continued, "I told him I was buying Wendy's, thank you, sir. I like their stuffed pitas, especially the chicken with the ranch dressing. Can't eat real estate."

"Did he tell you he was my financial advisor?" Mary Alice asked.

"Said that's how come you're so rich."

"Damn." Sister turned to me. "Mouse, I think you and I'd better go have a talk with Mr. Alcorn Jones."

Don't ask why I was included in the "talk." But I was dumb enough to go and end up in the Birmingham jail.

"Has Al been investing any of your money on the side?" I asked her on our way downtown.

"A little," Mary Alice admitted.

"Lost it all?"

"A little. A drugstore chain he recommended filed for Chapter 11 two days after I bought the stock."

But as Sister explained to Debbie later (Alcorn didn't press charges; I didn't expect him to), it wasn't the money, or even the fact that he was telling everyone he was her financial advisor. What really got to her was the fact that he wasn't a gentleman.

"I told him politely, didn't I, Mouse, that I expected my money back, plus any that he might have lost for the investment club ladies, and that we didn't want to have any more dealings with him."

"What did he say?" Debbie wanted to know. We were walking to her car from the jail.

"He said all right."

Debbie looked at me.

I nodded. "He did. He said all right."

"And you hit him over the head, Mama?"

"She broke some spokes in my kitten umbrella," I added.

"But why?"

"Well," Sister admitted, "after I gave him my ultimatum and turned around to leave, he pinched me on the behind."

Debbie stopped walking. "And you hit him for that? It wasn't a very nice thing for him to do, but, Mama, don't you think you overreacted?"

"It was a whole handful, not just a pinch. And he whispered, 'Remember Ruffner Mountain, Mary Alice.' "

Debbie was totally puzzled. "Remember Ruffner Mountain? Why? What's that about?"

"Not much," Sister said, beginning to giggle. And then the giggle exploded.

People driving down Sixth Avenue that afternoon were rewarded with the sight of one bewildered looking young pregnant woman watching two older women laughing so hard they were having to hold each other up.

"I'm starving," Sister said finally, gasping for breath. "Let's go to Chick-Fil-A, girls.

And then we've got an umbrella to buy."

"Kittens looking through stained glass," I insisted. "They'd better still have one. It's already snowing in Warsaw."

And they did.

The employees of Thorndike Press hope you have enjoyed this Large Print book. All our Large Print titles are designed for easy reading, and all our books are made to last. Other Thorndike Press Large Print books are available at your library, through selected bookstores, or directly from us.

For information about titles, please call:

(800) 257-5157
To share your comments, please write:

Publisher
Thorndike Press
P.O. Box 159
Thorndike, Maine 04986